SHADOW SIGHT

Shadowed Steps – Book Three

Ken Hughes

Windward Road Press

LOS ANGELES, CA

Windward Road Press
11923 NE Sumner St Ste 879426
Portland, OR 97250-9601

Publisher's Note: This is a work of fiction. Names, characters, places, and incidents are a product of the author's imagination. Locales and public names are sometimes used for atmospheric purposes. Any resemblance to actual people, living or dead, or to businesses, companies, events, institutions, or locales is completely coincidental.

Book Layout © 2017 BookDesignTemplates.com
Cover © 2020 by Sleepy Fox Studio

ISBN paperback: 978-1-7350002-2-0
ISBN ebook: 978-1-7350002-1-3

Shadow Sight/ Ken Hughes -- 1st ed.

To Carol

— "Nobody" was better then, and he still is

CONTENTS

CHAPTER ONE

THE PLEA

"The first charge is Criminal Trespassing in the first degree, at the LifeLab facilities, Your Honor."

Of course it is. But I did that to restore the company's reputation, after I was tricked into framing them... at least until I got blackmailed myself...

At Paul's side, his new lawyer gave her head the smallest nod at the charge. But back a few benches behind them were Paul's father and brother—what kind of pain or shame had to be on those faces?

Focus. He kept his eyes on the judge up in front. At least that man's craggy, impassive face wasn't tightening in hostility so far.

Paul resisted the urge to Open and lock his sight onto the tiniest motions of the judge's face, or look beyond it to glimpse his thoughts. Those senses might still tease out some advantage for his plea, but not yet.

"Criminal Trespassing again," Assistant DA Oliver went on, "at St. Cedric's General Hospital. Also, additional counts of that will likely be filed soon."

Still no glower or scowl from the judge. This time Paul did steal a glance over at his father—no expression showed on his bearded face, even at being reminded how his "missing" son had never even gone far from the hospital he'd been last seen... The place that Paul had been so sure held the answers to his suddenly Opened senses. *But I was trying to keep whatever trouble I was in away from you two.*

Paul swung his head forward again. Even that motion felt like a wild wave of his arm in the coiled stillness of the courtroom, under the eyes of the painted judges hanging on the wall, and the flesh-and-blood man up front that was weighing his life. The bench under him felt harder than ever, and the chains were cold on his wrists and ankles.

"Criminal Trespassing in the first, and Stalking in the second, regarding Addamson Abbot Insurance." Richard Oliver laid out the words with elegant motions of his hands, one point at a time. Never mind how they'd ever prove the *intent to commit a crime* element of those charges—it was Addamson Abbot that had been cheating its customers for years, until Paul had exposed them.

"Electronic Eavesdropping…"

"Criminal Trespassing…"

"Criminal Impersonation…"

Paul tried to keep his eyes on the judge, and whether those thin lips really were twisting that crucial fraction of a scowl that could mark that he was turning against the parade of small charges. But now the assistant DA's manicured fingers were tapping a manila folder on his desk, a folder half an inch thick.

One of those charges could mean half a year of Paul's life, sealed away in stone walls. Another could add a year for every count, and another and another, and they still only listed *six* times they thought they could prove his actions. Only six.

"The People expect there'll be many more charges, Your Honor. We have a span of at least two years of Paul Schuman's life to investigate."

"That's quite a list." The judge leaned forward. "Quite a list of nonviolent offenses, as if you're dealing in quantity over quality. Criminal intent, but no actual thefts to make it burglary? And weren't there charges of previous assault on the arresting officer?"

Detective Reid stood up beside Oliver. "That would be me, sir. I asked the People to not follow that up, so the case would stay concentrated on the volume of Mr. Schuman's offenses."

He gave Paul a cold look, his infamous huge eyebrows lowering to all but cover his eyes. Those eyes that could be skimming through Paul's mind as easily as Paul could his, if the detective had been willing to use his own powers.

"Hmm. Mister Schuman, you've heard the charges, as they stand. How do you plead?"

The lawyer beside Paul—Celia Claire, "yes they call me CC"—whispered "It's too soon for a deal. Still, Reid's sure to bring Oliver more charges, and you might head that off now if the judge is friendly. Wouldn't recommend it, though."

It might stop them from reopening the death of that blackmailer Quinn, but his father said not to worry there—

Paul looked at the judge, tightened his thoughts around his own *need* to know, and Opened.

The world shrank, from five senses to something other than sight, that held only an image of the graying man up on the bench, and that "image" melted at the edges. That still, hard face tightened, features drawing together in concentration and body slowly leaning forward toward his prey, fingers reaching along the desk and curling ready to grasp...

Paul broke the trance. His other senses flooded back in, and he saw Reid's eyes on him. Just that one instant of watching the judge's thoughts must be enough for Reid to guess he'd taken a peek.

No mercy in this court. Paul gave CC a small shake of his head.

The lawyer raised her voice. "Not guilty, Your Honor."

"Of course. Yours is an odd case, Mr. Schuman. A list of misdemeanors and possible felonies, with limited evidence and a lot of promise that more will come out of the woodwork. You may want to think about what deal you can make."

Paul's throat felt dry as he answered "I will, Your Honor."

What they'd do was fight, against every piece of weak evidence Reid could produce without him revealing how Paul *really* got to the truth, and every accusation that Paul's work had been "crimes" instead of proper whistleblowing. Instead of what it should be.

The prosecutor said "The People request bail be denied. Mr. Schuman has shown himself a flight risk many times, including fleeing clear out of state."

"—and then surrendering voluntarily, Your Honor," CC added smoothly.

To take the blame for Sarah Gomez, and they still won't tell me what they did with her.

"And after they exposed—"

Paul's brother cut off that stage whisper, instead of going on to mention the police corruption out at Cedar Springs.

"That will be enough," the judge told Greg, then turned back to Paul. "Mr. Schuman's activity in this city is the issue. Bail denied. The defendant is remanded to North Penitentiary."

The single rap of the gavel could have been an inch from Paul's ear. Not because he had Opened to the sound, but because it meant *every* sound and motion from now on would be crowding in on him. And they'd make him serve every day of the charges they could, in the deepest hole they could find.

He looked over at his family again. His father leaned toward him, with what looked like sympathy trying to shine out on that face, cracking open his usual control and looking awkward to be seen in public. Beside him, Greg's face viewed his brother with much the same look.

"We'll get a better deal soon," CC promised.

Paul sagged on the bench. No more need to keep his eyes on the judge, the prosecutor, or Reid... Instead he Opened to the sounds, to fill himself with the sweet sounds just outside the courtroom's window, of people strolling and talking and gusts of winter wind. *I can still listen for those any time, all this means is more cages to reach past, and we might still beat or reduce the charges—*

Police arms hauled him to his feet. They started him for the door.

The chains on Paul's legs held him to a shuffling stride of barely a foot a step. Their rattle seemed to draw gazes from the people sitting behind him, making them look up from their own, separate whispers and worries. To wonder why a silent kid of twenty-three was chained up and led between *two* uniforms like he still thought he could run.

He heard footsteps close in. Someone trotted up to where CC walked behind them, and called out "About those LifeLab charges? First you helped expose the 'animal experiments,' then you disproved them?"

Paul glanced back as he walked on. That chubby older man wasn't a reporter, not with that casual tone and the simple but perfectly-kept suit.

CC said "And your interest in that would be?" Her tone was guarded, watching for any advantage she could get.

"To be honest, I'm curious how he got his information. Eugene Brandt," he added.

Brandt... that name had been...

Paul kept the shock off his face, and even kept walking without a shift in the chains' clatter. LifeLab's own owner, down here?

He stole another glance back, and Opened. Brandt's face looked the same, only peering forward an inch more—no angry gestures or eager staring that might match a serious interest in what Paul had done...

A moment later Paul fell back into step with the police. CC and Brandt had stopped to talk, and Paul wished he could drag her away.

I don't think Brandt has a clue how I really got his secrets. Please, please, let's keep it that way...

"Don't let it get to you!"

His father's voice called out from behind them.

"CC's the best lawyer in town for this, and she's just getting started!" He had to lean on Greg to catch up to the others' speed, and Paul could hear his wound tugging at his breath and his voice.

"Thanks," Paul answered. "Again. And, I'm really sorry for..."

He couldn't finish. Sorry for staying away, when he'd been sure it would keep his family safe? "Sorry" his father had been shot, when Ian Schuman already had his own dealings with the late Quinn—

What was that? I can't start to blame *them for what went wrong, it was my own years of secrets that made theirs so explosive!*

"Forget it," Greg said. "And, we'll find... whatever's behind this."

Meaning Lorraine. Meaning Greg's own wife, and how she'd hidden her own power from them all these years, playing dumb even after Paul had gotten it too by accident. She'd never used it to change the world like Paul tried to, but now she was the one in hiding out there somewhere.

One of the cops turned to Paul's family and waved them back. "Sorry. You want to see him, you have to put in for a visit."

The two fell back. His father stared after Paul, then called out "We'll beat this. And until we do, you'll get through it, I know you will!"

Paul forced a smile and a hearty voice. "Really not a problem."

Ian Schuman's eyes went wide.

Paul watched his family until the cops shuffled him around a corner, and wished he'd picked a different goodbye. Were they ready to *believe* that he'd spent the last two years learning to cope with jails?

By the next two turns, the corridor's number of police had thickened and the civilians had dwindled down to the few who made it past the checkpoints. Then Paul reached the room at the end.

His first thought was a locker room—it had no lockers, but it was rimmed with long benches where five men in chains and prison orange sat. Just waiting, under the eyes of three police. Stale sweat was thick in the air.

The others' faces—black and white, bearded and scarred and smooth—only glanced at him a moment. Paul sank onto the end of a bench, quiet as he could, chained hands resting on his knees.

He could only take this one minute at a time, never thinking about how many endless minutes lay ahead. Or those looks in his father's and brother's eyes.

His gaze settled on a stain on the wall, just a bit above the opposite row of prisoners. *I'm not a thief, I'm not like them. I spent my time stopping liars and threats that might never have been caught...*

The police muttered to each other, and outside the room voices and feet clattered along on their way. Paul tried to ignore the smell, and poke through what the prosecutor had listed.

Electronic eavesdropping? They'd never prove that, when he only used his senses instead. And they never mentioned the times he'd slipped into a home to borrow some fraud's ID, or just get out of the cold.

One prisoner nudged another, and whispered some kind of soft joke. Paul Opened and glimpsed one man's inner self sagging helpless on the bench, the other's fist rapping a leashed, mechanical thump against his thigh as if he barely noticed his own frustration, *thump, thump, thump...* At least they weren't looking at Paul.

Blend in.

The face of that LifeLab owner Brandt flashed in his head again— but the man really had seemed to have no idea how Paul had broken his security. CC didn't know, and his father and Greg still had only a vague sense of what his power was.

His fingers twitched, wanted to clench where they lay. Did Lorraine have the right idea? She'd kept her power hidden for years, even after marrying Greg, and she'd been safe. *But I had to run off and hide while I tried to find what had happened to me.*

Still, it had been working. Paul's power over his senses had been perfect for rooting out dirty secrets all over town. *I was* good *at it— and even way out at Cedar Springs I helped beat Chief Thiessen and save Lorraine...*

And look how that had worked out with Sarah. She'd been happy to report the stories he'd broken—but she got one word of what he and Lorraine could really do and all her appreciation turned to fear. Until she'd gotten past that, and taken on the police herself to help them escape.

I gave myself up to clear her... yeah, clear her from the price of getting involved with me. Her choice, his choice—either way he was stuck here struggling to keep his fists from pounding like the helpless thoughts of that man across from him...

The door opened. Detective Terrence Reid walked in.

The uniforms let him in with a glance, of course they knew him. Reid moved slowly over, jaw set tight, until he stood close in front of Paul.

That man's hands had pummeled him and made his head ring... but Paul refused to flinch away. No point in glancing at Reid's thoughts, not for a few glimpses of hidden gestures. But the cold way he looked at Paul...

"So we got you."

Because Paul had turned himself in. He kept his face still.

Up close, Reid looked more thin and drawn than ever, as if the fervor in his eyes was consuming him from inside. He went on, low and fierce: "I wanted to let you know... Everything you did, we're going to prove. All of it. At least what a court will believe," and he halted.

What was Reid up to? Paul glared back at him, trying to fill his mind with Reid's clenched eyes and huge eyebrows—*and no secrets about my work for him to pick up.* But no, Reid would never trick him, or use his own powers at all.

Sure enough, Reid added "But, I do get some of the pressure you've been under."

"Yeah. We did end up on the same side, against the chief—"

Paul cut off. He could feel the ripple of shifted breathing and eyes, as a roomful of criminals had to decide what that word meant. One more thing to watch out for now; if prisoners thought he'd taken on a police chief, would that make him safer or just more conspicuous?

"Don't you put me out there with you!" Reid leaned closer and his eyes narrowed to slits. "I know where the line is, and I stay within the law. You're a *cheat* who makes up your own rules, and you think you'll never have to pay for it."

Paul held his gaze. Reid couldn't hit him, wouldn't reach into his mind... *but if he did...* Something deep in Paul shivered, something down in his spine underneath all the excuses and the self-control.

Still, he focused on Reid's words. "So you came to gloat?"

"I told you. I'll find everything I need about you. But, I haven't started yet, so there's nothing you can get out of me."

Like Paul really could see exact thoughts from him? The shivering spread a little further.

"And, there won't be one step out of line. Not one," and Reid's eyes dug deeper. "I wanted you to know that."

So... the detective wouldn't use his power. What did that make this, Reid's *vow*—to the man who'd shown him that power—that he'd live without it? And he'd bury Paul to prove it?

Reid turned away and started for the door.

"What happened with Sarah?" Paul called after him. "I told you, she never hit you."

"So you don't know?" And he only kept walking, bastard—

"Did you charge her or what? What happened?" Paul had to keep asking, even with all the eyes on him now.

Reid was gone.

Paul let out a breath and tried to go still again, and not think about the moment one of the crooks could say something about him and the cop, and the girl...

Nobody did speak. But the shivering dug into his back, like some restless talon sinking in deep, deeper every moment he leaned against the cold wall.

Let the worry go. Sitting quiet is what I have to do. He had enough practice hiding and blending in, so he leaned out a fraction away from the wall and tried to let the trembling fade. Or at least keep it hidden.

The room had no clock.

When the door opened again, nobody looked at him. There were only the two new guards and the quick words between them and the others, and Paul and the other prisoners got to their feet together and lined up for the guards to run a chain between their cuffs. They trudged out in a line.

They stepped out into the parking lot, and the gray transport van was right at the door. Paul only had a glimpse of the outside before they all moved up the ramp to sit on the floor. The van's metal side was colder yet on his back.

The ride might have been an hour, most of it in shifting city traffic. Not so different from the hours Paul had sat in some spot waiting for some liar to let a clue slip, holding onto his hunter's patience. Except now he had none of that safe distance from anyone dangerous, and no option to pull back and change plans.

He kept still, and tried to push the shiver back down to the base of his spine. No choice.

The van slowed, halted. Voices called out around it as guards welcomed it in. Paul heard them here and there, and his hearing could begin building a picture of where they stood, but there were far too many of them to think of escape.

The van pulled inside that circle. The back opened.

As Paul stepped out, he got a good look at the gate, the walls and the guard towers, all surrounding the concrete yard and the great bulk of the building. He and the other prisoners got the same looks, every one of them.

On the outside, he would have been searching for every crack he might slip through. In a real prison, his senses only meant he knew better than anyone that there was no way out.

Because I just had *to dig up people's secrets*. The shiver in his back worked in deeper.

They moved for the door inside. Other prisoners around the yard watched them, and Paul tuned out the mutters and shouts they tossed at the new arrivals. Instead he grabbed for glimpses of the nearer minds, and tried to let the fiercest gazes slide on over him.

Anything could make an enemy here.

The shivering was spreading up his back now. His head ached already, trying to Open so many times without even slowing his step... but, stealing those looks in the middle of everything was what he'd need to survive.

He took one look up at the sky. The clear, endless winter sky that didn't even give him a cloud to remember...

He stepped through the prison door.

They passed through a quick check-in of sharp eyes and searching hands. Paul had expected they'd be split up and processed at once, but instead the group was only led on inside.

So far, the prison corridor didn't *look* so different from some run-down office space, if he didn't study the posters and the doors. The difference was the people: the navy-blue guard uniforms and the harsh looks, or the hushed, careful way some people in civilian clothes moved. The tired stumbling as one prisoner was herded past them. The darting glances another made. The louder, scattered sounds from deeper in.

Nobody spoke to Paul's group here. The guards' presence kept everyone quiet, and he couldn't catch any eyes singling him out.

The chill in his back only grew.

One sound up ahead pushed through the building's noise. A smattering of hard footsteps, grunts and growled words—the kind of small disruption that Paul would have swung wide around, or paused to analyze. Here, their guards didn't let him slow a step.

Two guards moved a prisoner into view. A push every couple of steps, some glowering looks between them... so that tall man must have given them trouble but it was already subsiding.

Their group trudged right past the three, without a word. Paul saw the prisoner's gaze flick over the newcomers, wild as his hair and beard, the kind of uninhibited look Paul saw more often in people's thoughts than on the faces they showed the world.

His gaze flicked past Paul, then darted back to him. Then the guards led him away.

The prisoner ahead of Paul muttered "There's always one guy. The one who screws up your vacation."

Blending in means more than keeping quiet. "Yeah. One guy," Paul chuckled back.

The man ahead smiled. The guard in front glanced back, but he let it go.

A wild roar burst behind them. The group *shattered*—men all around Paul jumping out of line and diving for cover while he was whirling around, guards fighting to push through the chaos.

The prisoner charged right at him.

Paul's feet caught in the chains, and he stumbled back against the wall—*don't fall, don't drag the others down and leave me exposed*—

"It's you!" the man bellowed. "You're the Escape Kid—and I bet I make it out before you!"

Paul gasped "You got it wrong—"

"You think I didn't hear about you??" Fury split over his face, and his hands lashed out.

Paul felt the wall behind him as the man closed in, a head taller and flailing at him. Paul swung out, blocked wildly, painfully—

Guards grabbed the prisoner and dragged him down, cursing and thrashing. Paul let his own arms drop, and another guard closing in on him halted.

Paul Opened to the wild man's thoughts. Under the mass of struggling bodies and the rat's nest of hair, those eyes stayed fixed on Paul, feverishly bright.

What did that mean? Obsession, hate, some kind of scheme? Paul pulled back a step from those eyes.

" 'Escape Kid'?" grunted the guard beside him.

Paul shrugged, tried to let his confusion show on his face. Better that than trying to look innocent, in here.

It only took them another half a minute to slam the prisoner down and get a grip that took the fight out of him. Paul and his group were already being herded away.

With all of their eyes on Paul.

Even with everything I did to keep under the radar... And those crazy eyes had been so *sure*. How could he have heard what Paul could do—had done, back in a normal and unguarded world? What did he want?

Just one moment of someone opening his mouth was too much attention. Before Paul had even seen his cell.

CHAPTER TWO

BARS

The visitor room didn't make people talk on telephones, or even keep glass partitions between them like they did on TV. Instead, Paul found himself at one of a number of small tables scattered around a room wide enough to give each some privacy in the middle of the chatter.

Something rancid lurked in one of the crevices of the room, where the stink soaked all through the space. Paul fought the useless urge to Open and track down the stench's source.

CC didn't seem to notice it at all. She only leaned across the table, with the same unruffled, understated polish that had to scream *lawyer* to everyone here. Her voice was low and firm.

"Since yesterday, they've found a few new charges for you. The first is Burglary at the house of a researcher for... 'Vitamintastic.' " She gave him a quick smile for the name, but at the next moment it faded. "This could be serious, if a jury hears you broke into someone's actual home. But nothing was taken, and their evidence is minimal that it even happened."

"Sounds like Reid is grasping at straws." Even though that house had been the only way to copy the test results they'd been covering up.

An angry shout came from two tables over. Paul's head twisted toward them, but the woman visitor there had already slapped her hand over her mouth, and the guards let it pass.

CC leaned closer, and pushed back a few strands of her styled hair that had fallen into her eyes. "The next is Coercion, when a certain bank teller testified against his boss. If that's anything but them 'grasping at straws' trying to connect you to it."

"It's not. I—no, not a chance."

He saw her eyes twitch when he hesitated, and her gaze sank to the table. One more hint, of how much he was keeping from her. She had no idea how much, but he couldn't lose her help now.

"The last charge is one more count of Criminal Trespassing at LifeLab. You've said everything you did there was to *restore* their reputation. I could sound out Mr. Brandt again about dropping those charges, or clarifying that there was nothing 'criminal' about the reasons behind your... work there."

"You could sound him out, sure. It's not like I haven't thought about some of these. But one thing: don't make him any promises about *how* someone might have beaten his security. Those need to stay my secret. I've already got rumors around here that I'm about to escape."

Her eyes clenched shut. *"Please* don't. Please don't tell me you're even thinking of—"

"Of course not. I'd never try to beat security like this. It's just that... after what I *have* done, there can't be any deals about my methods. With Brandt or anyone."

"Of course, if that's how you want it. But, that's one more thing you're holding back from me. Believe me, when a client doesn't..."

She wound to a stop. Her face sagged as she did, as if all her confidence had flickered away.

I shouldn't. But it's my freedom in the balance. He Opened.

In her thoughts, Celia Claire's head hung limply, low enough that he could just catch the glimmer of what looked like tears. So she was more tired than she looked, or actually ready to cry, or else he was seeing only some old regrets in the back of her mind...

He pulled out of the moment. Had it been an instant, or longer? Maybe let her take a rest?

He settled for a change of subject. "Say, is there any news about Sarah?" This time he dropped to a whisper. "She never knew what I did to get the stories she reported. She was the one who hit Reid when I escaped, but that was to help me—so I keep saying I did it. You know if they're still going after her?"

"I'll keep an ear out." CC's voice was the same steady tone it had been a minute ago, as if she'd never hesitated at all. "Your trying to cover for her is chivalrous, I admit. But you need to consider how that might backfire, against her and you. And…"

Her chair creaked softly, and she leaned closer, bringing her eyes and the worried lines around them nearer.

"Paul. Mr. Schuman. You want me to help you, but you keep leaving me in the dark and waiting to see how much more the police will get on you. Don't you think I should know what we might be dealing with *before* it comes out, all of it? I'm representing you—every word you say to me is in total confidence. Or were you thinking that I'd tell your father because he's paying the bill?"

Hard practice kept Paul from blinking, from flinching away from that question in spite of the tightening in his chest. Bad enough his family knew anything about his power—CC had no *idea* what she was asking. Or how every dirty dealer and power broker in town would want their hooks in him if they guessed what he could do…

One more person who knew was too risky.

"Sorry," he sighed.

For a moment the table was silent. In that stillness, a nursery song wafted in from down the room, someone trying to sing to his child.

"I was afraid of that," CC said. "It doesn't change the fact that I need to know your case better to represent you properly. And that does mean my next step will be to ask your father and brother what they know, for your sake."

Why does she keep bringing them up? The pressure in his chest tightened, but he kept it out of his voice to say "Go ahead."

Dad and Greg understood just some of what his power was. They knew what word getting out would mean, or they should.

He met her gaze and tried again. "Look. There are two years of my life that nobody knows about. Reid thinks what they're charging me with now is just a fraction of how I might have spent that time. What I can tell you is, he's not wrong."

CC only nodded. "Two years. What kind of 'fraction' is it that they don't know yet?"

Forty-eight cases. "Let's say it's more than they'll ever find. Even with Reid investigating, and he knows that. He's going to keep pushing, but..."

He stopped, took a breath.

"Everything I did, it was trying to bring out the truth. I don't steal. You can see that—I've been exposing liars and frauds, every time. And that should make a difference. You watch for any evidence they get. They might prove some of *what* I did, but there'll never be any proof that I did it *for* a crime. Because I didn't."

She nodded again, more slowly. "Possible. If the prosecution has to strike the 'criminal' from Criminal Trespass and Burglary again and again, that could put us in a better position to make a deal for the rest. I'll try to see how much leverage the whistleblower defense gives us."

"Thanks. It should make a difference. If they'd just stop charging me with thefts and things I didn't do..."

Then I'd accept the rest, and take my punishment? Is that why I really turned myself in? Maybe, if it meant anything besides staying in this place.

He must have kept his thoughts off his face, because CC only said "I'll talk with St. Cedric's, and LifeLab, first. They're the most recent offenses, and they never did show a reason that you'd robbed or harmed them." She started to stand, but halted and leaned in again. "But you should know, Mr. Brandt at LifeLab will want to know what else you might have seen or done there. And that hits the same wall as before: how you got through his security."

Of course it does.

* * *

On the way back, Paul kept his senses working. The thoughts of the guard beside him looked careful but bored, already convinced he was no trouble. But that left all the other guards and prisoners to watch.

A face leaning against bars. A guard and some stranger in a suit, that glanced at him. Whispers, talk, here and there and over there about a hundred subjects, every time he passed near enough or Opened to hear more.

None of those glances or conversations lingered on him. But his powers couldn't make him more than one man trying to catch what he could of *everyone* who might want a piece of the new kid. He had a whole set of alarms and no idea how to stop anyone who set them off.

His head throbbed with the strain of snatching moments of Opening between his slow steps. All he could do was keep going.

How long would the quiet last if they knew what he did? If CC attracted too much attention with her questions, or his family decided they had to tell her to keep her on the case? His chances of getting out only got worse without her.

Keep going. He had to hold on, hold it in, hide it all... He'd known it would be something this, from the moment he'd walked into the police station, thinking of Sarah and some notion of proving he was no thief.

And I don't even know if Sarah's locked up too.

"That really who Eckles grabbed?"

The voice behind him was deep, not quite a whisper. That had to be the tiny man in the cell he'd passed.

Paul Opened and caught a lower voice farther back: "Yeah, Schuman. Nobody making a break there."

Paul's feet stumbled, broke his focus—he should be better at Opening in mid-step by now. He started walking and listened again, but he heard nothing else from them. Not even a laugh for him almost falling.

"Eckles"? Was that the wild-eyed prisoner who'd "grabbed" at him?

Then he reached his cell. The same tight, steel-trimmed *sameness* that had been pressing into him since yesterday…

When they opened the door, Mickey jumped up, the same twitchy look on his cellmate's face as ever. He jumped again when the door clanged behind them, and flinched away as if Paul just being bigger was the same as growling threats.

Paul tried a quick "Hey," but the skinny, pinch-faced man was already pacing the cell and avoiding his gaze.

Whatever that was about… Paul settled for climbing up to his bunk and trying to lie still.

The thin mattress under him was less hard than many places he'd had to lie down. The smell of sweat and dust in it was worse, but that was nothing compared to the truth that he *had no way* to get away from it…

But, no more thoughts about that, or about what he might have to accept to get out some day. Instead he Opened to the farther sounds.

There they were. The rush of cars on the highway, large and small, droning into his range and passing beyond it again. The sweet voices that still proved there was a *world* bigger than these few cramped steps. But they were so faint, beyond the walls, beyond the yard, and his head already hurt to reach out to them.

He shifted on the bunk. The loose support under him rattled, that small sound that never went away.

The pain tightened around his skull. Listening outside took too much out of him, and he settled for taking in the prison's own sounds.

Grumbles. Jokes. Whispers. Footsteps that pooled in what must be one cell, or cut a line between rows. The clash of gates, and the rumble of the laundry room. The place had its own rhythm, and learning that *had* to be a help in spotting trouble.

Still, he strained to catch more of the sounds outside, until the pounding in his head grew and he had to pull in closer. Out, in.

Feet were strolling past his cell. Mickey's pacing drifted toward the door. Paul took a glance down toward them, at the corner of his eye.

A prisoner shuffled past the cell. The guard beside him looked away, and the man in orange held his hand near the bars he passed, near Mickey. Hidden within his fingers...

Metal.

Only for a moment, and then Mickey gave a quick motion that waved him off. The man outside moved on, keeping the weapon he'd been ready to pass to Mickey. If that was what it was.

Paul snapped his eyes shut before Mickey turned. He could hear him pacing, then settling on the other bunk... just below.

His cellmate hadn't taken the blade, if there had been one. But the quiet, nervous little man was *considering* one? Paul felt cold spreading all through him, tried not to think how long a knife would have to be to stab up through the mattress—

No. And he'd looked at Mickey's thoughts, again and again, and never gotten a glimpse that his cellmate was anything beyond scared. *I just need to be more careful.*

Paul lay still. One muscle at a time, he tried to will the tension away. He reached for the faint, free sounds of the highway again, and his headache only sank in deeper.

He stretched his head out, trying to loosen the pain. Even that motion made the loose support under him clank, one tiny sound.

Under him, Mickey started at the noise. Nothing more.

Next time it might be different. Or the time after that.

One muscle at a time...

* * *

"Are you alright?" his father asked.

Ian Schuman managed to make his low voice sound clear and natural for whispering at the visiting tables. Like it wasn't simply the shallow breath of recovering from a gunshot, like his refined features weren't showing some of the same sunken look Paul knew the street had put on his own face.

And Greg, the healthier, clean-shaven version of their father, only sat beside him as if it meant nothing to bring a wounded man *here*.

Paul felt his throat going tight. There had to be *some* words that captured a bit of how it felt here... if he could even say them in a room filled with prisoners and other strangers all chattering and muttering and watching for their own advantage.

"Mostly, it's worry, about what just might happen. And waiting, with always more waiting after that."

Greg said "CC's been asking us what you haven't been telling her. I'm guessing that means—" He tapped his ear, for what had to mean Paul's senses.

"We'll leave that to you, of course," their father added. "But Celia is the best in cases like this. She has a long history of taking low-profile problems that are deeply tangled, and making them go away. She'll protest, persuade, until she spots a real chance to negotiate. We'll have you out soon enough."

Except you weren't there this morning, when she hesitated with me. You can't see those tears on her inner face—why are Dad and Greg always so sure they're right?

He pushed that thought down, and swallowed to loosen his throat. They *had* to be right.

"Thank you," he said instead. "Thank you for getting her for me. For sticking with me after I ran off. For..."

The words faded as he eyed their faces, both of them glancing awkwardly away to hear talk like that in the family. The clamor of the visitor room raged on around them.

His father had been shot. And had to shoot Quinn.

"I can never say it enough. Thank—"

"I think you just did say it," his father cut in. "What else could we do?"

Paul managed a smile. None of this was easy, between them.

"On other fronts, Greg's getting business up again. I'm starting to think our clients don't know I'm housebound."

"Not that it's that different," Greg grinned.

Not different? That couldn't be true. Even a PR firm like Schuman and Son couldn't spin having their founder shot and then one of his sons arrested. Just how much were these two hiding, trying to deny how much more Paul had cost them?

Paul opened his mouth to apologize ahead, but the pain and frustration closed up his throat and left him silent. Greg and their father had nothing to fill the stillness either.

Finally, Greg said "Here's something new. It turns out all the charges against Sarah Gomez were dropped."

Paul blew out a breath of relief. One out of too many tensions actually separated from the rest and smoothed away.

Greg went on "They never had much on her anyway. I hear her lawyer got it all thrown out without even a word about you. Wish we could have afforded that guy—or that anyone could, for a problem that takes more than a day to fix. Anyway, she's clear."

"Thanks. Reid just left me wondering, when I asked him right to his face. Well, that's *something* good."

Paul stopped there. He could tell them how Sarah really had only a few contacts with him, until he'd gotten careless and she'd pushed her way into his life. How Lorraine, the woman they'd once known only as Greg's wife, had tried to bend Sarah's emotions to keep her at a safe distance from their fight. And Sarah still chose to put herself on the line, the same as when his father took that bullet.

And these two wonder why I wanted to disappear on them.

He felt the stillness stretching, the pocket of quiet in the shifting noise of the room. He should be able to tease out one thread from the tangle in his head that he could let them know. This was his one moment away from enemies and prisoners, to let his defenses down for once. But he still couldn't say a thing.

* * *

Sarah had her life back. Paul tried to hold on to that comfort, hidden under the same closed-off face he wore as he walked, keeping his senses out for which eyes to avoid.

If it hadn't been winter, they might have been out in the yard. Instead, Paul shuffled into an exercise room filled with scattered weights, two weight machines, and too many prisoners.

Paul edged around, past two men both striding for one barbell, watching for the guards, seeing how the inmates settled into their groups and patterns.

Far too many to watch. He'd glimpsed only a few of their minds, and *any* of them might pick a fight with him.

He moved around to the wall, just clear of the largest crowd that was passing free weights around. Not too obviously close to the guards, good.

With his spot picked out, he dropped down and began what many other isolated inmates were doing: sets of pushups, slowly and steadily as if he meant to stay there all hour. His arms ached and burned—his regular exercises were chosen for energy and flexibility, for endless walks and crawling through windows, not strength.

If his arms' strength gave out, how many of them would see him collapse? *Up, down… this is what I let myself in for… up… I cleared Sarah… down… I exposed liars, forty-eight times… up…*

Sweat beaded and fell in his eyes, as he stole glances around the room. He saw faces looking toward him, then away again, good. He pushed on and tried to hold the rhythm.

Another face turned to watch him, longer this time. Then another.

No good. Staying on the fringe itself was drawing attention.

Paul stood up and moved to the outer ring of the freeweight crowd. One orange-clad back shifted a step to close the gap and shut him out. Then two spots down, a pair of men eyed him and separated to make room.

Keeping thinking how Mickey refused that knife, not about how there are *knives somewhere.* Paul stepped into place and watched the little dumbbells being passed around the circle toward him. Nobody here knew him, nobody had a reason to start something. The guards were right over there.

The door at the far end opened. The wild man Eckles strode in.

He moved straight to two men with a barbell, and one skittered away to let him have it. When Eckles laid down under the weight, his head turned.

He looked right at Paul, before he hoisted the mass of iron up.

A *whoof* of breath sounded at Paul's elbow. The man beside him had finished his five reps with the dumbbell, a little thing half swallowed up by his hand. All Paul could do was take the weight and try to wrench his exhausted arm to curl upward, once, again, and more. Somehow he passed it on without letting it drop.

Another weight was circling up next. Paul worked his aching fingers, tried not to notice if more eyes settled on him. Eckles was still pumping his own weight, and eyeing Paul.

I put myself *here to help Sarah. To prove I'm not a thief.*

I'm a fool.

Across the room, Eckles marched straight toward him. His eyes looked more savage than ever, and his height and lean, iron muscle brought back all the times Paul had been in a fight and all the times he'd lost. He walked like he would have broken Paul or even Greg in half.

The crowd around Paul gave way—and fanned out behind him, hemming him in. The guards only stayed in their places at the walls, as if this was nothing. He edged a step to the side, and he heard a soft laugh from one of the men that blocked him.

No running, then. He turned to face Eckles.

The man walked right up and leaned down. Paul caught the sour smell on his breath.

"How you getting out?" he hissed. "One of the trucks? Over the wall?"

Don't move, don't flinch. "I'm not. I don't know what you heard." Paul kept his own voice low, and steady. "I'm leaving that to my lawyer."

Something swept over Eckles's craggy face, a tremor that shook his matted beard. "Think you can keep your plan all for yourself? I'll rip your head off."

"I'm Not. Trying. To Escape," Paul said. "I'm here because I turned myself in. Think, why would I—"

"Bullshit!" The roar climbed toward a shriek, no thought to keeping it between them now. "He said you beat the cops, here and everywhere. Everything they threw at you!"

He said?

Eckles's breathing heaved, ready to shout again or worse. Paul held his answer down to a private whisper within that storm: "He said? Someone told you about me?"

Eckles broke off. Was that embarrassment creasing his face?

Paul locked his own face still, and Opened to the convict's mind.

The shaggy head twitched—jerking one way and another, but only the smallest motions, and his eyes darted around with the freedom he didn't give to his head. Wanting to search around, not daring to.

Paul shifted to eye the man's real face again, inches from his. The harsh breathing struck at his skin.

Eckles turned away.

With one harsh grunt he spun and stomped away, without a glance at Paul or at the inmates he pushed past. A wash of cold swept through Paul and left his knees weak—only the sheer habit of hiding his reactions kept him on his feet.

Voices chattered around him, some of them almost like low, hesitant cheering. Paul kept focused on Eckles walking back to where he'd been. Was that just about rumors and paranoia, or something more? Eckles headed back to his friend with the barbell—

"What was that? What'd he want?" A broad man as squat as a boulder stepped in front of Paul. Almost tall enough to cut off his view.

"Just what you heard. Some talk about me and escapes. Rumors," and Paul tried to give the word just enough contempt to keep it casual.

Over the inmate's head, Eckles was just reaching his friend. Paul reached for their voices.

"He's nothing," Eckles sneered. "I bet I get out first." A rush of breath and a metallic clank said he'd hoisted those weights into the air.

"Sucker bet. How would you collect if you won?" His friend's higher voice sounded like he barely gave it a thought.

"Hey!"

A shove and a word sent Paul stumbling back, out of the trance. The stocky inmate closed in on him.

"Eyes on me! 'Rumors,' hell—I know that talk had to start somewhere. And if Eckles says you got something he wants, you deliver. You got me?" He shoved again.

Paul backpedaled and caught his balance. He glared down at the other man.

At that fierce smile that began to grow—

Paul kept his hands from curling into fists. His eyes locked on his attacker, his feet somehow kept from edging back. Voices around them dropped and settled into the same hushed, eager awareness. The guards *had* to be watching by now...

The shorter man sneered and turned away. Disappointment rippled around the crowd.

The group settled back into passing the dumbbells around, many of them rushing through their five reps with an extra competitive drive. Paul edged back into the fringe of the group.

When he could risk it, he watched Eckles again. The man's thoughts had glanced around for someone else when Paul had asked who told him, he *must* have. Someone besides his friend at the barbell—now those two did nothing but pump the weight.

Someone else was out there, someone with an eye on Paul and his history. Someone.

* * *

He lay in his bunk, searching for sounds. Eckles's cell couldn't be too far away since they exercised at the same time, but Paul couldn't seem to hear his voice, or any mention of his name. Or his own.

Mickey was pacing below again. Paul searched one cell after another, and the strain left his skull feeling drained and helpless as the headache grew.

Then a guard bellowed as his door. "Schuman! Phone call."

Paul stumbled out and down the corridor with him. His head hurt too much to try matching the cells he passed to the locations he'd listened to. A call… was it CC or his family, or someone else?

Where the visitors' room had tried to be large enough to give everyone some space, the phone room was a cramped row of chairs, and phones on the wall. Sounds spilled into Paul's ears—*"but you can't"* and *"so then I"*—as he moved toward his call.

The voice was Detective Reid: "So you're finally where you belong."

Paul's fingers clenched on the receiver. What was this, more of Reid's gloating about how well he resisted his own power?

Did he tell Eckles to watch for me? No, Reid wanted him locked up, not bullied. Or escaping.

Reid went on "We don't have laws for what you really did. But we've got enough. And don't you start thinking Sarah getting out means you'll have it as easy. You've been digging the pit you're in for years. Besides, I still know she's the one who hit me."

"You don't need her," Paul snapped. "You put me in here. That's what you wanted, right?"

Reid sighed. "I trusted her. She tried to keep me honest, about how dangerous having this... thing... is. She saw what you and Lorraine were, and she looked you in the eye and called you on your bullshit. And then you got to her anyway. Well, I'm *not* forgetting who I am!"

There it was again, Reid trying so hard—and so loudly—to brand their power as just a temptation. And Sarah's change of heart made her look like the worst kind of traitor.

Wait, I can give him something else to chase.

"Leave Sarah out of this. Listen, right now, there's a real—"

The voices around him... Paul stopped before he mentioned Eckles. How many words overheard would it take for prisoners nearby to guess he was passing a tip to a cop? That would do a lot worse than get him noticed.

To cover up what he'd already said, he finished with "—a real screwup. Can you just... listen to me, really listen at a hundred percent, for once?"

Yes, Reid *had* to understand that hint. Then, too softly for anything but Opened hearing to follow, he breathed into the phone:

"There's a dangerous prisoner here. Not just a danger to me: Eckles is fixated on escaping. So think about who else gets hurt if he gets out, or someone gets in his way. You're trying to be a real cop? Stop him."

Do I tell him there's someone who sicced Eckles on me? No, Reid mustn't make this about me.

In a normal voice, he finished "Are you listening to me?"

Reid gave a single laugh. "I didn't hear a word."

The receiver suddenly felt cold, fragile, like some toy Paul could crush between his fingers.

The detective went on "I'm not that easy. You think you can get me to use that cheat again, just by talking to you? I *know* you. Every time I'm tempted, I just remember what you did with this thing. And all your excuses."

Paul's breathing thundered in his ears, drowning out the voices around him—but not Reid's pitiless words.

Through his teeth, he managed to answer "You won't even listen? I'm *telling* you, it's *dangerous*. You can read it yourself if you look. Or see it with your own eyes. Just *listen* to me."

"No more tricks, Schuman. My job is making you and Sarah and Lorraine pay for crimes you've committed, real crimes. Not backsliding with you, or letting you distract me. That means all I have to do is…"

He hung up.

CHAPTER THREE

SCRATCH THE SURFACE

"You got another call." The guard's wrinkled face creased deeper as he looked at Paul. "You're new. Enjoy it while they keep coming."

Paul moved to the door, with Mickey edging back and giving him more of his nervous looks. The guard shouted for the door, and the guard up the corridor pushed the button to clang it open.

Stretching your legs, they call it. Every chance to move that wasn't circling the same crowded space was worth savoring. He tried to focus on that, not on the guard's promise that the calls would dry up soon.

Somehow the phone room was almost cleared out this time. The chairs on either side of his were both empty, and he found himself stretching in the plastic seat to fill a little of the space. "Hello?"

"Afternoon," came his father's voice. "I've got some news you'll be glad to hear."

"I could use some. But hearing your voice is a good start." Especially hearing it on the phone—his father shouldn't be pushing himself to make more visits in person.

"You think I'd let some time in the hospital stop me?" The words echoed Paul's thought, the one he hadn't said aloud. His father went on "Taking it slower is one thing, but there's no need to be stupid. It only means I spend more time running things without, let's say, *running* around."

For a moment, the sense of being on the same page, coming from the same place as them, shifted inside Paul. A sense from long before the years he'd kept away from his family.

"I should've expected that," he said.

"The news is: you'll be getting a visit from CC and then that prosecutor tomorrow. First you listen to her about what new charges they've dug up—it doesn't sound like they've got much. You work with her, and you come up with a plan for what to challenge and how you'll adjust your plea when the ADA joins you. That's what you wanted, right?"

"That's right."

Paul let the words settle into his mind, to push back the low voices and echoes of the prison rhythms that hung all around him. If the lawyers were ready, if it was *time*...

He let himself ask "You think there's a chance, to... change things, for real?"

"Not just 'a' chance. We'll fight them there, and then we'll fight them after that, and we'll keep fighting until you're out."

"Thanks." The word welled up in a sigh, longer and more awkward than he meant to make it.

"We have to." His father paused, and Paul could almost see him shaking his head. "I'm still not sure how I let it happen."

That damn loan shark Quinn. Even when he's dead... Paul swallowed, and kept his tone soft. "Quinn? Look, I'm sure when you started dealing with him again, you didn't have a choice." *And sooner or later I would have stumbled into it, and the man was just too dangerous.*

"No, not that. I'm thinking of how you ran off, and not after we had to face down Quinn, but two years ago... I should have stopped you, and instead I didn't know until you were gone."

Stopped me? You think it was your *choice?*

The phone quivered in Paul's hand. Fingers, jaw, chest, even his feet against the floor locked up, quivering. He willed the muscles to loosen, but this time they wouldn't obey.

"Now, some other news," his father added. "Detective Reid came by to warn us against raising any support for your case. He kept riding his one point: how easily rumors could leak out that the PR wins we've had might have come from you sneaking around. The prick insists it's not a threat about anything *he'd* start, only that what you've done has its own 'consequences' for everyone around you."

"Sounds like Reid," and Paul kept his voice even in spite of his clenched teeth. Sure, Reid would know every last bit of harm Paul's work could have done to them, and the cop would rub their noses in it.

"Not that it'll stop us," his father added.

Paul's teeth gritted tighter. Reid was a spider now, sitting in his web of rules and consequences and feeling every time someone triggered one. The Schumans were just more people trapped in that, so merely hearing the damage from his father's voice shouldn't drive the sting any deeper. Except, it did.

*　*　*

When the lights went out, Paul lay on the bunk and tried to clear his mind for tomorrow.

Distractions.

His father and brother, and whatever they said that didn't fit him right—those were like clothes he'd picked up that pinched or flapped around him, they didn't have to matter. And Reid's reminding him about the law, when Paul should be focusing on what the law actually said. Even Eckles—the best way to deal with him was to get out.

The prison. North Penitentiary... Paul could feel it around him in the dimness, whether he Opened or not. The scattered clangs and echoing voices, sounds that had no rhythm and struggled against falling into one. The smells of sweat and metal and the mix of other scents and cleaning fluids, that he already knew too well. He shifted on the bunk, and a finger reached down to brush the loose support.

Even that soft clatter made Mickey toss in his bunk below.

All distractions. Paul pushed them away.

The truth. The charges that held him here.

The police could only see one layer of what he'd done. Those times he'd crept inside a property to get the goods on some cheat, when looking and listening at a distance weren't enough. There were no laws against Opening.

There was Reid trying to retrace Paul's steps for something he could point the lawyers to. More blocks to build that case, *to build the walls around me and bury me here...*

A shiver wracked through him, from his toes to his finger on the stupid loose support.

He let it pass through him. *Hold on to the truth.*

The truth would be whatever visible evidence they had against him, from some few of the cases when he'd broken in somewhere. The more places they saw him sneak into out *there,* the longer they'd try to trap him *here.*

But the more cases they looked into, the more they'd see the other truth under them all. Again and again, he'd acted to expose fraud and corruption—his "crimes" were never tools to commit real crimes. *I don't steal.*

Even on the cold prison bed, that fact brought a warmth through him. He'd show them that: no matter what doors they might have seen him creep through, he'd done nothing more, and it was always to expose something worse.

The hospital... St. Central, St. Cedric's, had run up impossible bills on dozens of patients before Lorraine's mentor Curtis. His father and Greg had even wanted to let them cover it up—another chill swept through him, but he held on to his reasons. His own message to the media had put an end to that lie.

That was the start of my work, even though it was months before I could handle my power well enough to go back there again. And then he'd searched for whether the power itself had come from there, before he went on to search for other people's secrets.

The support rattled under his finger again.

Would they charge him about the health inspector who'd taken bribes? Or the drunken doctor... Paul had only gone into his files when no other clue appeared, and Reid would still want him locked up for that.

Mickey twisted and rolled down in his bunk. The prison pressed in again, but Paul pushed it from his mind.

The city planner and all his cousins on the payroll? That would be the most explosive case, but they'd never find Paul using bugs or breaking in or anything. Unless they stared at the question mark about his methods for so long they tried to prove he *must* have crossed some other line.

And if CC wants to point everything back to "But how could he have done it?" I may have to tell her why she can't open that door. About the power.

For one moment the clangs of the prison broke through his thoughts again. He couldn't risk her knowing.

But CC... As long as he could work with her, they'd show what he'd done *was* no crime, or it was so small that they'd bargain his time here down. Reid was wrong, about Paul and about their power. He could hear some of a liar's secrets as easily as turning his head—how could that power *not* be used for the truth?

He lay in the dark, sorting through his cases one by one for what Reid might have found. Now and then he looked up at the dim walls, or listened to the prison's echoes, but he could endure some of that. The free roar of cars was only a thought away, and so were all the whispers and mutterings around the prison itself. Once he heard a joke so dirty he had to shove his hand over his mouth to hold the laughter in.

I'll survive this, because I can. And I'll prove what I am is no crime.

His hand rattled the support again. Reid wouldn't care. He'd say knowing anything more, leaning across any of the lines people lived in, was the same as ripping the whole town apart... Paul shook his head.

The support rattled again, again, until he forced his fingers away.

* * *

Having real negotiations with lawyers got Paul out of the open visiting space and into a private room. Only a small, featureless spot with a metal table and chairs, too much like the interrogation rooms he'd seen too much of before. Still, he sensed nobody watching them, and it did have some space for him and CC, and the others that would be joining them.

When CC entered, he wrapped himself in all the confidence he'd gathered last night, and greeted her with a smile. "Thank you again, for all of this."

CC laid her laptop on the table and sank into the chair beside him, with a clumsy thump that made him wonder if she'd missed more sleep than he had.

Her voice was brisk enough, though. "Of course. Let's get started."

She slid the machine around to show him the file she had up.

"The prosecution is required to share all its evidence with us, and this is their latest. They're making another charge of Criminal Tres-passing, and you can see here how a witness reported seeing you here on the premises for the Health Inspector here..."

Those bribes I spotted. I knew they'd look into that one, it was an-other story I passed to Sarah. "Can't we keep building on what we agreed last time: is it 'Criminal' Trespassing if it wasn't done to commit a crime, besides my just being back there? And that's if they think this glimpse of me is enough to make a case," he added, but he didn't deny it.

"Perceptive, and we'll keep arguing that." CC reached for the keyboard, but then she sighed. "We need to be prepared, though. Detective Reid will still be looking into every aspect of the case for something to use against you."

"I noticed. He can look all he wants."

CC brought up a different file. "And here, they're pushing this case of you breaking up a charity fraud. There's another witness account of you there, and if you look here they seem to be about to claim electronic eavesdropping…"

"They can't find bugs that never existed."

He glanced at her, and CC's eyes were closed. He'd been wrong, she didn't have the sagging look of someone tired. More… reluctant.

He turned toward her. "Are you sure you can argue this?"

Her eyes opened, bright and alert again. "Is there a reason you're asking me that?"

"I know you took the case. But, can you really tell me that you think it's worth arguing? Or are you already writing it off?"

"Paul. At this stage, we're trying to expose the limits of their case, and looking for ways to bargain them down. So, you tell me—"

Her eyes locked straight onto his and pinned him in place.

"What would you accept here? If we could bring this down to fines, and years of supervised release and sentences served outside of prison itself? Would you settle for that?"

"Yes!"

For one moment he let himself believe that it was that easy, that the door out was only waiting for him to meet their terms. Even with him sitting unmoving, he could feel the word he'd said still swelling his chest.

CC shook her head. "I wish I could promise you that. We can make the argument, but I've seen… I've seen cases pushed to juries that decided them almost at random. I've seen a well-reasoned plea go to a judge who found every excuse to maximize the sentence. It could all rest on the judge here."

She swallowed.

"Paul, you have so *many* charges against you. Have you done the math about how much of your future depends on the difference between serving *concurrent sentences* where the times would be allowed to overlap, versus *consecutive sentences* that mean all of them add up to years and years of your life? That's just one decision in the process, that could ruin someone."

She halted, and the last sounds rang and faded off the hard walls and metal furniture of the little room.

Paul didn't move, didn't stir. He could only say "Look, it's a risk I can take. The thing I need to know is, are you wishing you could get out of this?"

CC's lip quirked in a tiny smile. "I took the case. And... I believe anything you've done was out of a desire to help. As you said, it's never been 'criminal' trespassing."

"Thank you." He grinned back, and felt knots in his muscles begin to loosen again. He added "I don't have a lot of allies. Who understand me, I mean. Dad and Greg are behind me, but they don't get it the same way.

"Not like Sarah Gomez?" CC nodded. "Or your sister-in-law Lorraine, from what they say about her own disappearance. It seems more that you do have allies, and you keep being cut off from them."

"That's fair." Even Reid would count—he only cut himself off when he turned against his own power.

"Then as your ally, here's a piece of advice." She leaned an inch toward him, and her voice grew softer. "We'll be trying to convince them that every action they find about you has the same pattern: limited offenses and always for a good cause. The risk will be how many more they keep dredging up, and the chance that one does give them a way to taint you in the eyes of the judge, or a jury."

"More of those random risks you mentioned."

"Exactly. So what I'd like to know is, would you be open to confessing to one or two more crimes that they haven't found yet, in exchange for them closing their investigation?"

"*More* crimes?" The idea had occurred to him, but...

"Not a tactic I like, usually. This will more likely be a straightforward push of ADA Oliver trying to make the most of everything he has, and us holding out about how little that would really look like to a jury, until we're able to make a deal about what's left. But, I wanted to clear this tactic with you in case he's holding out for more time. And only if I think it's just the right act of good faith that Oliver needs."

"Confessing to a case they don't have..."

Definitely a gamble. And yet, it felt oddly good to be gambling based on someone else's insight instead of his own.

And it wouldn't be all CC's choice anyway. I've got my own way to read the prosecutor. "If you think it's right, let me know and I'll consider it."

"Then we're ready. Please, use the rest of our time waiting to come up with any questions to ask me. Or relax—this will really just be you listening to the two of us go through it."

And CC looked over at her phone.

Waiting. Paul had too much practice with that lately, and he realized he hadn't asked how much longer they had before it began.

He swallowed the urge to ask. Better to stay in the moment, and not worry about the clock.

No distractions, remember the truth. He'd done only small "crimes," and never for crime's sake—no matter what Reid would insist. CC would use that. They could do this.

The door opened.

Instead of the prosecutor, Greg walked in.

"Is there a problem, Greg?" CC asked. "You didn't say you were coming."

Greg grinned back, his own hint of bad-boy-turned-good that he could flash around. "We're paying your fees—but really, I wanted to support my brother. Unless that *would* be a problem?"

Paul looked up at him. They'd wanted to limit the distractions... but Greg was too smart and committed for them to turn down. Unless he tried to take charge.

CC didn't lose a moment. "There's no time to brief you. Can you trust me to understand what's important here, and let me do this? I mean, stay quiet."

"Understood," Greg said. "Not a word."

"Good to have you," Paul added, as Greg moved a chair around the table and squeezed his muscular frame in at the corner beside him.

Just the presence of his big brother there... it brought an anchoring strength, even though he felt some of their control of the moment seeping away.

Was his father staying home? Paul opened his mouth to ask.

The door opened again.

Assistant DA Richard Oliver strode in, trim and elegant as ever. He took in the three of them with a glance, but his nod went straight to the lawyer. "CC. I didn't get to tell you in court, but it's good to see you back."

Back? And that bit of harshness in his voice, the narrowing look in his eye—Oliver was hinting she wasn't ready for a case.

CC only nodded in return. "Where else would I be? This is Mr. Schuman's brother Greg."

"Of course." He studied Greg a moment, just long enough to make them wonder how he'd use him. Greg didn't answer.

Oliver settled into the last chair, ignoring the Schumans to put himself directly opposite CC. On the table he laid a folder, not the bulging one he'd used in court but a slender one that might hold only a page or three.

CC asked "Do we wait for Reid?"

"The detective is more interested in knocking on doors, and then more doors," Oliver said. "I doubt he'll be joining us."

"Good," Greg muttered. The sound made Paul wince, when his brother had agreed to keep his mouth shut.

"Alright then." CC laid her palms on the table. "Impress us."

Oliver drew out a pen, and tapped it softly on the metal table. "Assaulting Detective Reid, and resisting arrest. Twice."

Paul heard the softest grunt from Greg at his elbow. Of what sounded like approval.

CC's eyes narrowed. "I thought you weren't charging him for those. One charge isn't even in this state."

"Does it matter? There are a dozen ways to get it in the record, so the jury sees what a danger your client is. He's already fled clear across the country."

"And then turned himself in."

Oliver sniffed, softly dismissing that. "To *claim* he attacked Detective Reid, when Sarah Gomez was facing that. And charges against her have already been dismissed, putting the focus back on Mr. Schuman. He can hardly have it both ways."

Paul's jaw twitched, wanting to answer that...

Instead he held still, and Opened to Oliver's thoughts.

The image that formed was the lawyer leaning back, brow furrowed and eyes darting back and forth between CC and the file with him. Guarded, careful—and even in his mind the file was still closed.

"Don't waste our time." CC had a small, knowing smile on her face. "I know you're not charging him with those."

"If we do, you'll find out soon enough."

Oliver had to be frustrated there. Keeping those off the list was Reid's one apology for how he'd felt his own power overwhelm him. *He almost broke my head too.*

The folder swung open. Oliver's motion made the few pages rustle and whisper across the cramped room.

"LifeLab. Burglary in the First—one to twenty years."

Greg gave a small, choked gasp.

"Not in commission of a crime," CC said. "Trespassing Two might get six months, if you could convince anyone that Mr. Schuman was there at all."

Oliver swung the first page of the file over. "St. Cedric's Hospital. Criminal Trespassing, four counts. That's four years just in themselves."

"Not 'criminal' trespassing, and not in the first degree."

Oliver's pen resumed its tapping against the table's metal. The rhythm clashed with the brisk slap of the page he turned. Paul gritted his teeth, telling himself he'd already worked out all the sentences' figures anyway.

"Addamson Abbot, Criminal Trespassing brings it to a minimum of five years, and Stalking Two to six."

The page turned, and the pen clattered on.

"Criminal Trespassing, to seven years.

"Criminal Impersonation to eight.

"Burglary… be grateful the Vitamintastic office was empty at the time, so it only brings it up to thirteen.

"Then going around a health inspector? Fourteen.

"And this charity—we'll have the electronic eavesdropping charge soon, but for now it brings it to an even fifteen years prison."

The metal chair felt like ice under him, holding him up and pulling the warmth from his flesh. He could hear Greg's harsh breathing at his elbow, but he couldn't look away. He tried to hold on to *there's no mention of who shot Quinn, that it was Dad… but how do I hold on…*

"So a minimum of fifteen years. And counting." And Oliver's pen ceased.

The stillness only had an instant to build, before CC said "You mean five. *Months,* as one concurrent sentence, once you stop pretending any of them were for criminal purposes."

Oliver leaned forward. "Now CC—"

"Sure, you're aiming for a total of five years, if you can convince the jury someone genuinely saw Paul at every single one of the ten counts that aren't obviously wrong. The 'Stalking' certainly doesn't apply, for one. And you'd be listing a parade of whistleblowings and hoping the jury would keep seeing them as crimes at all."

She motioned to her left, toward the end of the table.

"Imagine a waiter or a cook on the jury, who hears about Paul bringing down a crooked health inspector."

She moved her hand over, to where a second phantom figure might sit beside the first.

"Or anyone who's given to charities, and ever wondered if they'd been cheated. And then you tell them that Paul hit Reid once so he could escape and continue his work... they might stand up and cheer.

"And *then,* you're counting on the judge agreeing that he's enough of a menace that every charge you have left gets a separate, consecutive sentence. If the sentencing doesn't go that way, every point you've stacked up after the first is simply redundant."

CC leaned back in her chair.

Paul didn't move. He knew he shouldn't speak, shouldn't even smile, but...

Oliver caught at his files and thumbed through them. "We'll be gathering more charges."

"*Redundant.* You'll be wasting taxpayer money, and it will all go to strengthen the pattern that Paul Schuman was never the kind of criminal you should have been chasing. And then there's your arresting officer. Who knows what Reid will say on the stand, considering that the man is such a stickler for rules, regardless of their cost to society? All he's doing is digging himself in deeper."

The pen restarted its tapping. "So confident? I still have eleven counts, against a man who was able to run rings around the law for this long. That's a case the DA's office can't ignore."

"And how is it going to make you look? How many rocks will you keep turning over, trying to get just one more charge? Against a man who's already surrendered of his own accord?"

Under the table, CC's foot nudged against Paul's.

A hint. Oliver wanted to track down more charges, but CC had suggested heading that off, that he volunteer one more case to help them lock down better terms. If that didn't just hint at how many of his forty-eight cases they'd still missed...

Paul let Oliver's inner self form in front of him again. The man's thoughts squinted at CC, fumbled with his pen. He was on edge, but would that make him desperate for a deal or too dangerous to show weakness to?

"Say there's no crime intended," Oliver was saying. "Just eleven counts of trespassing, and a clear pattern of ignoring the law. I *will* get six years for that, and we should have more soon." The pen's tempo began building.

"Just more proof that you're chasing a hero."

CC's hands swung up from the table and slammed down, a single fierce *clang* in the narrow space that blasted the pen to silence.

"Remember who we're sitting in here with, Oliver. This is Greg Schuman, of Schuman and Son publicity, and you're trying to bury his brother for making the city a better place. I can only hold the PR blitz back for so long."

Greg didn't move. But he *smiled.*

"I'll... give you fifteen months." Oliver swallowed. "The time might not be prison at all, and he could be out in a fraction of it. But we're still looking for more evidence."

CC turned to glance at Paul.

There it was. Shutting down that search for "more" was the point of volunteering other crimes, and it might bargain them all down further. He opened his mouth.

The door swung open.

Heads turned all around the room, as Detective Reid shoved in.

Reid ignored their gazes, and moved straight behind Oliver, holding out his phone for him to view.

"Found them at St. Cedric's."

Oliver's lips crooked in a sly smile.

"Storming in late, Reid?" CC asked. "Is that meant to impress us?"

"No. The 'impressions' are these."

Reid swung the phone around. On the screen were close shots of two file cabinet locks, both surrounded by a smattering of bright lines in the metal.

"Scratches. These locks were picked," the detective said.

"You... didn't tell me." CC's voice was weaker. Paul had the sudden thought that she meant him, even though her eyes were on Oliver.

"What did I say, again and again?" the prosecutor said. "We were looking for more evidence, and you waved that away as tainting our own case. This is hardly our concealing findings and then springing them in court."

"It's more circumstantial claims. More charges that my client is barely tied to."

"It's clear enough," Reid said. "I have a witness who gave a solid description of him lurking around the records room. And I have a whole hospital of other locks to check."

Paul's gaze bored into Reid's, where the bastard stood there with that cold grin.

I went through St. Central for clues to the power I'd discovered there. I could barely hold the picks steady back then. You know what it's like, when you got your power you almost cracked my head open with those fists, trying to understand it.

Oliver chuckled. "Of course you can claim this isn't proof. Of course there has been a year since Mr. Schuman was seen there. But every time you argue that he's been some kind of public servant, I'll be presenting them with the image of how many locks and doors he might be going through, and how nobody is ever safe until he's behind locked *and guarded* gates. Detective, at the different times this man was captured, was he ever found with lockpicks on him?"

"He was. And there have to be marks at other sites too, no matter how much practice he's had," Reid added.

"Of course there are. Now, CC, what were you offering again?"

CC's gaze sank toward the table. "I... need to talk with my client."

"Six years, and I'll try not to make it in maximum security. Or, we walk away and keep adding more to it. Going, going..."

"Just go *away,*" she sighed. "I told you, we need to talk."

"Of course."

Oliver scooped up his file with one smooth motion. Reid gave them a last look, before he and Oliver stepped outside.

CHAPTER FOUR

FIRST TO BREAK

Picking locks. Paul watched CC, how she still wouldn't look up.

Was it that simple, was just that change in how his case *looked* enough to turn everything upside down? *But the more they look into those two years of secret work... they'll ask more and more about how I got all my answers, when they can't find me using any bugs, and Reid knows the truth...*

Greg muttered "Did that just happen? He jumped from fifteen months to six years?"

"He thinks he can." CC was still staring at the table, not looking at them. "It gives him a whole strategy, and there's no earthly way of knowing what that'll lead to. There's always something that happens."

"Strategy. They're reframing Paul as a threat." Greg shifted his weight on the chair, and its legs scraped on the floor. "Dad and I can counter that. We'll start promoting all the good he's done—"

"Not yet," CC cut in, but her voice grew weaker with each word. "Still too in flux. Can't contaminate the jury."

Greg leaned across the table to her, stretching right past Paul. "No, we can—"

"Will you *listen* to her?" Paul burst out. "Better yet, shut up and let me talk to her."

Greg grimaced. "I... okay."

Was that *hurt* in his voice? Paul's jaw moved uselessly as he watched his brother squeeze around the table and walk out.

He turned back to CC, still sagging in her chair beside him.

Carefully he said "A few locks. Does that really make that big a difference?"

"You didn't tell me. I should never have stopped asking you what you were holding back. You picked locks. What else could they find? Wiretapping, or coercion to get your job done?"

Not until I bullied Koenig to come clean about his LifeLab lies... and behind all of it there's the power itself... He said nothing.

CC's head sank even lower. "There's always something that comes up. How many other people did you help? A dozen?"

He said nothing.

"Two dozen?"

Forty-eight cases worth of seeing and hearing what nobody else ever could. And just a few scratches on a lock changed everything.

The silence stretched, with every second hinting at more and more secrets.

At last he said "Would they really put me in maximum security?" His voice cracked.

"It's a bluff... except, I've seen it happen..."

She sat almost doubled over on the table, eyes blind to the laptop that sat in front of her. Strands of her hair fell against the pins that held it.

Here it was. Paul had seen CC hesitate before, but now she was simply deflated, helpless.

"You said you'd taken my case—" No, this wasn't about him anymore. He leaned closer. "Are you alright—"

"People depend on me. They say 'But you took the case,' every time something goes wrong. Every time."

She looked up. Her face was still, calm, but her voice was as soft as a little girl's.

"People say murder and rape and drugs are where all the high stakes are. As if all the smaller crimes can't have lives on the brink waiting for one decision to destroy them.

"My last case? Shoplifting. A simple crime, a complicated story of being with the wrong crowd, in the wrong room when an assault broke out. No deaths, no weapons, no premeditation. A promising kid—who deserved a few promises, yes. But still, five years in prison. Actually guilty, for all the difference that makes."

Paul studied her still, too-calm face.

Maybe he could shock her back into focus. "Um. If that was a client, should you be telling me this?"

CC laughed, a tiny, brittle sound. "No difference now. She was killed in her cell."

He opened his mouth. No sound came out.

*   *   *

The clangs and shouts and murmurs of the prison had never been so loud. Paul let the guard lead him back, and his eyes could anticipate every gate, every stain on the wall, before they came in view. How long before his feet were counting out those steps, drumming the measurement into his head no matter how he tried to free his thoughts?

Walls like these might be all he *ever* knew, always one slip away from another knife. Unless he found some way to give CC an edge against what was coming.

Like tell her about my power?

A shiver rose up and swept through him at the idea. The image of her bowed head and then her blank face hovered in his memory. If she let the secret slip, he could wind up on a dissection table, or whatever else the worst of humanity came up with.

And telling her wouldn't help. This was about two years of what he'd already done.

"You still here?"

Eckles. Paul's gaze darted to the doorway, to the dining space beyond it and the tall man staring out at him.

"Yeah, I see you there. Who you think you're bullshitting, walking around like you aren't planning—"

Eckles cut off as a guard stepped in front of him.

How had he seen Paul in the first place? Did he just hang around the doorway and shout at anyone he knew?

Paul Opened to his thoughts. The image of the man shifted to even wilder glances around him, and his hands reaching out, grabbing at Paul—

Paul lurched out of the trance with a shove at his back. He stumbled on past the doorway, his own guard herding him onward.

"Just you wait!" Eckles yelled. "I'll show you!"

Paul could only keep walking. No choice, no way to make the guard slow, nothing he did made a difference and he was still trapped...

When he reached his cell, he stomped into it the moment the guard's shout slid it open. He marched in so fast, he sent Mickey yelping *hey!* and dodging away to crouch in the corner.

Great. Now he was panicking Mickey, or even pushing him closer to getting that knife. Paul shook himself, tried to clear the frustration out of his head.

"Not your fault," he offered his cellmate. "I just came from talking with a lawyer."

Keep it natural, head off tensions or problems before they start. He'd settle for getting a lawyer joke back.

Mickey only said "Yeah, yeah," and sank down to sit on the floor. His eyes peeped up to watch Paul.

And Mickey's thoughts looked the same: always nervous, always scattered. No way to know if he was on the edge of more or not.

Paul retreated upward and threw himself onto his bunk.

Did he even *have* a way out? After years of trying to make a difference and follow where his power led... Was that it? Two years of damning history, that Reid would never stop sifting through to prop up the cop's fear of his own abilities...

Paul stretched his hearing out to the rush of the cars outside. All the sounds and motions he couldn't touch.

His hand reached down to rattle the bunk's loose support.

He listened around, searching through walls and corridors for some useful whisper. He'd broken frauds and corruption of all kinds before, so there had to be *some* clue here that could give him a weapon. Sooner or later.

No use. His fate was in the hands of people that weren't within a mile of these walls. Nothing here would do more than help him adapt to the dangers here—even if he pieced together enough of some prison rumor or secret to trade on.

Not like how Lorraine used the power, came the sudden thought. The woman who'd unlocked his power didn't deal in whispers, she reached deeper into thoughts to make people trust her, overlook her, or even hate her when she needed. Someone with that gift could be running this place by now.

Except she'd run away faster than he had, at one thought of facing any police attention—and then the Cedar Springs police chief gave her enough reason to keep running and disappear. *And I put her on that truck myself.*

The bit of metal rattled under his finger again. How could it be so loose and yet so completely locked into the bed's frame? Rattle, rattle...

"Mail!" A guard at the door waved an envelope.

Mickey rushed to the bars, faster than Paul had seen him move.

"Not you," the guard added. Mickey sagged and shot a glare up to the bunk.

Paul climbed down and took the letter. A plain shape with no return address, a neatly typed mailing label with his name and the North Penitentiary address.

Mickey was still watching him. He slipped back up the bunk to sit and open the letter.

The LifeLab letterhead glowered blue at him.

And at the bottom—*T Johnston, Chief of Security*.

Security, at a place he'd skulked through.

How much did they suspect? Paul felt the sour tightness closing in the back of his throat.

Mr. Schuman, we regret your current circumstances...

...heard conflicting reports about whether you've spread misinformation about our animal testing or tried to promote the facts...

...my professional curiosity about your sources of information...

No, no, no... The page shook in his hands, and he had to clamp his fingers tight on the paper to still it.

Then:

We might see a way to reduce our charges against you, if you're willing to discuss what you've discovered about our security. Please contact...

Paul blinked, stared again. The words were still the same.

The leap of hope inside him wouldn't settle down. Of course it was only a chance to change *one* of his charges, and it was another case of security experts taking notice of what he'd done...

No, they'd be expecting to trade knowledge of how he'd planted bugs, or what insiders had been passing him information—like James Koenig had framed them in the first place.

They were *asking*. Someone else was starting to wonder how he'd gotten so many secrets, and Oliver's prosecution was already seeing it. All questions they could never un-ask, no matter how long he'd tried to work quietly and leave no hint that different cases even had the same person exposing them.

When had he lost control there?

And he still wanted to scream to this Johnston to get him *out*...

He stretched out flat on the stiff mattress. Fists curled. He filled his mind with the picture of himself strapped onto some dissection table, or a lifetime of questions and demands and abuses it would turn loose on him and everyone he knew. Even on Lorraine, wherever she was trying to hide.

The fear should be cutting deeper. Forcing him to find another way. Anything but risking that.

CC. He'd talk to her again, line up the plea to cut back on his sentence. If she was still up to fighting for him.

A tiny sound stirred down in his throat.

No, if she wasn't ready he'd beg her to pull herself together and get back in the fight. Or even tell her about the power they had to hide. No, not that, if CC couldn't stop asking he'd get a whole new lawyer, rebuild his whole case from Square One.

Something trembled in his feet, his hands. The sound moved in his throat again.

Think of your father, your brother. They were standing with him, lawyers and publicity and everything.

Some voice muttered in the next cell, but the whimpering in his mouth crept outward and began to drown it out.

He lay still, trying to force the trembling out of him. He had his family. Sarah was free. He had all of his power—maybe he'd catch some useful secret out among the clangings and whispers around the prison. Or learn to bend people's minds like Lorraine did.

And after that failed? He'd have to keep searching, keep holding on.

The sound inside his mouth was swelling. Not a whine, not a moan, this would become a *scream...* he shoved his hand over his mouth and waited for the urge to end.

End? How could it end? He'd be *still in prison—*

Shaking ate through him. What breathing came was ragged, straining through his nose and the spasming hand he kept locked on his mouth. Sounds faded, all but the scream fighting to be born.

I'm here to show I was only fighting for the truth—

But his eyes locked onto a gray stain in the ceiling, he knew he'd be staring at that pear-with-a-bite shape *forever*...

The shakes swept over him, tore through him. No plan, no thought, just *hold on, hold on, don't scream*...

Thought blurred away. And will. Strength faded as his lungs grew too worn out to launch the scream. He sank into darkness, with his hand on his mouth the last thing to fall.

* * *

Somewhere in the haze of sleep and exhaustion, a voice found his name.

"Schuman! You got a call."

One foot after another, he shuffled down the corridor. One numb thought stirred in his head: *Don't let this be Reid again.*

"Hi," came Greg's voice in his ear.

"Hi." He slumped against the wall's coldness, waiting for thoughts to come together again. *I'm not up to this now, any of it.*

Greg finally said "Still no word from CC. Tell me you two have some plans in the works."

"There's... no word to me either."

"Great. It didn't look good, how she left things when Reid blindsided her. Dad and I wondered how fast we could get another lawyer up to speed."

"Don't." Paul tightened his fingers on the phone, tried to force his mouth and his brain to work again. "Just... ask her to talk to me, soon."

"Okay. But... Paul, are you alright?"

He worked his lips—still sore—and tried to balance words and reasons for what to say. Was there any point in lying?

He settled for "As good as I can be."

"Okay then. We've been working on ad copy about your work, and possible contacts. Not easy when we don't know which charges you're admitting to."

And all of that just brings more attention to how many lies I've exposed, and we're closer to the time they see I'm doing the impossible... "CC said not to start those yet."

"We're not starting. But it's not like it has to be her decision every time. Or yours," Greg added.

What was that, a tremor of anger in Greg's voice? "What's that mean?"

"Paul, I asked you if you're alright."

"Of course I am, I told you that."

"You're lying to me. You—" Greg stopped, and Paul heard him take two heavy breaths. "You sound like someone who'd have me grabbing for their car keys when they tried to leave a party. Whether they were drinking or not. But who cares, every last step about this has to be a step *you* take, right?"

"Huh?" Paul knuckled his forehead. *Think, think!*

"This is all your world. You stepped into it, so you ran off and did what you did, all for reasons we don't get to know. But it gets better, it turns out my own wife was—" He broke off.

"I didn't ask for this."

No, those were the same words he'd thrown at Chief Thiessen back in Cedar Springs, and they hadn't calmed her down.

He tried "Look, Greg—I didn't plan this. And she didn't cheat on you, or plan it, or anything."

"Look, I get it!" Greg said. "Anyway, will you just let us help you already?"

"I..." He should be asking him more, following that chance to clear the air. Instead he said "Just let me talk to CC again, that's the first thing. And if you think about promoting me, try to point it away from just how many secrets I've dug up. Or *how* I did it," he added— Greg had to see the risk there. "How's that?"

"Good enough, to get us started. Anything else?"

"I guess not." Or, he could apologize, there was something—

"You hang in there." And the call ended.

Paul let a guard lead him back to his cell. Little prickles of anger and doubt swirled in his head from the clash, but they only swirled and shifted with no sign of gathering into real ideas again.

Either way, it came back to getting through each minute.

He made his silent way back up to the bunk. He lay there, trying to get something to happen.

The loose support rattled when he touched it.

Greg and his strategy were out there.

Rattle.

We're insisting I'm no criminal. Like I always said. But they still put him here.

Rattle, rattle.

Over in the corner, Mickey snapped "Will you leave that thing alone?"

Paul growled down to him "Deal with it!"

"Look…" Mickey took a step toward him, eyes as wide as if they'd crack his whole face down the lines through it. "Please. Just stop it. I don't want trouble. I mean, have I done one thing to you?"

"No." The word, the breath, eased out of him and took some of the tension with it.

"Then just stop clinking that thing. Come on—I'm almost out of this place, but don't take that out on me. You know I can't risk fucking it all up over some stupid noise."

Paul pulled his hand back from the support. "Okay. Sorry."

Mickey stepped toward him, looking up from below.

"I keep seeing it getting to you, man. The little things a guy can get stuck on. Or sounds that you can't hold inside. Or you start staring off, and hearing things that aren't there."

You have no idea what I'm hearing. But the others were right, and Paul smiled. "I guess."

"So just stop! If you get your head into those, you don't come out."

"Easy to say." He sighed, then thumped a fist on the mattress. "They're talking about six years and counting for me. And it was five months this morning, all for doing the same thing."

"Shit." Mickey shook his head. "Well, then you *know* you can't let it get to you. Even if everything you did was all the other guy's idea, and you're innocent too."

The word *innocent* had a soft sardonic twist in his mouth. That was the prison joke, that nobody here was guilty—Mickey couldn't even say it with a straight face, but at least he meant well.

"I... well, I did turn myself in. To prove that whatever I did, it wasn't a real crime."

"That's a new one." Mickey gave a sad little laugh. "Guess they didn't give you a vote then, after they grabbed you."

"Guess not," Paul sighed. "Oh, and I did it for a girl."

Mickey's eyes widened. His jaw shook, and then the *laugh* started, filling his face and warming it and sweeping his whole body into it.

Paul's fists trembled. But the sound rang on and on, a sheer belly laugh of helpless absurdity that echoed off the walls, and the shaking in his own hands was laughter too that caught him up and bounced off Mickey's and built more and more until it left him gasping and rolling on the bunk.

Slowly his breath came back. The cell lay silent, broken by only a few wheezes and the sense that the silence could be filled at any moment.

Then the guard's voice came from the door. "Alright, clowns. Visitor time."

Mickey's head jerked up, then looked away, trying to hide his eagerness.

The guard added "One for each of you. C'mon."

"She's here?" Mickey rushed to the door.

Paul followed him out, with the guard at their rear. Mickey moved with a spring in his step, that even the cautious prison pace couldn't hide. Right, he'd said he was getting out soon.

When the visitor room opened, Mickey rushed straight toward one table, with a single gasp of *Mom*. Paul found himself taking a curious step after him, toward the graying woman in the stained business suit he ran to. But of course, the guards would never let two prisoners gather at any one part of the room.

And Sarah Gomez was standing at the room's other end.

He moved toward her table. The reporter's face shone with that same fierce smile, that kept him too willing to think she understood a little of how he lived. Right now it was enough to just walk into that glow.

"They finally let me in," she said as they sank into seats.

How long had she been demanding visiting rights? He said "I guess after you were... Sorry. I never wanted you to..." *To dent Reid's skull trying to help me escape.*

"But you're the one paying for it now—"

She stopped, and pulled her hands in along the table. They'd been reaching across toward him.

"I know, I know," she said. "You said I got it wrong to think there was some other kind of connection between us. Either way, I still say it's crazy that they want to lock you up."

"Even after I..." He stopped. What was that, suddenly asking for reassurance? He settled for a quick grin. "That's good to hear. I've got a fight ahead."

"I'm counting on it." She nodded slowly. "The next round should be soon. Your lawyer, CC, said she'd be meeting us in—" She glanced at her phone. "Any minute."

"Oh?" Of course the two ladies were talking now. And what did *any minute* mean? Paul reached his hearing out, but nobody was walking up from the main visitor corridor, and beyond the other door at the side—

"And Schuman's in here now?" That low, hungry voice was Eckles.

"Yeah. So it matters?" said the man walking up with him, closing in on the visiting room's door.

"You just get to your spot."

What is this? Eckles is making a move—he's got allies—and he's targeting me? *What's he know about me?*

Who else would get caught in the middle?

Paul fell back into his own head, like diving into cold water with the shock of fear's adrenalin waiting for him.

"What?" Sarah said. Just the one word, but a flash of trust and self-control behind it.

He held up a hand for her to wait and stepped away from the table. No time to run, no time to think, but at least she didn't have to be seen with him.

The door opened across the room, and he found himself looking straight into Eckles's face.

Those wild eyes opened wider to see Paul looking back at him. Then the gaze swept around the roomful of chattering people, and Paul had a moment to hope Sarah wasn't visibly watching him and another to hope Eckles wouldn't dare anything drastic.

Eckles marched straight for the table with Mickey and his mother.

Paul closed in on them. Mickey jumped up and gasped "Hold on!" but the tall man shoved past him and leaned down next to his mother.

Her sudden paleness and the way Eckles held his hand next to his body made it all clear. *The bastard's showing her his knife.*

She clambered up from her chair, with her son staring fury at the man twice his size. She and Eckles started across the room—him not quite touching her, but walking so close anyone could think *hostage*. Guards started toward them.

The murmur of voices went still. Paul tried to keep the rage off his face and let Eckles walk away. They'd never get far.

Instead, Eckles beckoned to him.

Crazy! Going with anyone was the last thing he needed, and now Eckles had special plans for him? Still, somewhere in his gut twisted the lone thought *this might be the only way out.* He backed away.

Eckles stopped with his back to the door outward, and brought the blade up. Whatever it was scavenged from, it had two whole inches of metal gleaming beyond his fist, and he held it right next to the frightened woman's neck.

The guards stopped. "You can't think that'll get you out," one began.

Eckles's other hand moved. A key card flashed, and the visitors' door buzzed open.

A rumble of shock swept around the room. Two guards moved to stop more prisoners from closing in, and several others grabbed for their radios.

The woman whispered "Please—please don't..."

Eckles dragged her out the door, standing just past the doorway with a hand locked on her arm. He motioned to Paul with the knife hand, and shot a warning look at Mickey.

The little man stared after his mother. The familiar, frightened shaking swelled and swept over his face, and he slumped where he stood.

Paul dove through the door.

Figures up and down the corridor were scrambling away from them. Radios squawked and guards herded people out of sight behind other doors—*was that CC disappearing there?* The corridor was almost empty already.

And I came with them, like I can really help—

Eckles yanked the door behind them closed. "I told you, you wouldn't get out before me," he laughed at Paul. "My turn: there's a truckload of drugs waiting to split with you, if you help me make it out."

And the hostage? Paul steeled himself to read the convict's thoughts.

The lights went out.

A quick Opened glance brought the light from the door's cracks out painfully bright, and showed they still had the "dark" corridor to themselves. Voices clattered and jostled behind those doors, probably locking down all over the prison. Mickey's mother whispered "Please, please—"

Eckles laughed "Thought they'd pull that. Try and keep up!"

He dragged his hostage down the corridor. His first steps stumbled the way any ordinary sight would in the dimness, but then he caught his balance and made for one of the closed doors' outlines. Mickey's mother he simply hauled along and held upright by brute force.

Paul moved after them. The dark could be the best chance he'd get to pull the woman away, but Eckles's grip looked too strong. And the thought kept prickling inside him, that whatever Eckles's plan was it might actually get him *out.*

They passed one door, and Eckles opened the second with his card. Another open corridor stretched ahead, dim and empty. Eckles shifted his grip to cover the woman's mouth, and started down it at a faster pace now.

Where were the guards? Paul stretched his hearing behind them, around them. Careful, clustered feet moved in different spaces nearby, but none of them close to their own location. Eckles plodded on ahead, as if he had no doubt he'd found a route that none of them would search in time. He might be right.

Somewhere well up ahead, between the huddling voices and the rumble of trapped prisoners, Paul caught another voice. The same man who'd let Eckles into the visitor room, and he was muttering "You better make it" to himself.

Eckles and his hostage were slowing up ahead. Paul rushed forward to catch up. They'd reached an intersection.

Mickey's mother said "Please! Don't, don't hurt me." She tried to struggle, but banged against what looked like a cart in the dimness.

"You don't need her now," Paul said. "This is about speed and silence now, right? She's just slowing you down."

"Slowing *someone* down." Eckles caught at the cuff of the woman's jacket. His knife slashed at the cloth.

What's he doing? But Eckles didn't cut her, he sliced a strip from her jacket. In another quick move he shoved her against the cart and tied her hands to it. One more slash gave him a broader wad of fabric, that he tied inside her mouth for a gag.

"Try and make all the noise you want," Eckles told her. "Maybe they'll stop for you, maybe they'll shoot first. Now we move!" and he headed on up the corridor.

Paul stared after him a moment. So she was a decoy now?

"Hang on," he whispered to her. He Opened to pick out the knotted cloth in the dimness. A simple knot, but Eckles had wrenched it so tight his fingers strained to work it at all. Finally it loosened and pulled open, easy for her to finish.

Footsteps moved, back down the corridor where they'd come. He spun and rushed up the corridor.

Which way, where would this passage connect to? He strode through the dimness, trusting a few dark-piercing glances to know the floor was clear enough to run across. He tried to picture how the sounds and movements he'd tracked over the last few days laid out. Eckles trusted that this way would lead out—

And I have to stay with him? Paul stopped, tested the sounds around him. Up where he'd heard Eckles's ally, a man paced nervously back and forth. Eckles picked his way toward him in the dark. He'd just passed another intersection.

That choice. Turning right instead would lead deeper into the section that had always been quietest, safest. Paul made for that turn.

So now he was racing Eckles after all? *Wasn't I trying to save the woman, stay out of trouble?*

But the guards would be closing in in the dark behind him. Maybe Mickey's mother had calmed them down. He reached back for their sounds.

They were still barely past the door. One was saying "I told you, I've seen it! Rubber bullets kill too, we can't—"

"Shut it. No lights, just the nightscopes."

And Mickey's mother...

Still grunting into her gag. She was still bound, still in the guards' path. And they could barely see.

He charged after her. No time for Opening, he could only plunge through the darkness by blind memory. *Why didn't I stay until the knot was all the way open—why'd I leave at all?* His feet echoed in the dimness. He could be about to run right into her, how fast was he closing in?

Gunfire exploded. *Behind* him, said one desperate thought. Catching Eckles, not the helpless woman.

"Incoming!" "Move, move!" roared the guards in front.

Paul bellowed out "Don't shoot—"

In midstep he Opened to split the darkness. Armored shapes advancing with rifles coming up, Mickey's mother in their way and thrashing against the cart.

He leaped.

Every line of it was clear: the barrels of the guns, the lines of the woman's face so much like Mickey's, her wild staring back and forth—

He caught her, and they slammed to the ground together in a crash of the cart's metal down against his side. The blasts and the rubbery hailstorm against the cart came an instant later.

Then he only had to lie still and let them take him.

CHAPTER FIVE

HEARING

They grabbed him. Clumsy hands scrabbled in the dark, hauling him away from the cart and Mickey's mother. Paul stayed limp to let them shove him down along the floor, while she begged "Let him go! Don't hurt him!"

Finally the guards gave up fumbling around by their low-light goggles and switched on their lights. They helped the woman to her feet, surrounding her with a forest of light beams and more awkward questions about if "he" had hurt her, until they settled in and the words eased back into "are you alright."

Paul lay in the dust and reached his hearing up the corridor again. Up where the other shooting had been, swirled a muddle of curses, warnings, and the thumping sounds of another takedown. So guards had gotten ahead of Eckles after all, and their capture bullets had brought him down. His "plan" and his partner had only gotten the prisoner so far.

Paul's guards pulled him to his feet. They marched him back down the corridor, with only a few quieter *move it*s and pushes. He wondered how many embarrassed or apologetic looks were hiding under those armored visors.

The lights came back on as they neared the door, and they moved out into the main corridor Eckles had first led them through.

"Paul? Are you alright?"

CC. He got a glimpse of her with two other visitors, being led off to a door far down the hall. Guards with her were already moving to block her rushing to him.

"Fine, fine! I think it's over!" he yelled back, before they herded her out of sight.

Two of Paul's guards led Mickey's mother away. The rest brought him past a few doors to a large waiting room—now holding a half-dozen prisoners waiting out the lockdown, under the stern eyes of the guards that must have corralled them here.

They put Paul in a corner, with two of them separating him from the rest of the inmates. He leaned against the wall.

It's done. I'm back, she's safe, nobody's hurt... The realization softened his knees to mush, and he sank to the floor.

No, not yet. He forced his hearing to Open again and search for the spot CC had been taken. If she was still there.

"Yeah, he came running out of nowhere. Stopped us from plugging—" The speaker cut off with the grunt of a man who'd just gotten a shove from his neighbor.

CC's voice answered "The hostage? You were going to shoot at a helpless woman?"

"Not *at* her! And we've got protocols for this, no live ammunition. 'Sides, we were about to catch Schuman anyway."

"Oh, you're so sure of that?" And CC chuckled, stretching the sound out.

Then her voice sharpened. "Tell me about these 'protocols.' Someone needs to look into your shooting, and Mr. Schuman's turning down a chance to escape to help a hostage. And how the other prisoner got out of—the visitor room, was it? Who was the last to see him there?"

"Van Howe, maybe—"

Another man cut in "Of course we'll be looking into it. No need to worry on that count, *counselor,*" and he made the word a warning to the others there.

"Someone does need to worry. Either this is a massive display of failures, or someone like you there was in it. Van Howe, you said?"

"Hey! I don't have to talk to you," barked another voice, a familiar one.

"I said it will be investigated," the guards' leader said again, but Paul heard the man she'd accused stomping away. And from his voice, 'Van Howe' *was* the guard who'd led Eckles to the visitor room, and been waiting for him further on.

Paul tracked his heavy footsteps, up the main corridor. So this man had been part of Eckles's plan, even helping him time it to pull Paul in. And now he was closing in on Paul's own room.

The door opened.

Don't stare. From the corner of his eye he spotted Van Howe's face. He'd seen those dark, doughy features before... yes, the stocky guard who'd been "blocking" Eckles when he shouted at Paul from the dining area. They'd both been watching for him, together.

Paul Opened to his thoughts. Van Howe's true face curled into a grimace of rage, and his fists clenched and jabbed quick punches all around him. He glared at Paul, but a moment later his thoughts changed to shoot a savage look back behind him. Where CC had been.

Then he stepped over and took his place with some of the other guards watching the prisoners. His sunken eyes stole one more glance at Paul, but no more than that.

Paul huddled where he sat, folding his look of exhaustion tight to avoid their gazes. Van Howe had been part of Eckles's escape plan, and they'd fixed on Paul as the third component of getting out... And right now the guard was holding onto his temper by his fingernails, right when he only needed a few steps and one cheap excuse to drag Paul away for whatever he wanted. Or he could come to the cell and seize him at any time.

The sweat on Paul's skin felt colder than ever. *And I've got no way to prove what he is, and no way to use it if I did—I'm still caged.*

He reached past the room to search the prison's sounds again. Here a corridor was silent, there men in cells grumbled and called out guesses for what had set the lockdown off. He even heard what sounded like Eckles himself, being dragged to the infirmary surround-ed by guards.

In a space one room behind the visiting room, he heard Mickey chanting *she's okay, she's okay!* From the callous voices around him, the spot was full of prisoners that had been pulled back from where the visitors were. He shifted to search for those.

"I said, *is anyone dead?"* Sarah's voice caught at him.

"I… it's too early to say, miss," a man answered.

"You have to have a preliminary report on that radio by now," she said. "You give me one word now, yes or no, and I'll keep what I write about today friendly. That's all I need."

"But…" The guard swallowed. "From what I hear, the word is no."

"No deaths. Thank you," and she let out a deep sigh. "I am sorry for that. I just needed to know."

Paul could have sighed himself. That covered everyone in the pris-on he knew, so he was free to release his power and go back to hoping Van Howe left him alone…

"Everyone's alive."

Sarah's whisper stirred under the agitation of the room.

"You did it, Paul. You even started by pulling the danger away from me—again. And I hope you can hear me… or else that you es-caped and they're just covering that up and I'm talking to myself. But that doesn't sound like you. I think we owe you again, and I won't forget that."

Paul felt a flush trying to prickle on his face, a sensation that dragged at his focus on sound. *I didn't do it because of some debt, and I'm still the one who owes* you… He let his concentration fade.

* * *

"Mister Schuman, I'm disappointed in you. Days of no trouble at all—and now you're trying to escape."

Paul kept his voice calm, as he looked up from his chair at the guards' captain. "That's not what happened. Eckles took a woman hostage. I had to go along to help her."

"That's right, you went. And you left her tied up and ran off." The captain leaned down an inch, looming over where Paul sat. His scarred face was still steady, and his voice quiet.

"I tried to untie her. When I realized she wasn't loose, I came back to help." *And because your guards were trigger-happy,* but he didn't mention that. The last thing a prisoner needed was to point fingers at their keepers.

"You left," the captain said again. "With Eckles. And you turned around when he got caught."

"With Eckles? He's tried to pull me into his plans since I got here, and I kept refusing—your guards saw that. Until he took my cell-mate's mother hostage."

"Where'd you get the keycard?" The captain's face was suddenly inches from his own.

"Not me. Eckles had it, from somewhere."

Van Howe. It would be so easy, to say Eckles had mentioned a guard or even some ally... but that would only lead to questions even harder to answer.

The captain held his glare. Paul Opened to his thoughts.

The scarred man's look didn't soften. Instead his head turned, shifting between watching Paul and panning around the room and the prison, and he gave everything the same look. Fierce, determined, but fair.

"I'm watching you," he said. "You think you're some kind of hero, for staying here instead of escaping? I don't buy it."

Paul didn't answer. What could he say, that wouldn't make it worse?

I could still mention the guard... but, too risky.

Finally they led him back to his cell. The walk dug its own fingers of worry into him, watching faces turn toward him the way they never had before. One inmate yelled through the bars "What, you wuss out on Eckles??" and another shot back "That was Mickey's mom he saved!"

So they knew him now, and he could still only trudge back where they led him. At least he'd helped a helpless woman... or he'd meant to, rubber bullets were a long way from a real danger, and the guards might not have fired at all if he hadn't rushed in...

Cell after cell passed by him. *Maybe she needed my help, maybe not. I'm here to prove I'm not a criminal, so I stayed.*

Except for the one thought he couldn't get rid of. Just maybe, he could have made it out.

When his cell slammed shut behind him, Mickey was waiting. "You alright?" His eyes shifted around, not quite meeting Paul's gaze.

"After Eckles? Just a few bruises. And then they had to sit me down and find out if I was in on his plan, or I knew anything. I should have known they didn't have me down as a real threat when they didn't isolate me first thing." A lot of the guards must be embarrassed by their performance, but maybe he'd impressed some too.

Mickey looked up at him then, slowly. "You saved my mother. But... why'd Eckles go after her?"

There it was. Mickey had to have seen it.

Paul's sigh left him slumping where he stood. "Because he saw her with you. And he must have heard you're here with me, so he saw taking her was a chance to pull me in."

"Yeah. I figured."

Mickey edged back a step, and his gaze shifted away to eye the walls. Like he'd been when Paul first came—was he back to itching for a knife of his own now?

Then Mickey looked back. "Well, you still saved her. That's more balls than I had there, too. But you've got this target on you, this something... Just stay away from me."

"How?"

Paul nodded toward the walls, mockingly close. The space felt tighter than ever, and the farthest he could move would be to sink into his bunk again.

Except for one thing he couldn't keep to himself. "You may be right. I heard Eckles might be working with some guard—" no need to start any more specific rumors— "so you want to keep your eyes open. I'm just hoping they don't go after me again."

Mickey whistled. "Paranoid, they call it. Like 'they' ever know."

Paul collapsed on the mattress. But he held his eyes open: there was still a whole prison to watch, more dangerous than ever.

His hearing stretched out. Cell by cell, section by section, he listened for any trace of Van Howe's voice, any mention of him, or anything new about the escape. Or anything.

Hours passed. Random rumors, bets, petty voices crawled through his head.

And once Van Howe himself walked past his cell.

Paul lay still on the bunk, eyes slitted... but the guard only gave him one glance and moved on. Even Opening to Van Howe's mind only showed the same agitated glancing around, no particular attention to Paul as he passed. What did that mean, that he only saw him as some obsession of Eckles's, not a threat to himself?

But the guard *could* just walk by any time, or find a hundred ways to get at Paul. That was the hell of it.

Paul held his focus on Van Howe on into the afternoon, waiting for something useful. He monitored hours of angry steps and curt conversations where fellow guards gave him a wide berth. But about his scheme with Eckles, there was nothing.

*   *   *

It was late afternoon when they brought him out for a call.

His father's voice in his ear was slow, earnest. "Paul... you saved a woman in the middle of a prison break?"

"I guess I made a difference, Dad. Seems like everyone has to ask me about it today," he added.

"And you stayed behind to keep making your case. Even when it looks like someone there is targeting you. Of course you did."

Warmth trickled within those words. Paul held onto that sound, picturing it like a hand on his shoulder. For a moment, the simple plastic chair was a soft, perfect shape to lean back in.

His father went on "You know, Detective Reid called me."

"What?" He jerked upright.

"Reid said that if you'd tried to warn him about the break, he should have listened. Or else that you should have said it clearer instead of playing tricks with the message."

"He *would.*" Reid wouldn't even use his powers... but would he stop and listen when Paul used his? *Maybe he'll listen about Van Howe this time.*

"Of course he still thinks you're a menace," his father said. "But the rest of us are certainly impressed. We can make this work."

"This?" Paul's throat was suddenly dry. He swallowed, tried to keep his voice the same. "There's a plan?"

"The plan is the same. But for right now there's a new goal."

* * *

Suddenly everything was moving. The afternoon had almost ended, Paul was sure of it, but CC's visit was still squeezed in to the tail end of the visiting period. And yet it felt like hours sitting in the cell before they brought him out to her.

This time they had the meeting room to themselves. And CC dropped straight into the chair opposite him, with barely a nod before she began:

"Paul, I believe it's possible—*possible,*" and she held up her hands in caution, "that we can get you out of this place tomorrow. At least for the moment."

What?

Some part of him wanted to leap to his feet, grab at her, demand to know more. The Paul who'd lived through the last years settled for leaning closer and saying "You can?"

Her hands sank to the table and brought her hunching forward over them, taking a nervous glance around. "Again, possible. And also, it's important that we do this soon. Please, hear me out."

He nodded. The worry in her eyes sent fear tightening inside him.

"This won't be about your plea itself—let me be clear, it won't change the evidence or whether you confess to any charges. If you do that, it'll be in later negotiations. Instead, right now we can ask the judge to reconsider letting you out on bail, based on your history and your actions this morning. And…"

Her hands twitched against the table.

"And, because you could be in danger here. That man Eckles seemed to have plans for you, and now he may want revenge when the escape failed. Also, he may have friends among the guards. It could be a man named Van Howe."

Oh. Paul sagged in relief—*this time, the problem's nothing new.* "It's him alright," he said.

"You *know?* You learned that in the escape? Then you're in even more danger if he finds out. Please, exactly what did you see? I have to use that in the hearing… and I can't get it wrong or you'll…"

Paul weighed his choices. It didn't take long.

"Not much. He brought Eckles to the visiting room where he made his move, and I think I saw them whispering."

She closed her eyes. "That *isn't* much. I don't know if I can use it—but I'm sure you're right. Your whole case is about how much you've done with so little information.

"That leaves us with the arguments that you're in danger, and that this is the second time you've come back to accept your punishment. You're ready to pay your debt to society, and you deserve better than to be attacked for it."

"My debt." Did people actually call it that?

A line edged down her brow. "Paul. You may want to work on that frustration you're showing, before we get to court."

He frowned back. Of course he had some frustration about being stuck in prison. *But letting it show?* Me?

"Anyway," she added, "this will be about whether you're a flight risk, compared to how you're at risk yourself. You think you're ready for tomorrow?"

He glanced around at the walls, the same shade of paint he was starting to see when he closed his eyes.

"I'd better be."

* * *

No matter how he lay on the bunk, there was always another metal clang or an even sharper voice ringing out somewhere. Nothing he did blocked them out, and he needed to sleep.

His hand kept reaching for the loose support on his bed, just to throw some small noise of his own back at them. But he held his fingers away—he'd promised Mickey. And the thought whispered that if he touched the thing tonight, he'd never get away from it again.

Instead he lay there hearing the cell block's rhythms shift as the night dragged on. There was always something else.

Every sound in the corridor outside sent a jolt through him: this could be Van Howe using the last night he had to come after him.

Covering ears with his hands, his arms, shifting on the mattress did nothing. There were only more hours to crawl by, and the threat of years after that. The same damn piece of loose, trapped metal waited right there...

Until morning came.

Until they led him out—really *out,* past the corridors he'd tracked, on and on past them all until he stepped into the yard... crunching through actual snow, not just the remnants that visitors tracked in. And the sky—

He pulled his gaze down. No good staring at what he might just be giving up again.

Then they put him in the car, and every lurch and turn around him swept away more of the illusion. He was outside, but only as a lump of baggage they were ready to stuff right back in.

The courtroom looked just the same, elegant wood paneling and chairs full of its vast variety of people doing their best to all fit within the same rules. He sat with CC, watching Oliver with Reid beside him—of course Reid would be there himself too. Paul's father and brother were nowhere in sight.

And it meant waiting, yet more waiting while other cases ground on, and he could only sit upright and vow not to get in his lawyer's way.

Finally:

"Your Honor, we're requesting bail be granted on the grounds that Mr. Schuman's life is in danger. And also that it's unusual to deny bail for offenses on this small a scale."

"Unusual? You disagree with my decision?" The judge's eyebrows drew together.

That small, *angry* motion, focusing within less than an inch of space... Paul went rigid where he sat.

Reid added "He has a 'small,' longtime history of avoiding security and authorities, sir. I think you have a list—"

"I do." The judge held up a sheaf of papers.

CC said "And a history of *choosing* to face punishment, that Mr. Schuman demonstrated again yesterday. At the risk of his life."

"And Your Honor?"

That was *Greg*—when had he slipped in at the back? Paul glanced over and saw his brother advancing across the room, with Mickey's mother shuffling up beside him.

"Your Honor, I have the woman who was taken hostage in yesterday's incident, that my brother saved—"

"Mister Schuman," the judge boomed at Greg. "This is a bail hearing, not a trial. And I don't remember asking for character witnesses, or interruptions."

CC winced. Her hand actually trembled, as she waved Greg and his "witness" to sit down. At least Greg had the grace to sit without a murmur, and Paul saw him whispering to the woman, some kind of reassurance. If there was any chance left at all.

"I apologize, Your Honor," CC said. "I didn't plan that. But the fact remains that my client has become a target in prison."

Oliver shook his head. "Hardly this court's job to fix, is it?"

"He's 'targeted,' " Reid said, "because he has a reputation for escaping. We're in the midst of investigating just how many locks and security systems he's beaten over the years. Your Honor, this is a man who thinks the law doesn't apply to him. If he's given one opening he'll be long gone, again."

"·Locks, is it now?" The judge frowned.

Paul Opened to his thoughts. The judge's eyes *blazed* at him, he glanced between Paul and the papers in front of him, no hint of softness in his face. Paul dropped out of the trance.

"—ter Schuman? I *asked* you, do you think you're above the law?"

Oh God. Paul clamped all his control down over his face, his voice. "I did turn myself in, Your Honor."

"And you didn't answer my question." The judge's frown deepened.

Above the law? There was only one sane way to answer that here—but the *no* in his throat caught and choked, on how many hundreds of ways he'd seen people cheat and trick each other, inside the law and outside it, and someone like Reid *still only cares about what* I *do...*

CC's voice slid in: "Your Honor, shouldn't bail be a question of whether the person is a danger to the community, or a risk of flight—"

"In my courtroom I think I can decide what the question is." Those eyes locked onto her.

Paul swallowed, flailed for something to say.

CC nodded. "Of course, sir. It's your decision, and we're simply bringing you the evidence about what a young man is claimed to have done."

She motioned to Paul.

"And how every accusation here admits it's been done in the spirit of serving the community, and how he's now chosen *twice* to face the charges against him. In spite of all the fearmongering that the prosecution has presented about what he *might* do."

She gestured to him again.

The judge gave her a long look. "It's still my courtroom, counselor."

"Yes, Your Honor. It could be his life, in your hands." CC let her own hands fall to her sides, finished.

Paul found himself leaning toward her, nodding. When had he started that? The seat felt harder than ever, but now he didn't dare move.

The judge laughed.

"Good to have you back, Ms. Claire. Mr. Schuman, until your trial, you will be transferred to house arrest—"

House arrest. House, *he really said it. Real air, a real chance to breathe without worrying who's standing behind me.* His head swam, his blood pounded in his ears and swallowed the next words.

Then, "—required to wear a tracking device. And, since you have so many separate counts against different victims, bail will be set at…"

The judge glanced down at the papers in front of him. *One* glance.

"Sixty thousand dollars."

A low gasp came from CC, that could have been "For *burglary,* if it even counts as that?"

"Counselor?" The judge shot her a sharp look.

From behind them, Greg called out "That... shouldn't be a problem, Your Honor." His voice sounded strained, but he added "If it means we can take him home."

CHAPTER SIX

CHALLENGES

"Home" would be Greg's house.

Paul let them lead him through the processing and drive him out. He let the minutes wash over him, sitting quiet in the car and then standing in the living room... all he needed was to stand still a while longer, and the police would finally be gone. Even Reid.

His brother led them around the house, and his father too. He'd missed that point—his father was already staying with Greg while he recovered from his wound.

So it's all three Schumans under one roof. Or the men of the family, before Lorraine joined us.

Reid and the other cops clomped and poked their way around the rooms, looking for... Paul tried not to wonder what security issues they were looking for, not when they were so close to done. They worked their way through each room, thumbing through the odd mix of Greg's older, familiar possessions and the ones Lorraine or the last years had added.

Then Reid clamped the tracker on. A block of blue plastic and metal—probably a few tiny scraps of electronics sealed in a mass of armor—all fused to the heavy nylon band that locked in place around his ankle. It clung coldly to his flesh as if it refused to warm.

Outside the police were setting up other electronics in Greg's token space of a yard, all the overlapping transmitters and receivers that would fence Paul in. He could hear neighbors muttering at their windows and watching them work.

"The rules." Reid handed him a set of heavy-duty papers. "Simple: you stay in. This isn't a set of alarms to avoid tripping, it's one alert that's only quiet as long as it senses you're within the perimeter. Except if we bring you out again."

"We understand," his father said.

Reid tapped the keypad they'd fastened into the wall. "If anything happens, sign in here and speak into it. How fast you answer might determine what kind of response you see from us. And we'll be coming down here when we see fit, to check on you."

"And of course, you protect this." He leaned down to tap the anklet. "Most of these have some resilience to them, but this is the most sensitive model."

"Because you insisted, didn't you?" Greg said.

"Oh, you think I'm enjoying this?" Reid stepped back, to study Paul and the room. "Did you really expect anything different, when you live like you can simply walk in and out of anywhere and never face the consequences?"

The warnings, the prodding, all the cops watching even at the last moments of leaving... "Just leave your forms and go," Paul sighed. "Or lock me up again."

Reid eyed him a moment.

Then he nodded, and turned away.

Police gathered and tromped out the door—when it closed behind them he could *feel* the soft thump. They climbed into their cars, every last one of them, all clear to his Opened hearing. Engines roared to life.

They drove away.

Paul staggered over one step, enough to sag down and sit on the big yellow living-room sofa. Just the sound of the cushions rasping as his weight settled was a piece of his childhood. No wonder Greg had brought it to his own home.

Greg asked "So, do you—"

"Shhh," came their father's voice.

Paul let himself breathe, in and out, slow and deep. Letting the muscles in his neck unknot, trying not to feel the strangeness clinging to his leg.

They were gone.

Probably gone. Would they bother to bug me here? Plant something during the search or inside this anklet, or send someone outside with a long-range mic? Would anything they heard be usable against him? Still, Reid wouldn't want some casual mention of power getting on the record...

Even when I've come home I keep thinking about secrets. I should be able to scream, laugh, hug the people who've stood by me...

"I'm about ready for some dinner," his father said. "Do we want to keep this easy and order it?"

Greg laughed. "Three guys living on a pizza app? We can do better than that. I'll whip up a celebration—a small one, anyway. Unless you want something else?" and he gave Paul a belated look.

"Sounds fine. Show me how good you are. And how fast, too. You should know, I did work as a cook for a while, out there."

Greg looked at him a moment, maybe taking in the concept. Or the whole idea of Paul's years of *out there* that had dropped into the room.

"Challenge accepted."

Paul leaned back and closed his eyes.

Slowly, slowly, he waited for his muscles to pop free of their tension, to slough some of the prison off of them. Now and then he played his hearing around, in a haphazard search for the faint buzz that might mean hidden electronics. Only now and then.

He didn't look up often—better not to learn the look of his new shrunken world too soon. Outside the house, cars and voices settled in to the rhythms of where this little suburb squeezed into the city. Greg rattled and rustled in the kitchen, spilling scents into the air. And Ian

Schuman settled into an opposite chair, and began clicking on a laptop as if he'd been juggling files there forever.

By the time dinner was served, Paul could guess the whole menu without Opening any of his senses. Spaghetti with some new twist on the sauce, one of their salads, garlic bread. The food was a pleasure to dive into, and almost tempted him to Open to taste even with his family there to see.

"So, how is it?" Greg asked. "Does it stand up against the professional here?"

"Way better than anything I did," Paul said. "Really, I was only working a grill in a diner for a couple of days. It just happened, and it was a way to make some quick money."

They looked at him a moment. He wondered which part of that story was the strangest to them, out of all its hints about how he'd lived.

Greg grinned. "So that was a bluff? Still sounds like you've got a few kitchen tricks worth trading."

"The way you compete with Lorraine?" their father said. "Have you heard from her?"

Paul set his fork down. Did he have to bring that up, right then?

Greg said "You know I haven't in days. And those were just teases that she was fine, always cagey about if I'd see her again. Something she learned from you, Paul—oh, I know it goes back to before you and the..."

He stopped, looked around the dining room. Thinking of bugs, Paul realized.

"Anyway, do *you* know if she's coming back?" Greg's voice should have been hurt, or angry, or eager. Instead it was calm, with any other feelings hidden.

Paul met his gaze. "I... wish I knew. She said she was thinking of talking to you. She also wanted to get away from Cedar Springs, and any charges Reid might have for her too."

"She made her own choices," his father said. "She did what looked like the best option, to her."

"Or *for* her," Greg said.

Their father opened his mouth. Then he cut off, and clamped it shut.

What? Ian Schuman never hesitated, and he certainly didn't get *caught* doing it—

The next instant Paul was Opening to that mind.

The true form of those sharp eyes stole a nervous glace at him, the whole face and body of his father tilted uneasily away from him—*like he thought running would have been my best option too... does he wish* I'd *stayed missing...*

He dove back into his own head. Was it *that* easy to start grabbing at people's thoughts? With family?

Guilt had to be splashed all over his face. His peek, his father's fear, how they'd all just dropped into Lorraine's nightmare of people finding their thoughts were wide open. How Reid said the power was too corrupting to have at all. *But my father wants me to disappear, or I'm just wrong—*

"Now, how's the Nickelson ad coming?" his father said.

They didn't know.

Greg stepped right in with "On track. A good response there and it'll help our whole quarter pick up, even with the delays."

Back and forth the two went. Of course, they could always talk about the firm—the mistake here was in bringing up anything else.

Paul listened, nodded, tried to ignore the rage coiling in his stomach. It couldn't be just the business they cared about. Besides, most of their news sounded like Schuman and Son was holding on, in spite of their worried clients and time helping him and the bail they set aside.

Or they should *hate me. Or I'm reading it all wrong.*

When he took his last bite he jumped up with "Need a shower." He'd left the room behind before he realized he hadn't even cleared his plate from the table.

He shut the bathroom door behind him... and found himself alone and free for the first time since he'd taken that step into the Cedar

Springs police station. No, not free, not with the thing that was clamped to his ankle. But ohh, he needed to be alone.

The clothes—his own torn, grease-stained clothes that they'd let him put on as he left—stripped off as fast as his fingers could pull at them. At least until he had to work the pants off over the anklet, the bulky, threatening block he'd had to bring in among his family, of *course* he was putting everything they had in danger, even with all their support…

He couldn't even stand in the shower. Instead he had to tinker with faucet levels and wrap towels around the plastic, and trust that all its bulk wasn't just waiting for one drop of water to work through the seam and start the whole system screeching for the police.

How's anyone supposed to scrub the memory of the prison off them while they're stuck with this?

They aren't.

He stabbed his sight at the thing, then the same hearing that could hear the current buzzing in a hidden microphone. Some of that power ran just behind the case's seam. More tendrils of sound showed wires inside the strap, all waiting to feel any break if the prisoner forced it open or cut it off.

Reid said the anklet was tamperproof. But against true senses and day after day of wearing it? Or, none of that could stop him from simply slashing it loose and using his skill to disappear…

None of that mattered. *Do Dad and Greg* expect *me to bolt and leave them on the hook for that bail?* He'd come back to face down the people who called him a criminal. Face them, and win.

Or go back to that cell.

No. Paul locked his eyes on the lump of blue plastic on his leg. Reid couldn't get more than scraps of proof about his work—and the cop *couldn't* prove he'd robbed or cheated anyone, ever. He and CC would keep smashing through those accusations until he walked free. Or beat them down to just a list of fines.

Or back to that cell.

Its voices clashing, the doors clashing closed and how it echoed off the whole mass of concrete... those sounds were still waiting in his ears. The crawling of his skin, every inch of him screaming *danger* against every direction... *But I'm out, I'm out, I'm crouching on Greg's own bathroom...* The shaking swept through him, pulled him in, made him press down on the tiles fighting not to curl up into a naked ball.

And the anklet caught against a foot. He glared at the thing again. Just a bit of plastic and humming power clamped around him, not some rattlesnake about to strike. And, it was never the only thing holding him here.

When he tried to sleep, they let him take the big yellow sofa that had always been part of the family. Its cushions weren't nearly enough.

* * *

The new day finally began. Paul wrapped himself in some of Greg's too-large clothes and parked himself in the kitchen, turning every heightened sense he had into frying up the perfect eggs and sausage.

Greg wolfed his down and raced off for the office as fast as he could say *delicious*. Their father savored his, then settled in with his laptop.

Until CC arrived.

The lawyer had a broad smile and all but bounced on her feet, even before she unwrapped the carton of coffees with her. "Are you settling in alright?" she began.

"Sure. And I owe the whole thing to you. Dad, I wish you'd heard her speech yesterday. The prosecutor never had a chance."

"You're too kind. But we need to keep our momentum up now." She dropped into a chair and cued up her laptop. "You know Detective Reid must be out combing through every report they have, in hopes of getting just one more glimmer of proof against you. We need to take every case he can make and crush it."

"How?" It always felt strange to speak it, to ask someone else for a whole world of ideas in one word.

CC smiled. "We look through these events, and we bring out the message that can keep your narrative on track: how clear it is that anything you did do, you did for the good of the people involved. That means getting some of *your* promotions ready," she nodded to his father, then back to Paul with "and practicing what *you* might tell a jury.

"And more than that, Paul. We consider taking the offensive, with a list of other Good Samaritan moments they don't know about. Anything they can't charge you for, that makes it clearer it's all part of a bigger picture."

Paul felt the frown starting to dig into his face. Of course he'd never meant his work as a crime... but CC had no idea how deep that hole went. Or what made it possible.

His father said "An ambitious plan, of the kind that risks backfiring. Paul could end up accused of every whistleblowing that's ever happened here."

"I understand that. But we can win this, by using the scale of how ambitious Paul's work already is."

"No, he's right," Paul said. "It's risky. Reid will only keep watching for more charges to add. He knows too much about my methods already." *Even without using his own power.* "And Eckles went after me just on the rumor that I might be someone he could use. Van Howe's still there in the guards, isn't he?"

"Is that fear, Paul? We *need* to take risks now. Reid will keep digging no matter what we do. We need to show we have something that can outweigh what he finds, if they ever take it to a jury. Tell me, do you think the evidence he's finding will simply go away?"

"No." He met her gaze, reaching for words that would get through to her.

"I've lived in fear." CC leaned toward him. "But when I look at your case... the LifeLab frame, the charity fraud? You chose to bring those into the light, and you risked more than anyone did to make a difference. It's time to embrace that."

"Is that worth it? It's also set off Reid, Eckles, Van Howe—and they'd just be the start."

"Let me tell you something, Paul. Just on the way here, I saw a car that I thought was following me. I actually let myself twist through a few streets and sat parked, until I was sure he was gone. I couldn't stop thinking it might be Van Howe. That he was chasing me because I asked the prison to investigate him."

Paul shifted on the sofa. She couldn't be sure, he couldn't know—

"That seems like a stretch," his father said.

"You see!" She laughed. "And I admit it, those were some of the same fears I've felt since that other case I talked about. The client I lost. So, it's time to get past all that and deal with what's real."

"And if the danger is real?" Paul said. "You've met Van Howe too, what if he *is* that vicious?" *The way the guard's thoughts had clenched and lashed around—*

"Still an unlikely idea," Ian Schuman cut in. "But CC, let's look back at the legal strategy here, before we jump to what we're willing to risk or not."

Paul held up a hand. "Hold on. Did you see that car again?"

"No. I told you, I was wrong. But what we need—"

The doorbell rang.

A lash of shock had Paul's feet shifting, ready to leap up.

His father started, then let out a weak laugh. "They got me. One moment," he called out.

He stood up—slowly, still a man recovering from being *shot.* Paul stepped past him to the door, ignoring the irritated look. He checked the peephole.

Not Van Howe. On the other side stood Eugene Brandt, from Life-Lab. Plump and ruddy-faced, as if he weren't quite in condition to come visiting, and smiling as if staying away never occurred to him.

Paul stepped back, and his father opened it.

"Mr. Schuman, isn't it? My name's Brandt."

CC crowded in behind them. "This is a surprise, sir. We spoke so briefly. What brings a company head down here?"

"Ms. Claire too? Good that you're here, I only have a minute."

The three of them stepped back to let him in.

He went on "Call it a lucky guess of mine, or you just being on my way. Anyway, I thought I'd make a personal appeal to our whistle-blower here. You did get our letter? We're hoping you'll consider explaining how you got past our security, in exchange for LifeLab dropping charges against you."

Paul forced a smile. Behind Brandt he saw his father's head dipping in a deep nod. Didn't any of them understand the dangers here?

"Quite a generous offer," CC said. "Of course we'll consider it. I don't suppose you have any influence with St. Cedric's Hospital, to suggest they make a similar deal?"

"Sorry."

Alarms, binoculars, a stolen badge? Paul fumbled through his list of tactics. There had to be *something* he could tell them.

Brandt took a step toward him. "Paul? No offense to your lawyer, but I would like a word with you alone."

CC shook her head, a tiny, fierce little warning against it.

There had to be a way. "Alright."

Paul led Brandt a few steps to the kitchen, keeping his eyes away from the others' worried looks.

Brandt leaned close, to whisper. "Full disclosure about that offer. I was curious about you, and we paid that Van Howe guard to keep an eye on any security skills that you showed in prison. So he may have brought the convict, Eckles, in on it—I swear I never expected any of what happened then."

What?

Paul stared, but Brandt was silent now, waiting for him to take it in. Paul reached for his thoughts.

His face barely changed. The same downcast, ashamed look, the same struggle to force his gaze back up to meet Paul's. Only a few more nervous glances away than his outer face showed.

If those signs were right, Brandt *was* the regretful businessman simply trying to face up to his mistake.

But Van Howe— "Van Howe has a history like that?" Paul hissed. "CC thought she was followed on the street today. And he already saw her call for an investigation into him."

Brandt spun around to walk back toward CC. "You said someone followed you today?"

"What do you mean? I said it was a mistake."

Paul glared at her. She just *didn't get it.*

Brandt said "You might consider that perhaps there's something to this. There was a prison guard, Van Howe, that just got fired today, and you were one of the first to accuse him? Ms. Claire, I'll deny this if you ever say it—but I paid him to keep an eye on Paul. Then matters spiraled out of control. I knew the man was corrupt when I had him approached, but he could be dangerous. I mean, dangerous to you."

"You make it sound so ominous." CC pursed her lips and blew out a breath. "I don't believe that makes a connection to one moment on the street. Would he really dig himself in deeper by going after me?"

Van Howe shouldn't, no. Still, the way his inner self had been glaring around after she accused him...

CC added "I appreciate your concern, believe me. Now, you came to talk about Paul and your security? What is it you'd like to know?

*I can't tell Brandt, I can't warn CC—*Paul took a step between the two.

But Brandt edged back to eye him and the lawyer together. He said "Frankly, who you contacted in our organization. Please," and he raised a hand, "we're not looking to fire anyone. As I said, we think you were trying to help save LifeLab's reputation. Still, once someone goes behind our back once, we do need to consider how much confidential information they can be trusted near. And, we'd like to know what other methods you used. You can help us patch any weaknesses in our system. I'll talk to my security chief about the details."

Paul was opening his mouth when CC said "Excellent. You can send the terms to my office. And we do appreciate your interest in working out an approach that could give us all what we want."

"You'll have a draft soon. Mr. Schuman, I honestly believe you were trying to help us. You shouldn't go to jail for that."

Paul Opened to Brandt's thoughts again. The man's true face softened to a regretful smile, nothing more—

Paul yanked his focus back. "But, I never agreed..." Too clumsy. He tried "That is, I don't know if I have anything you'd want. Or what it might mean to anyone else."

Brandt didn't even slow down. "Just look at the terms, and we'll take it from there. And now I really am running late."

Then it was Paul's father pushing in. "Thank you for stopping by. We'll call soon—"

And Ian Schuman was walking Brandt out. Paul stood there on the fringe as the master publicist led the executive to the door, with just the few words and smiles that might help Brandt remember him, never a fraction more. Then the door closed.

He turned back to his son. "What was that about the guard? You were warning us *just* before the man who hired him showed up with the same message? How are we supposed to interpret a coincidence on that scale?" His voice had only one tremble in it, one hint of what he thought he'd glimpsed.

This wasn't part of my power, Dad. Or, this is just what my power brings out of the woodwork.

Paul looked at CC. She might be in actual danger, and it all started with people like Brandt wanting a way to know his secrets.

He said "Look, Van Howe really did look like a ticking bomb to me. What if this is simply me and Brandt seeing the same thing, and you too? Even if he wasn't following you today, what if your instincts are on edge because he's a real threat?"

CC's brows lowered. "Are you trying to scare me now?"

"I think…" He forced out the words. "I think it could be unsafe to represent me. Maybe you should rethink—"

"Don't you finish that sentence. If that's true, it's an enemy I've already made. And I'm not convinced it is." She shook her head, like the threat was no more than a distraction from her cause. "I'll keep it in mind, but I want you to start thinking about what Mr. Brandt said to you. That's what we want everyone connected with your work to think: that it's not something you should go to jail for."

"I know," Paul sighed. "I guess I'll see what they're offering."

"Of course. And we won't admit to anything without full confidentiality and protection. And now, I think it's time I started preparing." She scooped up her laptop. "Any questions right now?"

So that was it, the meeting was over?

"None, not yet. But thank you," he managed to say.

And then she was walking out.

When she was gone, his father rounded on him. "You're making me ask a second time now. What's that really about?"

Paul flinched away from that gaze. "Can you just—"

"Don't deny it. A man just walked through that door to hand you one piece of your freedom, and all you do is worry? What's going on here?"

Paul glanced around. The police *probably* hadn't bugged the place, but…

He reached for his father's laptop. He typed out the words *Can't risk more attention about,* and then he tapped his ear. As the only way he could mention the power itself.

Ian Schuman looked at him, and slowly nodded.

Paul sat down onto the sofa, on suddenly tired legs. One thought spun around and around his head: *it* was already starting.

It had from the moment Reid targeted him, then hauled him in... Brandt had only been curious, his thoughts made that clear. But his poking around had put Van Howe on the track of something that snagged Eckles's interest, and now CC might be in danger too?

And Brandt wants to know more *about my secrets?*

Paul let himself grow still, muscle by muscle. The same calmness that could let him sit for hours waiting for some clue. He watched his father thumb through the laptop's files, and played his hearing around the neighborhood outside. A few voices, a glimpse of snow through the blinds. Peaceful.

Whatever came...

I'll handle it? How? His fist pressed down on the yellow cushion, digging deeper and deeper. If CC were in danger, how would he know? He couldn't watch over her, couldn't go outside after her. Or tell her why Van Howe worried him.

At least I warned her.

Slowly his hand relaxed. The sounds outside played around him, and minutes flowed and streamed on. He let himself think about the LifeLab offer—was there anything he could give them? If he claimed he'd used bugs on them, would that confession get to the police? Or would it just reduce the pressure on CC, on his father and brother, and bring them all closer to finishing...

Bang!

The blow on the door jolted him to his feet, all sense of safety shattered—if he'd ever trusted he was free at all.

"Police, Schuman! Inspection, now!"

They stomped in before his father reached the door—of course Reid had a key. Paul stood at the edge of the living room, but the first two cops moved right past him like some dark blue tide. They paced from room to room, yanked open drawers, searched and poked and prodded through it all more fiercely than they had when they'd left him there.

His father faced down Reid. "You couldn't give us twenty-four hours alone here?"

"We inspect whenever we have a need," Reid said. "And a state senator just said we have a need."

What?

Paul swallowed the word. Reid brought out a tiny keypad and crouched down to play it over the tracker on his ankle.

Paul Opened to the sounds. That dimmest hum might be its current shifting, useless—

Reid was already squinting at the plastic with a magnifying glass. Looking for more of those lockpicking scratches he loved to find, and Paul could only stand still and be poked over. When he'd just started to feel he was *out* of that cell.

His father said "So who's twisting your chain this time, Detective?"

"A picture of Wallace and his mistress. You seen the Gazette?" Reid held up a shot on his phone.

A tabloid cover of a man in a coat, a strange woman leaning against him, outside the entrance to the Selene in all of the motel's grimy glory.

Seriously? Paul pressed his lips shut. Reid had to know his case file enough to know he tracked people for cheating on bigger things than their own marriage. *So now I get the blame every time the paparazzi get lucky?*

"What do you people think you're doing?" Greg stormed in the front door.

"That should be my line, for you." Reid showed him the picture. "This might be yesterday morning. Your brother was still in custody, but where were you, Mr. Schuman?"

"At court getting him out," Greg shot back. "You saw me there."

"And the night before? One tip to embarrass someone powerful, while Paul Schuman is in a cell—might be a good way to make your brother look innocent. Someone sent the Gazette vultures out there, and Wallace wants answers—"

"*He* wants?" Greg laughed. "I don't know why anyone bothers to run a picture like that. Everyone knows about Senator Wallace and his women. The only thing different from any other week is that your witch hunt found him someone to blame it on."

That's exactly *what it is, and you saw it right off.* Paul gave his brother a quick grin, not caring what Reid saw.

The detective kept his gaze on Greg. "Heard from your wife lately?"

"Now *you're* asking about—" Greg stopped cold.

Oh no. Paul caught at Reid's thoughts—they held a sharp glare at both Schumans, a careful stare that was more searching than certain. But, Reid couldn't think Lorraine would snap that kind of cheap picture like that just to give them a distraction.

Greg's fingers flexed, in and out of fists. "Lorraine would... she'd..."

He took a step toward Reid. Paul caught at his arm.

But Greg wasn't pushing through him. Instead he stopped where he stood and growled "She'd be here with us, if you weren't chasing her and Paul all over the country!"

Reid glared back at him. "They're the ones who ran. Your brother is facing time for a long list of very real crimes, enough to raise some legitimate questions about her too."

Their father stepped in between them. "I think that's enough," he said.

"It'll be enough soon," Greg said. "Or any time you can remember the laws about harassment, Detective. Each time you open your mouth, something more goes on my list."

His arms fell to his sides. His fists stayed clenched, but his anger was leashed.

Reid said "I do remember the laws. It's your family that forgets them. And your wife just melts them with a word—are you sure you know her at all?"

Says the man afraid of his own power. Paul kept his eyes on Reid, and listened to Greg's breathing seethe but hold steady. If Reid was trying to shake something, or someone, loose from the family, he was failing.

Greg didn't open his mouth again, until Reid and his men finished up and drove away.

Then he said "What if it *is* Lorraine?"

CHAPTER SEVEN

OUT THE WINDOW

"It *could* be her," Greg went on. "Lorraine's first moves in trying to weaken their case, say. If she's not ready to show herself—"

"Greg…" Their father shook his head slowly. "Are you going to let Reid tell you what to think?"

"But he could be right. She could be out there—" Greg's hand waved toward the window, and it trembled— "reminding them all that people get their dirty laundry shown all the time, they can't just pin everything on Paul. I bet she could find dirt like this with—"

"*We all* want it to be her," Paul said, before Greg could go on about powers and secrets. "But you said it yourself. This is the kind of everyday scandal that's always going on. If Senator Wallace is the type who sneaks around all the time, he must get caught all the time. It doesn't need anyone more to make this happen."

"I *know!*"

Greg stared at the floor. He could have been a statue, with even his breathing choked off.

Then, "But, what if it still—"

Paul said "It's not her. Look, she's under suspicion herself. If she got involved it'd be to meddle with the sightings at LifeLab—"

Because Lorraine wouldn't put herself in danger again, for anyone except herself. Paul kept it off his tongue, but that was the woman he'd gotten to know at Cedar Springs. And finally, the way she'd limped away with her injuries, just wanting to be safe now...

Greg's eyes were locked onto his. He had to have guessed some of that, from how long she'd kept her secret from them all.

Then Greg snapped "I'm going anyway."

Their father said "Is that so? That's a state senator trying to bully the police. Do you want to get yourself locked up?"

"Of course not. I'll just look around, is all. Ask some questions at the hotel, and the Gazette. Maybe I'll learn something. Or she'll still be around there, and she'll see me asking." He started for the door.

Paul stepped in front of him. "Slow down. Maybe I can—"

All of Greg's strength shoved into him, past him, sent him spinning aside to catch himself against the wall.

Beep beep beep—the anklet chirped, a harsh sound that came faster each moment. Like a heartbeat gathering speed at the thought of it catching him. Greg didn't even slow down.

Paul lunged around to the keypad the police had stuck in the wall, and the display counting down. His fingers fumbled at the combination. *Did Reid even get out of the neighborhood yet?*

He stood in front of its camera and wrenched his voice into steadiness. "False alarm. This is Paul Schuman, right here, still in the house, can you see? I just bumped the thing, that's all. You need anything else from me?"

Silence. Was someone even listening there?

"Got it, cancelling the alarm. Try being more careful." The voice almost sounded *bored*.

The beeping ceased, and the wall's display cleared. He reached his hearing out, and heard Greg's car roaring away. "He's gone."

"Of course he's gone," his father said. "Did you have to remind him how much there is about her that he doesn't know? He had to leave."

Paul slumped down to sit, feeling that glare on him. But, those pictures just didn't seem like Lorraine's work... *and I keep telling Greg that her power and her choices aren't my fault.* Or her fault, not completely. But the message wasn't reaching him.

Lorraine, out there or on the road somewhere. Van Howe—Brandt said he'd just been fired? The guard's thoughts had looked furious enough already. And now Greg running off.

And the damn tracker was still clamped to his leg. He closed his eyes, and let the sound of its current fill him. For what little his Opened hearing could make out... still, it told him something about its inside, and there were only so many ways to build a pressure sensor or a circuit to interrupt... he could feel the wires running inside the nylon strap around him, sensitive as a spider's legs...

He dragged himself out of the trance. They'd take the tracker off *in prison,* if he couldn't beat Reid's charges. And make CC understand that her moves were drawing more trouble.

* * *

An hour later his father got the call.

CC sounded more confident than ever. "I'm on my way back. We should have LifeLab's terms soon. And there'll be something else," and her voice had a hint of teasing to it.

They didn't have to wait long. Paul tracked her gray coupe driving up, and watched her walk up to the door.

Sarah pulled up behind her. She started up the walk, actually moving slower than CC had hurried in.

"Hello, all," CC said when she stepped inside. She nodded over her shoulder. "I thought it was time Sarah added her voice to some of what we're doing."

Sarah halted in the doorway, eyes on Paul.

She hadn't hesitated in the visiting room. And before that she'd supported him, then feared him and his power, then defended him...

Then a quick step brought her inside. "Good to see you again. And out of that place too." Her face had a glow to it.

His father beckoned her in. "And you. In fact, we could use a reporter right now. You heard about the Senator Wallace picture at the
Gazette?"

Sarah wrinkled her nose. "The Gazette isn't reporters. It's only
trash floating downstream."

As they moved to sit, Paul stood and went to the blinds at the window. He stretched his hearing out, along the quiet street, the isolated
footsteps scuffing along the snow. A slow peek outside confirmed
each one: no sign of Van Howe or anyone following her.

"About your defense." CC waved him away from the window, and
when he didn't move she turned to Sarah. "I've been telling Paul that
he needs to take more credit for the good he's done, if he's going to
stay out of prison. You helped him break some of those stories, and
then of course he gave himself up to clear your name."

She paused at that, and shot a glance between Sarah and him. *Is
she* matchmaking *too, besides running my defense?*

"So, can you tell my client that he needs to stop hiding what he's
trying to do?"

Sarah closed her eyes. A long moment later she opened them to answer "First you were wondering about some dirt in the Gazette. Now
you want to link Paul with every secret you can find? The more important you make him, the more trouble will come after him."

She knew. She'd seen what his power could really do, and she
knew how big the risks could get, where CC didn't. Paul clamped
down the urge to give CC a smug grin. Sarah's fainter smile had to be
enough.

"That's what I've been saying," he said. "Isn't there another way to
do this? You've already gotten a man fired and thought you saw him
following you." He nudged the blind back to peep out again.

Opening cut through the distance to where a red pickup truck sat
far up at the end of the block, with its driver at the wheel.

Van Howe. Training binoculars on them.

He heard Sarah saying "I really should go. You probably want to go over this without me—"

The ex-guard's face was just a speck in the distance to normal sight, out of range for reading thoughts too. All the same, Paul steeled himself and reached out, grabbing for the image with all his strength.

The face stayed tiny. Instead he felt his power ripple around the car, and the driver's rage flared out within the headlights flashing, and a throbbing like he could *feel* the engine revving.

Paul fell back into himself, blinking and shivering. To his regular eyes it was still a far-off car parked, unmoving.

"I... think that's Van Howe there," he said.

Shouts and footsteps erupted around the room. CC was the first to the window, squeezing past him to peek out herself. "Where? I don't see him."

You can't. "He was just there. Must have turned out of view."

"Are you sure? He was there a moment ago, and now there's nothing?"

"I saw him, it was him."

CC shook her head. He reached for her thoughts, and saw her face blur and turn awkwardly away from him, closing off in doubt. Not good, not good.

He looked out. CC pulled back, and he saw Sarah watching him with the beginnings of a crease in her brow. At least she knew what he could be seeing.

"LifeLab still hasn't sent that offer." CC glanced up from her phone. "But I want to try something."

She drew herself up as she faced him.

"Paul, imagine I'm ADA Oliver. There's a jury sitting right behind me, and *you need them to understand* how you did the right thing. So right now: 'Mr. Schuman, the LifeLab corporation had just been exposed as abusing animals in their tests. Why did you try to defend them?' "

Paul frowned. CC wanted to start this now, with Sarah here? More of her thoughts that she'd "encourage" him?

"Right now!" CC said. " 'Mr. Schuman, why did you try to defend them?' "

He made himself say "They didn't do it. A former employee named Koenig faked those tests. And he used Sarah to spread his lies." *And me.* "So of course I had to get the truth out there."

He stopped, and the words sank clumsily in the silence. Only the last few sounded like they had much force in his ears, even with the volume of him already on his feet. Sarah gave him a nod.

"A good start," his father mused. "We want to keep building on that."

CC said "Let's try again. Remember, they need to believe you're fighting for the truth. Don't be afraid of that word now."

Sarah stood up. "Then it *is* time I left. You don't need me anyway. This is about your story, not what parts of it I can corroborate."

"Another time, then," his father said. "Always a pleasure."

"Hold on," Paul said. "Are you sure…" He peeked out the window.

Van Howe was gone.

He smiled in relief. "Okay. Anyway, watch yourself out there."

Sarah looked at him a moment, and glanced at the others. *Like she might say something more, if they weren't there?* Then she walked out.

"Again. 'Mr. Schuman—' "

"Let's just be sure," Paul said. He stayed at the window until her blue hybrid drove out of sight. Nothing moved after her, on the street or around it. Van Howe really had moved on.

CC's voice cut in, " 'Mr. Schuman, you were seen inside the offices of one of the oldest charities in the city. You took it upon yourself to spy on it?' "

"Oldest *cheats,* you mean." She wanted emotion from him? Fine. "That outfit had been a mix of real causes and sending money to front corporations, from the beginning."

" 'And that justified bugging their phones?' " She advanced on him, the way a prosecutor would pounce on a weak point.

Wrong move. "I never used a bug on them."

"Paul..." CC's voice softened. "It's in the list of charges. Do you want to keep saying that, when you're staring at some of the spyware or the electronic traces they found?"

"There won't be any. The prosecutor's only guessing that they're about to find something, but I never bugged them."

CC shook her head, but her worried look was more thoughtful now.

And how long before they find how I do *get my answers?* LifeLab was pushing for details too.

Or if Reid learned how he'd finally bullied Koenig into confessing, or they reopened the Quinn case... Paul glanced at his father. *When Dad took that bullet, and shot the loan shark, it wasn't self-defense. He was saving my secrets from Quinn.*

CC kept drilling him, and the longer they went, the less Paul could look at his father. Each question tried to bare more of his drive to expose frauds—as if that could outweigh how her "prosecutor" questions threw around words like *spy, intruder,* and *vigilante.* Each word chipped away at the hope that someone would still see the good in what he did.

Paul kept his face controlled. But sweat gathered and pooled under his clothes until it soaked him all through.

And CC only pushed harder. With each question, Paul heard a fiercer and fiercer edge in her voice. Was this actually steeling him for all the cases Oliver had a chance to make... or did she *assume* that he'd have to defend dozens of crimes to justify even one of them?

She raced him through the charges again and again, still arguing the initial *why* and not digging into the *how.* So far.

Then her phone vibrated.

"There, it's Mr. Brandt's offer. And there's the Confidentiality for us to sign before we see anything. A good start; this won't be some casual promise."

She scrolled through the file—two pages, that she and Paul's father took in at a glance. The form had multiple spaces for signing, so all three of them sent it back.

The offer itself appeared just seconds later.

CC began thumbing through it. "The question is, how well would this protect you from prosecution—and lawsuits—over anything you reveal..."

You still think that's the worst that my secrets can do, don't you? Paul tried to read over her shoulder, but she scrolled casually through the legal mazes.

"Confidentiality... indemnity for you... looks good in general," she said. "Now here: essentially you'd be safe from legal consequences for *anything* you gave them a full description of, excluding bodily injury, sabotage, selling their secrets... All of those are well within the code you lived by."

"I wouldn't call it a code."

"We'll work on that." She tapped the screen. "Now here: what they want is a full description of your methods, including a walk-through with their security. Oh here, this looks like a hint that they might hire you as a consultant there. They *do* value what you—"

"I can't do it! Any of it." The words tore out of his throat.

She looked at him, and her jaw tightened.

His father added "If you think they're requiring the job, they're not. And it's not so uncommon for security to hire burglars, hackers, or anyone with related skills—" He cut off on the last word. There was the Pandora's Box itself.

Paul said "They want me to walk them through everything. But the tricks I used are..." Impossible? Unmentionable?

"It's all covered there," and CC nodded at the screen again. "If you didn't break someone's bones or any of the other limits here, they can't use it against you. Just look at it. They're giving us until 5 tonight to send an answer."

She passed the offer to his father's laptop.

Paul sat beside her. The words barely held his gaze, but his eyes kept stealing glances at CC above the screen. Minutes inched by, dragged out by hopeless glances at the text, or Opening to the sounds outside.

Did it all come down to this? How long could CC keep dealing with his secrets and dangers, without knowing about the power at the root of them all?

The offer was the same as it had been ten minutes ago. The street outside…

Tires squealed.

He reached along the street outside. There, a car roared up the neighborhood, too fast—

He jumped to his feet and nudged the blind aside. Van Howe's truck tore along the afternoon street, gathering speed and already racing past their house. Not attacking, but escaping.

Seconds later a police car pulled into view. It rolled casually up to Greg's driveway, like they had no idea who they'd chased off.

"What is it now?" CC asked.

"Police again, here. And Van Howe was here, and bolted so they wouldn't see him."

"But *you* knew…"

CC's face softened into a smile.

"I shouldn't bother being surprised any more, Paul. Look, if the LifeLab deal bothers you so much, I'll see if I can talk to them. I might be able to loosen the 5pm deadline so we can negotiate more. Once we see what the police want this time, anyway."

She started to the door.

"Wait—" he heard himself saying.

The door opened. "Inspection!"

Uniforms trooped in, eyeing them with the same *casually* suspicious look Paul was starting to hate. This time Reid wasn't among them.

"Two inspections in a few hours?" his father told them. "Don't pretend that's following your standards."

"The *standard* is a *surprise* inspection," the cop in front said, the biggest of them. "Shouldn't be that big a shock, after you had an incident with this." He waved to Paul's anklet and raised one of their testing remotes.

CC said "So it's routine. Let me know if 'our good officers' do anything stupid." She reached for the door.

"Hold on! Please!"

But Paul had to lock his feet in place; the cop was about to grab at his ankle. The man's teeth flashed in a warning.

At least I can tell them this much. "Listen. I saw a dangerous suspect out there. Van Howe."

"No stalling. We've got a job to do." The cop grabbed his foot.

"I'm serious. He collaborated in a prison break—a *real* crime," he had to growl at the cop. "He's got a grudge against CC now. He drove off when you came up, but he could still be hanging around. Go look—it's a red truck with a crack in the windshield. CC, you have to give them a chance."

"Of all the…"

"He's talking about an attempted prison break, or a suspect in it," Ian Schuman said. "How will it look if you ignore it, and then Van Howe grabs Ms. Claire as she leaves?"

"Oh, for—I hate inspections anyway," a woman cop in the back said. "Once around the block." She pushed past CC and marched outside.

Paul let out a sigh, while the bigger cop pulled up his pants cuff and went to work on the anklet. He gave it only a couple of beeps with his tester, then a single long look at the plastic casing.

Then he stood up, and the police spread out and began tromping through the house. They moved like part of their "search" plan was for their feet to shake the floorboards for anything hidden in them.

But for a moment, the cops were in the next room or upstairs. The three were almost alone.

"Now I do need to go," CC said. "Paul, don't worry so much about your tricks of the trade. With these terms you could pretty much have read their minds and they couldn't touch you."

God. I get one chance to say it...

Paul darted toward her, two quick steps to reach her side. She startled back a step, but he whispered "But, what if I did..."

His voice went hoarse. He swallowed.

Feet stomped up behind him. All three police, right behind him. "That just leaves the basement," one said, and they headed for the stairs.

His father called "Careful down there!" and moved after them.

To slow them down, so I can finish here.

He looked back at the surprised lawyer. "I mean, what if I *can?* Listen—"

"What are you talking about?" Her voice tightened, suspicious.

"About spotting Van Howe out there. And explaining to LifeLab. You just said—"

The front door swung open.

"No red trucks lurking out there," the woman cop declared. "Alright, Mr. Schuman. You and I need to have a talk about the Home Incarceration manual."

"And I need to go," CC said.

Paul grabbed for a breath. *She has to understand this.* He called out "What if I *have* been doing what you just said? It's all in the mind." Her eyes went wider. "I mean, it really is that simple. And that tangled up."

She stared, her eyes slowly filling up wider, wider...

"Now you're insulting me, Paul. Whatever it is, I said I'd buy us some time to work out the right deal. Just leave that to me."

When she left, the door didn't slam behind her, but he still felt the *thunk* in his bones.

That sound was swallowed a moment later, as the police continued marching and poking through the house. The woman cop broke out the house arrest instructions and led him through their points, and he nodded blandly at each. Not one of the warnings mentioned brothers shoving him into walls and setting off the alarm.

Then at last, the police drove away. There was only Paul, his father, and the silence.

"Thanks for following them to the basement there. I tried to tell CC to... remember what our case is about." He tapped his ear.

"You did what you could. It might be what she needs." His father settled in his chair again, and Paul saw him wince. From his wound.

"Dad, I'm sorry you had to sit through all that. The cops, and CC's hitting me with all their accusations. And all that after getting you..." Paul could only gesture to him, to the chair he was all but trapped in.

"You did what you did." His father took out his phone, began thumbing through messages.

No. I can't leave it at that.

Paul took a step toward him. "Look. It's just that everywhere I looked I saw liars and cheats that needed stopping. And I know I should have done more for the family than just saying I was alright—"

This is crazy, I put them through so much and I'm so afraid of bugs I still can't tell them what it's like having the power tearing my head up. Say something, anything—

"I tried so hard to keep all of you separate from—"

"Do you mind?" his father growled. "I'm trying to check for messages from Greg."

"Oh."

"Someone needs to check on if he's okay," he added. "Oh. Sure."

Greg's fooling around had started most of the family's trouble. Paul had kept them out of his own risks for two years, until he'd come back to clean up Greg's mess—

Paul dropped down to the old sofa, hard enough to hear springs squeak.

With CC and her records gone, the next real copy of their case and LifeLab's offer was on his father's machine. *And there's no damn way I'll ask him to take his attention off Greg now!*

Instead he mentally ran through the cases they said they had on him. LifeLab. St. Central, with multiple counts out of all the months he'd searched it for answers. Addamson Abbot. The inspector, the charity, the vitamins, the several others. Extra risks like the charity, where the prosecutor would assume he must have crossed the line into wiretapping... and they *couldn't* know what bits of proof Reid might dig up.

Ian Schuman just stayed in his chair, typing his way down his own rabbit-hole. The way he always was, him and Greg. Paul reached out to listen to the street outside, the chatters and clashes of families that weren't locked in.

The tracker clung to his ankle.

And I've just felt it being tested again. Its current hums so much softer now than when it's being tested... that wouldn't be true if it had a big busy mic capturing sounds as well as location all the time. Or did he have that wrong? The case had no holes or gaps that could let sound in.

Wires whispered inside the band around his leg. More current pooled across the opening of the plastic housing, maybe another circuit-interruption alarm. *The strap could be cut if its wires stayed connected, or the casing opened with the same kind of bridging.* Cutting off the exposed band would be much less delicate, but there'd be no hope of hiding that afterward—

Paul gritted his teeth. The whole thought was idiotic, no better than him rattling the loose support back in his cell.

He pushed his hearing to the street outside again. Cars and a few people trundled through the snow outside. When had the snow begun falling again?

LifeLab. St. Central. Addamson Abbot. He had to be ready, for anything…

And the anklet was still stuck to his leg. Its outer wires lay around his skin like alien veins—but it would all come off some day if he faced those accusations down.

That hum. The wires beside his flesh, the buzz of the battery, the softest sounds of their radio tracker, the system's tireless little ear. The alarms, sleepy fingers stretching around him and touch-sensitive teeth lurking just inside the living mouth that held all the rest…

"Hey—" The sound trickled through to him. Something jarred his shoulder, drawing him back to himself.

"What?" he told his father. His face flushed—he knew better than to get pulled into Opening to anything.

A look of concern lingered on Ian Schuman's face, but it faded as he handed Paul his phone. "For you. Of course."

The name on the screen was *Reid.*

He felt *that, Reid felt me probing his tracker—*

The wash of fear only lasted an instant. Reid was probably miles out of reach, and he didn't use the powers he had.

"This is Paul. What do you want, Detective?" No point in tiptoeing around it with him.

"Getting two inspections in a day? You need to be more careful." There was that same smugness, thicker than ever.

"Greg was right, you're begging for a harassment charge. What do you *want?"* He tried to stop there, but the words kept pouring out. "You really think I'll stop fighting and throw myself on the court's mercy, and start seeing it all the way you do? That everything I've done is wrong?"

"Everything you've 'done' affects everything around you, Schuman. You think there are no consequences?"

"I know there are!"

Oh God, *do I know! They shot Dad, Greg's off chasing Lorraine…*

"And there are some for you too," he flung back. "That's why you're obsessed with beating me. The more you can make me pay, the more you can convince yourself you can't use your own gifts, ever."

This time he bit down the rest of his challenge. But he knew, each time Reid called him out of the blue, it had to mean the detective was wrestling with his power's temptation.

"You think you know everything. I suppose you really could think that, couldn't you?" Reid actually sighed, a sound of *pity*. "But, there has to be a way to teach you."

And he hung up.

Paul stared at the screen. The cop was only using him to yell warnings at himself… So Reid would never stop until he buried him in a hole as deep as his own fears. *And I have to sit here while he shovels more dirt on.*

The door rattled open.

He jumped to his feet. All that time straining his hearing at the locator and he didn't even spot someone in the driveway.

Greg stalked in. Paul stole a peep at their father, bracing for some look of sheer relief at having the 'good' son back. But Ian Schuman only gave Greg a simple smile.

"No sign of Lorraine," Greg reported. "She might not be in this at all. Or I missed her, so she might hear later how I came around."

And that would convince Lorraine to see him when nothing else had? *But I know how hard it is to find her, or me, when we don't want to be.* "I'm glad you're back alright. Since Van Howe's been lurking around the streets," he added. "I think he's gone now."

"Okay. So what do we want for food? It's after five."

"Five? There should be a message from CC…" Their father took the phone back. "Nothing."

"What's this?" Greg said.

Paul said "We had a five-o'clock deadline to take LifeLab's deal, and CC went to them trying to push it back. She might have called to reassure us by now."

Greg frowned. "So you're saying…"

"Let's find out," and their father snapped off a quick email.

Minutes ground by, and then he sent a second one.

Finally he looked up. "LifeLab says she never showed up."

I should have stopped her. Paul felt the certainty, as Greg said "No? What does that mean?"

"They found a gray car like hers at the edge of their lot, empty, where it might have been forced off the road. And there's no sign of CC."

CHAPTER EIGHT

ONE LIFE

That rage…

Paul could feel it again, Van Howe crouching in his truck and fuming as he watched them all, fury that had reached clear down the block.

Of course he had CC.

The sounds of the room were another world, far off and meaningless. All he felt was that anger, and the certainty, and the trembling in his fingers just when he needed them under control.

Then the voices crashed back in. "I don't care if they reported it! You check with LifeLab, you start a search, or I'll make it my business to tell the whole city—"

His father. His family, people he couldn't put in more danger.

"Sarah says she made it home fine." Greg looked up from checking his own phone.

It doesn't have to be me. There's still the police. There's Reid, he'd understand that Van Howe is that dangerous when I tell him…

I tried to tell him about Eckles too.

Softly he said "I'm… going upstairs. I think it's best you stay inside tonight. And down here."

Greg looked at him, and understanding stretched across his face. "You can't!"

"He can," their father said. "If he couldn't, he'd still just be sitting here."

If only it were that simple. The shaking in Paul's fingers stretched and spread as he stepped into the kitchen. The tiniest and sharpest knife there, a handful of flatware, a couple of dishcloths. Those should cover the basics. A few more steps brought him to Greg's room up-stairs—at least he could give them some deniability.

When he put it all at risk.

He grabbed a lamp from the wall. Opening to touch let him clench his fingers into stillness again, and he sliced the insulation from the lamp's cord. Then he settled on the floor, with his legs twisted to let him bend over the tracker anklet.

Electronics... he'd never had enough free time to study them. Most of what he'd learned was matched to how his power could hear the current itself. *They built this to run power through where they ex-pected any tampering would interrupt it. I just have to keep those points connected.*

If any senses, any touch, could be delicate enough. There were on-ly three wires running through the strap, he could bridge those with loops and cut the strap under the loop...

And find CC and then keep running before the police came to check on him again? The moment he put a visible cut in the strap, he'd have to abandon his father and brother, and the bail they'd put up.

His family's voices broke through from the floor below. Hushed, talking about ordering dinner.

Was CC even still *alive?*

Van Howe wanted revenge, and she could have been missing for hours already. What those hours could mean...

Paul glared at the thing on his leg and forced those doubts away. CC had believed he did it all to help people—he couldn't simply cut his ties to her, or anyone.

Instead he brought the knife over to the lamp cord's wiring. His fingers shook again, and he forced them still. Just cut a few strips from the strands of copper...

The knife slipped. A thin line of blood welled up on his thumb.

Yeah. Good start.

He Opened deeper, deeper into touch, to reach past the twinge of pain and root the shaking out of his muscles. Shifting to hearing let him plot the sensor between the plastic's edges. Sight measured the casing itself.

Slowly, moving in the blind precision of Opened touch, he scraped the knife inside the plastic seam... just enough to widen it and make room. He eased the loops of copper inside it, slowly, working each of their tiny tips into place, like positioning a massive twenty-fingered hand by using only the two digits that were alive.

If it wasn't too late.

Work the knife in again. Hold it all in place, while prying the case just enough. The plastic eased apart.

He took his sight back and looked at the open casing. Battery, tracker and transmitter, the web of wires he'd laid over the lid. And the jaws that held the strap in.

Poking and studying from one angle and another, he at last fitted more wires in to keep the current connected, and worked the fastening...

Open.

The strap slid loose. The anklet lifted away to be placed on the floor, silent and harmless in its new nest of wires.

Let's see Lorraine and her mind-twisting do that!

The nightstand clock said he'd been working almost an hour. His foot cramped and ached from being sat on so long—but that melted away when he stood up, free.

He dug around Greg's room for extra clothes to borrow against the winter. The window slid up.

The fierce night cold slashed at him. For one moment he thought, he could turn back and click the anklet on again, and nobody had to know he'd beaten it...

He shifted his weight out onto the sill, sliding over until he could drag the window closed behind him and dangle by his fingertips. Kicking off the wall let him drop—he made it past the strip of grass to reach the driveway. There a bit of scuffing his shoes on the pavement hid his more obvious tracks, and they could shovel the walk to get the rest later.

One more long glance around the dimming neighborhood, and he was off down the street.

He was most of the way down the block, when he glimpsed a police car pull into view behind him.

Steady, it only feels like the thing's picking up speed. Paul kept walking, despite the wash of utter cold through him. He was just a guy out in a sweatshirt, maybe a too-stubborn jogger. *Please don't be Reid in that car.*

The police car rolled on by. Only a patrol.

He shifted to a proper jog when it was gone, anything to try to keep the fear from settling into his flesh. He'd risked everything in the hope that CC still had a chance—now he was out on the street with just his senses.

The LifeLab facility lay far across town. His lungs began to ache and his legs were stiff, from too many days stuck in one small space or another.

But the *streets*...

One building, one block at a time, they slid by. Even in the white winter and the graying night, people sifted and flowed and passed by each other, each one on their own business. Cars and trucks rolled past, flashing company names on their sides or simple bumper stickers as they passed. His home, again.

The nearer he drew to his destination, the deeper the dark thought burrowed into him: *Could I go back and be locked in that box again? Did I ever think I could?*

The LifeLab building was a single broad square on the street. It and its parking lot stood a bit apart from the industrial complexes around it, but they'd said CC's car had been forced off nearby, not at it. Paul moved through the side streets, running enhanced sight over the snow.

One turn, one corner after another showed nothing. Only passing cars moving through the evening.

Then he saw it: one car parked at the edge of an alley, with a man in a security guard's uniform sitting in it. His attention shifted between his phone and brief glances to the main street in front of him, and especially up the alley behind him.

Back there, then? Paul swung around the block to enter the alley from the back. So LifeLab was keeping the site guarded—still waiting for the police?

Or else Brandt or someone in there was covering something up. They'd been the ones who knew Van Howe in the first place. The thought came to Paul all too easily.

He peeped around the back of the alley. CC's nimble gray coupe sprawled in the snow, at the end of a swerving track. He could just picture CC ducking off the road to check if Van Howe was following her, and then fishtailing to a stop when she found herself cut off. Where its license plate should be it had only twisted bits of metal.

Nobody else was watching. He eyed the bored guard in front and chose his moment, then slipped forward to crouch down behind the car's hidden side. The car itself looked undamaged, apart from the missing plate.

To cover his fingerprints he wrapped his hand in the hem of the sweatshirt, and tried the door. Unlocked.

He leaned inside, keeping low beneath the guard's view. The inside was so neat and empty it could have been brand-new, if the new-car smell had been replaced by coffee and the scattered nicks and scrapes of a car in use. The glovebox was empty too—another step to slow down confirming who the driver had been.

Paul Opened to scent.

Coffee and more coffee roiled against the heater's fumes, cut by the brisk air outside, all tangled together... The coffee could have been the mix CC brought to their meeting... Was that a trace of the perfume she used? Was that gun oil?

He wrenched back into himself. Scent was always the hardest sense to keep clear—he had to have better options than that.

He had to.

He slid back outside and peeped under the car. Opened sight traced the heavy, jagged treads of what could be Van Howe's truck tires in the snow, and two sets of hours-old footprints. A man and a woman.

The dimness made it easy to slip back down the alley and around to the main street again. An Opened glance brought Van Howe's tracks out of the darkness to his eyes, twisting around and heading back and away from LifeLab. Only to be swallowed in traffic.

Paul shuffled along the sidewalk. He raked the street with his sight, but cars slashed through his vision and splashed snow around, grinding any hope of making out a single track down to slush. *Please, just let me find one trace that survived.*

Once in the crushed snowscape he found two inches of tread that hinted Van Howe had driven down the block. But then at the intersection... he stared and stared up one way, up another, then the third way. Nothing.

His eyes watered and ached. All he could think was to Open to scent again.

Deep-baked stench flooded in from years of the factories... car after car burning by, all with the same burned smell...

One whispering wisp, one droplet of a scent spoke to him... no time to marvel at his luck, he could only take a step forward and sniff again, but the smell only grew fainter. A backward step, then to the right...

Behind the sidewalk, a scraggly attempt at bushes clung to the ground. In the snow underneath them lay CC's phone.

There was no other scent of hers. Its long track in the snow told the story: it had been tossed here from the street. Its SIM card was gone, and Paul left the phone untouched. Dead.

He looked up, around the dim, churning, cold-lashed streets. Of course the trail was dead, he'd never had much hope of finding something that was hours old.

Never much hope.

He dug inside him for some small faith that tonight would still end with him finding CC. That it had ever been more than an excuse to run.

Now, I can run.

The hitching was gone from his lungs, after too many blocks of pushing himself on. The streets shone where lights glinted on snow or asphalt, stretching and turning before him, waiting for him to vanish in their midst. All that was left, wasn't it?

He spun away to shut that sight out. Behind him were only more streets—

And the LifeLab building. Its people had visited him, written to him... with their help he wouldn't be one man alone on a corner.

He took a step toward them. Another.

It could be worth the risks. Part of LifeLab had a connection to Van Howe already, but any dealing with them would raise more interest in the secrets he kept. But they already wanted his help.

Walking. Faster.

Was that it, he'd bang on their doors and try to get someone at this hour who'd help him search for CC—and hope they wouldn't tell the police he'd escaped? *I have to take every risk, or else it means my breaking out was never about finding her at all.*

Faster. The car and the bored guard sat up ahead. Beyond him were the LifeLab building itself, the only people left who might help find her...

He skidded to a stop.

These weren't the only ones.

* * *

He thought he remembered her street number right. "Sarah on Carrow" was easy, but the rest had faded in the months since he'd considered coming by to leave her some paper note.

But none of his family had the skills to keep the search alive. And he'd endangered them enough.

The apartments were a simple two-floor box above the parking lot. Sarah's hybrid sat in one space. One of the mail slots said *Gomez,* but with no apartment numbers. He could only search for her by sweeping his hearing through the rooms, and hoping.

He heard silence. A TV blaring news. Kids fighting over a bath.

"—appreciate you taking the time," came Sarah's voice, more subdued than usual.

"I always have time for you." A man's voice—something prickled in Paul's gut, before he pulled back.

It would be easy enough to leave them alone...

Idiot. This is still a life in danger. He marched up the stairs, ignoring his footfalls ringing in the night, and rapped on the door.

"Who's that?" Suspicion thickened the man's voice.

"Friend of Sarah's. Sorry for the timing, but I do need to talk to her."

Seconds crawled by. Then the door cracked open.

The young man there gave Paul the kind of stare for someone he'd caught beating on the door with a stick. "Is this him?"

"It's him." Sarah moved up behind the stranger. "Sorry, I do need to see him. Can you leave this to us?"

SHADOW SIGHT · 121

The man studied Paul a moment, and the watchful squint in his eyes didn't soften. Paul looked past his tailored shirt to take in how he had the same dark sheen of hair, the same shape of his nose—Sarah's *brother,* or near enough. A smile edged onto Paul's lips.

"I hope it's alright," the brother sighed. He scooped up a coat and walked off without a word to Paul.

Sarah waved him in. "Sorry for that. After Greg started asking if I was alright, I wanted someone to sit with me. And he guessed I was nervous over something."

Paul stepped inside and took in the apartment. Neatly laid out, surrounded by shelves of books and nicknacks and so many spots where they stacked or grouped up, as if fighting a losing battle to put them back in order. A Morning Star music poster hung in one corner.

But, no more stalling. "You should be worried. Greg called because CC was grabbed off the street. And the police *still* weren't down there," he added.

"So we need to make them... listen? I guess that's a joke." She dropped to a chair and caught up her laptop. "You want my help setting you up to find what the police can't. Of course you've got it."

"Thanks."

That wasn't enough. It was never enough, but he had no idea what else to say, after all the complications between them.

"What's first?" she said.

"I... don't know. CC got grabbed outside LifeLab. I looked at the site, but the kidnapper's truck just drove away. It has to be Van Howe, I've felt how furious he is, mostly whenever he looked toward CC. But, he got her hours ago." The thought kept eating into him, stripping down what he had left to hold onto.

"That's all?" Sarah said. "And you still snuck out of your arrest to deal with it yourself."

She met his gaze, with what could be appreciation or concern.

Then she said "Good thing I've got a head start. I've been looking into Mr. Calvin Van Howe here..."

Files on her laptop clicked open.

"Birth, school, Army, jobs... too many jobs, and too many police reports, mostly for his temper. But, if he kidnapped someone?"

Two clicks and another window sprang up. She only glanced at it a moment before she brought up another, and another. Paul had to remind himself, she was only reviewing what she'd already collected.

"For a place he could take her... nothing stands out. His apartment's probably too risky, maybe somewhere around his gym or a treatment center... Or even something at LifeLab. He used to work there, but the hints are that he was fired, and then they still let him guard convicts? And this is the man who has CC."

"Ominous, yeah, unless it's a reason he'd keep her alive. Let me see—"

Instead she swung the screen down. And grabbed for a coat.

"No! You can't—"

"It's my files, and my car. Who's letting who tag along here?"

He glared back at that teasing face. She *wouldn't* go off alone, he could Open to see if she was bluffing—

No, I'm not doing that to her again. And she wouldn't bluff.

"Well, nobody's just tagging along," he said. "If we do this, *you* listen to me. You, we, need to use my senses to stay out of his sight, and send the police when we find him. You don't want his kind of rage aimed at you, trust me."

"Trust you? I think that's always been the easy part," she said.

What did *that* mean? But it did sum up too much of their relationship. Even her being spooked by the power and still deciding to help him against Reid.

He scrambled after her.

* * *

They went to Van Howe's apartment first. No surprise it was empty, but Paul hung back up the corridor, and Sarah kept knocking until a woman peeked out of a neighboring door.

"I don't know where he'd be. He lost his job, so he could be at the gym, or even the damn off-road track."

And Paul saw the young woman's thoughts twist, and her face tighten and scowl when she mentioned it.

"Please, think a little," Sarah said. "Do you know anywhere else? Or which track it is?" Even without his hints, she knew just what to ask.

A minute later they were back in her car.

"She might know Van Howe more than she admits," Sarah said. "An off-road track on a winter night could be the place. But that's only a guess."

"Except it's her guess too. She was thinking the place meant too much to him."

"Of course, you would read that." Only a trace of bitterness was in her voice now; she might be getting used to the idea of his senses. "Is it always that easy for you?"

"Easy? No, just some moments are."

Mostly because Sarah had gotten the girl talking. Paul wanted to tell her that, but she was busy digging through her laptop for a location.

The ride there was a mixed blessing. The soft seats and heated air tugged at Paul's eyelids, and should have made it harder to stay awake. The thought of how thin the trail was—and how late they were—poked through all that to make him squirm where he sat.

Suddenly Sarah broke the silence. "You know, with a man like that... CC might never have had a chance. And it's not your fault."

"You think you're reading me now?" he tried to joke. "If you had the Sight, you'd know it."

"I keep trying. Power or no power."

She laughed softly.

"Paul... People tell me I have blinders on about some of what I get into. But I never threw myself into a ruthless police chief's prison, then surrendered to another cop, worked my way out into house arrest and then escaped *that* just for the chance of finding someone alive, and then went back to keep clearing my name."

"I never said…" The words soured in his mouth. *I never said I was going back.*

She looked at him. "You *see* so much. Thoughts, whispers, everything about what people really are. I wonder, does that mean you see every glimmer of hope out there and you have to throw yourself at any chance to protect it? Or is it that you can't let go of the thrills?"

"It's not…" He had no answer for that.

* * *

By the time they reached the edge of town and the track itself, the snowfall thickened and screened the night air. Paul needed all his night-piercing sight to be certain this "off-road track" had no buildings, no features where someone might be hiding. There was only a broad, clear space where people might have parked, and the path itself leading into the trees.

And one set of tracks leading in. Jagged, snow-blurred shapes that *might* be Van Howe's tires.

Sarah cut her lights and eased her car onto the path. The road was more than wide enough, and almost level, but it weaved and shifted through the shadowy trees to hold them down to a crawl. Her hybrid's engine made it a quiet hum of a crawl.

Paul cracked his window. He gritted his teeth at the rush of cold, and strained his senses through the night. No cars, no feet, no voices in the wood. The tracks ahead could have been from any truck.

If Van Howe had CC, if he needed a place to take her, if that place was here… the whole night was a fragile chain of gambles.

One dark, dim turn after another passed. Tires edged through angled ground and lurched where the path threw up its hills. Going on foot would be faster—all the car gave them was some lumbering sense of protection.

A sound moved in the wood. Far ahead, down the side and down the slope. A voice, sobbing.

Paul Opened to smell. Somewhere within the crisp, cold-choked resin and still air...

"Blood." One part of him had been sure he'd never find them, and now he felt that doubt turn over and die. "That's blood out there. And fear."

Sarah halted the car. She scrabbled around and pulled out a plain-looking phone, some disposable thing, to tap 911.

"I hear screaming... out at the track..."

"Miss? Please, are you in a safe place—"

Paul blanked out the words as he clenched his fists, steeled himself. Then he leaned over right to Sarah's ear and breathed "They're right. Please, *please,* stay here. At least you've got the car between yourself and him."

She turned, inches away. "Would you tell Lorraine to stay back?" she said.

Of course! But what he said, low and fierce in the instant before he twisted away, was "You're not my sister."

Then he was grabbing for the door and diving onto the night.

Where the voices had been, now he picked up only a rustling in the snow, somewhere far off the side from the path. He started through the trees, picking his way diagonally down a shallow slope. The open air and the muffling trees were the opposite of an echo, but each crunch of his foot still seemed like a thunderclap in the night.

No more wondering. No more delaying. Now it all came down to... could he decoy Van Howe away from CC? Or else he'd have to jump him somehow. He reached back, and heard Sarah still moving around within the car, good.

He edged between brush and around tree after tree, stark shapes that broke up the dim, snowfall-laden air. Opening to sight stripped that back to only a crowded view, bright as day down the slope.

Footprints. Two sets of prints headed down from somewhere ahead on the track—he caught a glint of metal up where they came from, where a truck could have been left on the path. The prints led down toward a gully, screened with trees.

The source of the sounds. Now he heard a weak... *burbling* from down in it.

He surged forward, and his feet slid in the snow. He lurched to a stop. *How do I lead Van Howe away when we're leaving tracks all over the wood?* He edged closer, straining to find some idea.

The gully cut across the bottom of the slope. Paul checked one more time that Sarah had stayed put. Then he edged around to the side of the gully, around to behind a patch of brush where he could look down along the trench.

A figure hunched over the ground. Opened sight picked out Van Howe's face lined with tears, and blood caked on the knife in his hand.

The figure beside him was a woman. Torn, slashed, over and over. CC's face was still as wax.

No breathing from her. Hearing found only the clumsy sound of the man gasping, swallowing in his throat, wheezing "Why... why won't you answer me..."

The truth soaked through Paul. CC was dead—she *had* to be long dead, if Van Howe took her this far away from witnesses and had kept her so long. All they'd been chasing was the ghost of a hope.

He took a slow step backward. *No, I can't leave her... but I have to.* She'd never had a chance.

Van Howe looked up.

Paul dove back behind the bush. A bellow of rage tore through the night—his own *motion* in the shadows had given him away.

He spun and dove through the trees. Shapes slid by around him, a maze of dimness he picked through with the benefit of nighttime experience. Behind him Van Howe roared again and crashed around, blind and clumsy.

The tracks. Paul was still leaving them—he was following his own tracks back, so once Van Howe spotted those—

He Opened to sight for a moment, like a flash of invisible light to plot his way through the brush. Then he hunched lower and trotted forward, soft and steady.

Could he just keep going, trust sight and the path he'd picked downward to keep him ahead of Van Howe?

No, that led straight back to Sarah. And Van Howe had the gun he'd captured CC with—*I have to lose him.*

The footsteps, the ragged breathing, came closer behind him.

Paul Opened for another glimpse through the dark. Trees, snow, and the shape with the knife burst into clarity.

He twisted sideways, from running diagonally up the slope to double back and run along it, parallel to the road and heading deeper in. He heard a spray of snow behind him, and the scratch-crash of a man tearing through branches trying to catch up.

Van Howe's first tracks down lay ahead. Paul reached those and swung around to run within them, up the slope, backtracking along how Van Howe had first come to the gully. *I'm leaving CC behind again, dammit.*

That mass of rage behind him followed the turn. Van Howe didn't need to see him, Paul's sounds and the tracks were enough to give him away.

Paul wove around one tree, saw a moment's clear space before a tangle of shadow ahead, and stole one more guiding glimpse through the night. He charged forward, then in the darkest knot of trees he twisted away off the trail.

He was ten feet clear of it when Van Howe charged past him, straight up the slope along his own tracks.

Paul crouched lower. He zigzagged to keep trees between himself and his night-blind enemy, and angled back toward the road where he'd left Sarah. If Van Howe made it all the way back to his own truck, he could drive back up the trail and find her…

The road had just come in sight when Paul heard Van Howe's scream of outrage. He twisted his head, saw the killer charging through the trees at him.

No more hiding. Sarah's car was just in view now, and Paul flung himself toward it with a shout of "Go! Go!"

She'd already worked the car around on the track, ready to escape, he realized. She had a door hanging open.

Paul dove inside and slammed down on the passenger seat. For one instant he thought *Why do I keep jumping into someone else's car to get away? Because I keep walking into danger alone.* Then the engine surged to life.

The car skidded, bounced over bumps and obstacles on the path. Sarah twisted it around bends, with huge trees swaying into the headlights and sliding aside when she swung the wheel back on course.

Van Howe only kept running behind them, waving the knife. His mouth was open, screaming out from whatever had broken inside him when he'd cut up CC.

The path broke into the open. Sarah rammed the pedal down and left him behind.

A quarter mile later they saw the police cars. *And I should still be "locked in" back at Greg's...*

Paul had to dive outside one more time, to slip into the night before the police came to Sarah's rescue.

CHAPTER NINE

LOST AND FOUND

Paul lay hidden in the snow a stone's throw from the road, until the police dragged the exhausted Van Howe down.

Sarah insisted she'd been tracking him down on her own. The story might have been harder to accept if Van Howe hadn't had that dazed, deflated look on his face.

I didn't mean to break her, he kept saying.

The words hung in Paul's head as he trudged back to town. Where they should be grinding inside him with anger, instead he felt only hollowed out and tired. *Tired* of how an unstable man lashing out could destroy a good woman... *tired* of coming in far too late to help, tired of the police ignoring what should have been their jobs, not that they could have done much better...

He pushed on through the darkness, the trees, and then the streets. *I always go after liars and frauds, and never wanted any bigger trouble.* No attention from the authorities, no maniacs, no life or death stakes. Every part of that plan was crumbling now.

Paul found himself on the street to Greg's house, before he'd noticed his feet taking him there. Chasing Van Howe and CC had been so hopeless, it had felt like only a thin excuse for running out and giving up on the courts—hadn't he *accepted* that? And yet here he was walking back into their box again. *I guess I should be proud.*

The house's lights were on, even this deep in the bitter night.

Only Greg and their father were moving inside. He worked his way around the block searching for police surveillance, before he headed in. Of course his family was worried about him.

When he opened the door, both of them jumped to their feet.

Then the relief on their faces pulled back, reined in, of course. What Greg said was simply an eager "Any luck?"

Hell. "I found them. Too late. *All* too late to save CC."

The heavy words slipped from him and hung in the air, leaving him slumped on his feet as if he were leaning against the message they left.

His father said "You need to get some sleep."

"I think I'm too tired for that. I mean..."

And then he couldn't stop:

"Sarah's safe and the cops got Van Howe red-handed—bloody knife and all—and I never had one chance to stop him. I couldn't make them listen, I couldn't find him in time even with Sarah and my powers. And CC's gone, *dead,* because she tried to defend me, and because a ticking bomb like Van Howe got aimed at us. I knew he was out there somewhere, and I couldn't even make her listen!" His fists slammed into the wall.

The sound echoed around the room. Then it faded into the plaster, and Paul could only hear his own pounding heart.

Softly, his father said. "Are you going to blame yourself now?"

"I—"

He stopped. That was pain wrinkling the edges of that face. *Dad's done more than any of us, he shot Quinn himself for our sakes...*

Carefully, testing, Paul said "Is it that easy not to blame myself? She's dead."

"Yes. But that doesn't change the facts." His father waved a hand to brush it aside. "You did what you did, and you say it couldn't have made a difference. Alright; now you face what's next and keep on pushing yourself to get every inch of leverage you can. All three of us know, that's the only way to face a challenge with no regrets." He sat back down in his chair.

Paul gritted his teeth. No surprise the man had nothing worth hearing, even now.

Then his father sighed "And if you see their faces every day, that's the price you pay for caring about anyone. There'll only be more, every year." His eyes closed.

He did feel it after all. Paul breathed "So... I just..."

Greg said "We know you did everything you could," and his gaze lingered between both of them. "Anyway, none of us have ever been much for guilt. Do we want to talk our pains out at 1 AM, or can we get some sleep?"

Ian Schuman looked up. "What I want is to hear more about your idea, Greg. Where do you think Lorraine is?"

What? We were talking about us, or finally going to pack it in, and then he brings up...

"Um. I told you." Greg turned to Paul. "While you were out, I started a list of the places and people that are charging you. Lor could be looking into any of them, trying to clean up your—"

" 'Could be'?" Paul snapped. "You mean you want her to be. But, did you ever have any way to find out, with the cops watching those cases and me trapped here, when even if you were right she'd be trying not to be found? Or is it just based on what you *want* to be out there? Because I just spent the night finding out what that kind of wishing leads to!"

Greg stared at him. *"Whaaaat?"*

Paul jerked his gaze away from those eyes, that looked too shocked to be angry. "Sorry! I'm *tired.* But she's more tired," he heard himself go on. "Tired of all of it. You didn't see her when we split up. Chief Thiessen had been running through old grudges and trying to break her knee—"

"What?"

This time the word was sharper. *I never gave him those details—*

Greg lunged across the room. His hand caught at Paul's collar. "And you let her go?"

"She asked me to. Greg, she was fine, she spent our last hour showing me her power could still handle anything. After all the trouble we got into, she was just... tired," he said again.

I know how she feels right now. He met his brother's gaze, and saw the anger start to smooth away. Better.

He waited. He'd said too much already—no point in keeping them awake any longer with talk of how many years Lorraine had had her power and used it for nothing but helping people around her smile. *And you really think she'll come back and help us now?*

Greg's eyes were no longer studying his brother's face. His hand fell away from Paul, and he sighed "You let her go, with an injured knee. Paulie, sometimes I get sick of this little club of yours, and you thinking only you can understand each other."

He turned to look at their father.

"Any more air you want cleared, when you think Paul and I are too worn out to shut up? Or can we call it a night?"

Oh. Was that what was going on? Paul forced out "I think we're done. And... sorry. Sorry for worrying you. Again."

"It's alright," Ian Schuman said. His voice had no trace of an apology for his trick.

Greg added "Yeah. If you live thinking about how many people worry about you, I guess you can't do much living. Funny thing: I used to tell *Lorraine* that. Funny."

With that, they began turning in. Paul scavenged more clothes that could replace the sweaty, snow-soaked layers that he'd dragged around on his doomed search.

The anklet was still upstairs, still waiting to go back on him. And the police could still show up tonight and find it on the floor... but worrying didn't help when his fingers had no strength left to put the thing back together. One touch tonight and he'd probably set it off.

He was heading for the sofa when his father held out his phone. "You should call Sarah. You haven't asked if she's alright."

Is Dad still *trying to pick our brains while we're worn out?* "I'm sure she is. Or she's busy fielding questions from the police and she can't pick up. It's just too late—"

His father waggled the phone. "Believe me. After what you must have gone through, she wants you to call."

It would be so easy to turn away, to just slump down and go to sleep. But, he put the call through.

"Yes? Mr. Schuman?"

Sarah actually yawned as she said it. Regret knifed through Paul, but he said "It's just me on Dad's phone. We all wanted to check in. You... said you were looking for CC?" That should give them all some cover if someone heard.

"Can we talk tomorrow? I'm fine. But the police are deciding what to do with me—can we save the rest for later?"

He could picture her, stuck at one of the stations, able to talk but in no place to open up about losing CC...

But she can still mention police, and that there's more, and she knows that I've shared most of it. Our secret.

"Okay. Right now I don't have much to say that matters."

"Oh, never say that." He could hear her sudden grin through the line. Then she hung up.

What did *that* mean now? Paul shook his head. But, it had been good to hear her voice.

*　*　*

When the morning came, he woke up aching and haunted, but some of his luck was holding. At least no police had stormed through the door.

Carefully Paul worked the anklet back on, closing it up and withdrawing each wire. His care had left the plastic clear of visible scrapes, good. That left only the wires he'd used and the shoes that would match any of last night's footprints, and Greg took those away when he left early for work.

The traces were gone almost an hour before Reid arrived.

This time the detective only said "Inspection!" and went straight to the locator on his leg. Paul stood as still as he could be, silently reliving every touch he'd given the device, while Reid poked and peered over every trace of its surface for some betraying sign. The control device ran one test after another, while two uniforms looked at the panel on the wall.

Paul's father gave them a few minutes before he said "Another inspection? What's the bill to the taxpayers up to now?"

"You're pretending you don't know?" Reid stood up and fixed him with his gaze. "Celia Claire is *dead.*"

He was testing for a reaction, or a lack of one. But Paul simply said "We do know. Sarah told us."

"That's a good story." Reid spun and advanced on Paul, a slow, unflinching stride that forced him back with every step. "You're saying she found Van Howe all on her own? We found another set of footprints there—and all she says is she didn't recognize the other man who just happened to be there."

Paul's back hit the wall. *Don't react, don't show him one crack of anything about losing CC or that night or anything...*

Behind Reid, Paul's father laughed bitterly. "We warned you. We called the police and begged them to investigate the attack on CC's car. You people could have found them hours ago. It must be embarrassing to have a reporter care more about a missing woman than you did. And doing your job better."

"You do *not* want to start that. I know she didn't track him down herself. And you—"

He glared straight at Paul.

"You really did it. I told them, I told them every time that they couldn't let you out of that cell. But they put you on house arrest, and you still snuck out."

"How?" Paul looked straight back into that burning gaze. "How are you going to prove any of that? You just went all through the tracker, and came up empty, right? So how did I get out?"

Reid only glared back. For an instant Paul thought he *would* tell them, and show the police and the whole world what they could do.

Or those eyes could be probing his thoughts right now... but that temptation was the enemy Reid hated, even more than Paul.

"Every scrap," Reid hissed through his teeth. "Every trace you left, every door you should have stayed outside, every scratch on a lock that shows nowhere is safe from you. You gave us years of evidence to sift through. And now this is a murder."

The word hung in the air as he spun around and stalked away.

*   *   *

It's not a murder case, Paul kept trying to tell himself. They knew Van Howe killed CC, Reid couldn't charge Paul or Sarah with that. Having a death at the periphery of what was still a mass-trespassing case might even pull attention *away* from Paul.

Even if had been his secrets that put CC in the killer's path.

And he was still trapped, struggling to counter whatever Reid was closing in on.

His father called CC's law firm. From what he told Paul afterward, her loss left her colleagues with a deeper hole in them than they'd admit, along with dazed promises that they'd finish his case.

Greg stayed out at Schuman and Son, juggling their own business and what updates they got about Paul's case. From his voice on the phone, Paul suspected he was still looking for Lorraine too. *He doesn't get it, she's long gone...* but Paul couldn't blame Greg for wanting to believe.

And every minute, the charges against him circled in his mind and dug even deeper tracks into it. LifeLab. St. Central, Addamson Abbot and the inspector and the charity and the rest, and how many more of the forty-eight Reid might be onto now. Was there *anything* left except rotting away in prison, or being picked apart by whoever paid the most for the secret of his powers, or simply abandoning his family and everything?

Then a call came in from Brandt.

"Have you had any news about Ms. Claire? The police won't talk to us here." He sounded so *unscarred,* for a moment longer before he learned the truth.

And Paul had to deliver it. "She's dead. Van Howe took her and killed her."

"Oh. Oh God…" Brandt's voice cracked, for one jagged moment. "I'm so sorry. And she was coming to meet us. We kept telling the police that it couldn't be just an abandoned car, but they took so long… I, I can't help but feel a bit responsible."

And you pointed Van Howe at us in the first place. But of course Brandt wouldn't admit to that again. Paul could hear the shock in his voice, the gap between LifeLab's simple curiosity and where Van Howe's revenge had ended up.

"I… I do have some other news," Brandt resumed. "James Koenig—the ex-employee who first tried to frame us—he said he was approached by the police. About one of the versions of his stories, when he said someone coerced him into confessing."

Coerced.

The word dug into Paul's mind, right at the memory of Van Howe's rampage that was all too recent. He slapped a hand over his mouth to hold his breakfast down.

Just weeks ago, I was standing over Koenig in his apartment in the middle of the night, feeding him lies about someone manipulating him. For Paul to push someone that far… Reid would call it worse than Van Howe, or on the way to it, when his powers made it so easy. He might be right.

"I see," Paul managed to say.

"Koenig said he didn't tell them. LifeLab already made a deal with him to stop him talking about his history with us."

Reid *didn't* know?

Dizzying relief washed through him. At least that one episode could stay buried. He'd told himself he did it for Sarah, who'd gotten the blame for his story, and his family had been caught up in it too, but—

"Why did you do that?" he asked. "Why are you telling me this?"

"Koenig and all the publicity he brought had given us enough trouble. Of course we paid him to keep quiet. Besides, if someone else had been trying to stop Koenig, there's no reason for them to suffer too."

So that was why LifeLab had shut Koenig up. And why Brandt told Paul—they had no doubt who had gotten to Koenig before.

"I... see."

"And, I suppose that makes this the wrong time to mention the terms we offered you. Still, Koenig was actually happy with his fee, and there's nothing nefarious about agreeing to end an episode that had only hurt everyone. When you're ready to look at your own offer from us, I hope that's the lesson you take from his example."

"When I'm ready..."

CC had thought LifeLab's offer was fair. *What next, do I start telling myself that my saying no was the reason CC went out into Van Howe's hands?*

His father leaned in, almost over the phone. "We have been looking at that offer. Could we meet about it? I'm sure your schedule's crammed, but Paul does prefer to see people in person these days. Trust, you know."

And reading their minds. His father was setting up the perfect circumstances for safe bargaining—but he was also starting to pull it under his own control.

"I'll see if I can do that," Brandt said.

"The key is in agreeing to reveal details about how Paul— allegedly—accessed your information, in exchange for dropping the charges?"

"Yes. Though I suppose our charges amount to only one share of what they're 'alleging.' "

"But," Paul forced in, "we appreciate it. We'll try to work something out, but we can't promise anything right now."

"Of course not. And I won't take up more of your time."

When Brandt hung up, Paul's father stared at him. "What was *that*? We had the company owner on the line, and I was starting to connect with him."

"I'm sure you were. You asked for the in-person meeting just to let me bring my talents in, but you still had to take over?"

"Take over? So you're the master deal-maker, now that you can do one thing?"

"No—"

Paul clamped his mouth shut, and bit down the rise of his temper. *It's just my father, why let him get to me now? I only have to tell him once, and make it clear.* He stepped over to peep out the blinds, then sweep his sight and hearing around the neighborhood.

There could still be police listening. But he had to say it:

"Dad, it's my deal to make. Brandt doesn't know what I can do, and that's exactly what he's trying to learn. He's a decent man I'd like to trust. But just a bit of his curiosity already had Van Howe poking around me, and it got CC killed."

"So that's *Brandt's* fault?" his father snapped. "Everything comes back to you and your secrets?"

"Not yet—but it could, if one thing went wrong. Just, please, stop and think. Think how much more trouble we'd have, if just one more hint got out. Think who'd want a piece of it. I've had years to think about that." *CIA 'recruitment'... or Homeland Security throwing me in a hole... the demands to find how the power worked... hell, LifeLab might end up first in line to dissect me...*

"Maybe you've had too long to think," his father said. "But you'll have even longer, if you keep holding onto a defense that lands you in prison."

Paul could have let that pass, and simply settled in to more silent fuming. But instead he jumped up and walked away to the kitchen, just to get out of his father's sight for a moment.

He took a slow breath, and a long stretch of his arms. The sense of cabin fever pressed in closer today. He'd felt it before whenever his life off the grid had shut him in with strangers, but this was *family*. And no way to walk away.

After one night free on the streets, he was still just one step short of being back in prison.

He squared his shoulders and walked back to the living room. His father only glanced up from his laptop, nothing more.

What *could* Reid use against him? LifeLab was the most recent, but they had the most counts of him snooping around St. Central, from all the months he'd been sure the hospital had some connection to his power. Even though he'd never taken or hurt anything.

But only if he made the court believe that. He drew a deep breath, and mouthed what he might say: *I never stole a thing. I didn't sabotage. I don't care how many people think they saw me, I never did any harm...*

No, CC would want him to own his reasons—

CC. The loss slammed into him, made him gasp for breath. He sat still and rode it out until his chest steadied again. At least they'd caught Van Howe.

He'd never called Sarah back again. But they'd spoken just last night, better to let that cool for a while.

"You think Greg has any news?" he asked his father.

"You'd know if he told me. We can always check," and he held out his phone. Letting Paul make the call himself, a peace offering.

Two taps put the call through, but it went straight to voice mail.

"Just me," he said. "Of course you're busy, and I'm just getting antsy looking for an update—"

"Good timing," Greg's voice came on. "I just heard from a friend at Addamson Abbot."

Now Greg was investigating? "A friend?"

"I've got a few, yes. He started working there after the whistle got blown on them, and he says that the way they operated before, it wouldn't have been a frame. And today he saw the police come in to check on the witnesses who say they saw you there. Get this: this time they're not so sure who they saw or if anyone was spying at all."

"Thanks."

"Had to happen. They're talking about something more than a year ago. Allegedly," he added. "Listen, I'm on top of something else right now."

"Okay, what—" But Greg had hung up.

His father took the phone back. "You've got some good news there. But remember, that 'something else' of his might not be about your case at all."

"Sure, it's still business hours. And I know this is just taking time from that to check on what you can do for me. Nobody's expecting miracles."

He leaned back, thinking what Greg had said. Just to *hear* it, that people were starting to doubt or forget a face they'd glimpsed months ago…

The case against him always came back to volume, the pattern of how many "glimpses" they had of him. Reid and Oliver kept saying that was enough, but then they'd been eager to add a few suspicious scratches on a lock to make it all more solid. And they had to want the most reliable proof, his most recent run through LifeLab and the sheer number of times he'd been through St. Central.

Again and again he went through the cases in his mind. How much evidence could they have? Until Koenig and LifeLab, he'd worked only by observing at a distance—nothing they could prove there—and by slipping in to get at the truth. Reid might look all over the city, but he'd never find more than vague witnesses, plus some traces from locks and any cameras he'd missed.

The day edged by. Paul checked on Greg a few more times, but he never answered. His father was buried in his own laptop, and only glanced up at noon when Paul brought him a sandwich.

Is it just the newer, clearer charges, and any mistakes that left solid proof? Was that really most of what Reid had? How much of that was just LifeLab?

And LifeLab wanted to trade. Paul tried to picture it: sitting with Brandt or their security experts and showing he could beat their systems through sheer stealth. One slip might show them the power behind his moves and ruin everything... but if he didn't slip?

What if one of the others wanted the same deal, security advice in exchange for dropping old charges? If just one or two were interested, what would that do to Reid's "volume" of vague evidence? Undermine that enough and he could live with pleading out the rest. Maybe.

If they found someone to bargain with, if nothing went wrong...

The thought flickered and shifted inside him as the day went on, like a piece of sunlight he'd somehow swallowed, still warm. If they could keep the secret.

There was still no answer from Greg, as the afternoon wore on. His father had no reaction when Paul couldn't reach him. Finally Paul put a call through to the office itself.

"Sorry, Paul. We haven't seen him since lunch."

Only minutes later, Greg walked in the door.

Ian Schuman was on his feet at once. "Where were you?" he said, in a voice that just tested the edges of how it could rise.

"I said I had a lead. And I found one." Greg's smile stretched wider every moment. "That snake oil shop Vitamintastic? They're still fuming about it. The police wanted to check their locks for lockpicking—and they just noticed the main interior one got broken. So there are no clues left to find there, and it must have happened after you were in custody!"

"I see," Paul said. *And I see who you think did it.* "How'd you find that? What were you out looking for?"

"I went around town to the sites you were at. Just looking for the quietest ways I could ask if a strange woman had been around lately. I bet she got that lock."

"All around town," Ian Schuman repeated. "Looking for Lorraine."

"That's right. And like I said on the phone, people are starting to forget what they saw. You know what that means."

Paul felt a growl somewhere down in his throat. Greg had started him hoping that witnesses would forget his face... but all along his brother had only believed it was Lorraine's power at work?

Greg went on "I stayed out of the way, sure. No interfering, just looking and asking where I got a chance. And *being* seen—if she's anywhere around she has to see me looking for her, and know she can come back."

"I told you..." Paul cut it off. No point in telling him all over again, how Lorraine only walked away from problems.

"I told *you,* she has to be here, and she's trying to—"

"So your answer," their father said, "was to tear around town asking who'd seen her? You ever think the police might notice that?"

"I'm trying to help—"

"Help who? Paul?" The voice swelled, just enough to resonate off of the walls. "Not him, not by flirting with interference charges to get some fragments of information. Not Lorraine, if you walk around telling everyone she might have been working behind the scenes. Not even work, if we need you on-site and you run off for the flimsiest—"

"You sent me there, you deal with my decisions. Finding Lorraine is the best thing for everyone, and that's including work."

Don't move, don't say a word to join in. One hint of a two-on-one will make this even more ugly.

"Decisions, Greg? That's your idea of a choice?"

"My choice. The only chance we had. And someone had to make it—someone who's healthy enough to walk outside, that they still let go out there."

"That's right. You're the only one who can be our eyes and our face out there now. So you spend the day running around like you lost a puppy? On the day after we *did* lose CC, and you never left us one word about you?" His gaze narrowed, stabbed through his son. "You wasted half the day, and now you're throwing away the last of it by coming here, for what? To brag about your 'choice'?"

The front door rattled.

Greg snapped "Would it be so bad… so end-of-the-world awful…"

The door opened.

"…if I made one choice that wasn't yours?"

Their father's mouth opened, and froze there. All their heads were turning, toward the sound from the door.

The woman was still pale, injured, with mismatched clothes nothing like what she'd worn the last time Paul saw her. Where she normally looked like a piece of jewelry to match her trim golden hair, now she looked like jewelry that had been picked out of a pile of sand.

She stood half in the door—her body was swaying back a fraction, one inch toward slipping away from the clash she'd walked in on. Then her knuckles tightened on the doorknob, and she stepped in.

"Sorry, but I'd like to hear that answer myself," Lorraine said.

Greg's voice was a hoarse whisper, a throat afraid to let the word out.

"Lor?"

She smiled. "I got your message."

Greg shuffled, stumbled, caught himself, and made it to her to pull her into a desperate embrace.

CHAPTER TEN

THE BEST DEFENSE

Greg half-pulled and half-carried his wife toward a chair. A stream of *here, here, get off your feet* and *how long have you* and *get you a drink* poured from his mouth.

Paul let him and their father move in ahead and surround her. And when Lorraine's face showed between the two, he sent her his own welcoming grin, and she smiled back to him.

Greg caught the look between them, and crowded even closer to her, not quite touching her now.

"Your knee," he pleaded. "They said it got... how bad is it?"

Lorraine curled her skirt up, just enough to show a glimpse of purpled flesh. "It's okay. I can walk fine if I pace myself."

"That bitch Thiessen—that's the same leg you broke as a kid. Did she know that?"

Of course Greg knew Lorraine's past. As much as anyone could, without hearing about how her power had shaped so much of it.

"Oh, the chief knew, believe me. Then we shut her down, and I just wanted to get away... away from her, and Reid, and all their persecutions."

Just a fraction's delay before the last words, and then she added them with the tiniest rush behind them. Which was the truth and which was her misspeaking, her leaving her enemies behind or leaving everyone?

"Forget it. You're here now." Greg's hand began inching toward her arm, hesitating at the last distance between them.

"Sure. I needed to be here."

Their father added "You're still under suspicion by the police. Though it's more a set of questions they have for you, so it may not be serious at all."

Lorraine's eyes shifted. For a moment her gaze turned away, not meeting the others.

Then Greg started in. "Easy to fix. We look over the details on what they want—it's all mixed in with Paul's case—then we know how you have to come forward—"

Words burst out of Paul. "You think you can just squeeze this into your plan? You keep throwing money and 'friends' at it?"

Greg whirled around, eyes locked on him. "Back off! To the cops, she's still just someone on the fringe of this. Of course we'll fix it, we'll do anything to get her out of it—"

"Except listen to her?"

"We have to head this off before it gets out of control. I don't think they've got any real charges—"

Lorraine said "I *know* what they have." Her voice rose just enough to push through theirs. "I know they want to see if I was part of what they're putting on Paul. They're mostly interested in LifeLab, since it's the most recent. And then there's what I saw with Quinn, and how I ran away from the police. Twice."

Greg knelt down beside her chair. "Of course. And this is nothing like Paul's problem, it'll be easy to stand up to them. Even for your escapes. I'm sorry, but you do know you'll have to turn yourself in—a formality, it won't mean a thing if we set the stage for it right. You'll be in and out, no problem."

His father added "First we grab a lawyer. With the right support, it shouldn't be much more than confronting the police with how much you didn't do."

"Oh?" Lorraine raised an eyebrow. "You're so sure I wasn't Paul's partner in this from the start?"

Greg let out a soft laugh. "Of course you weren't." His voice had the beginning of a waver in it.

Lorraine leaned over to where he knelt. Paul didn't need to Open to hear the whisper: "Not until LifeLab. When he broke in there, I started a fire in the lot to help him escape."

"What? You've been—" Greg choked the words off. He pulled back, stared at her, face pale. "How long have you—"

"No!" she said. *"Listen* to me, Greg. Whatever Paul might have been involved in for those years, I had no idea. But don't you see? I *could* have done the same thing, starting years before I met any of you."

Greg's head turned away from hers. Like he'd just remembered she read thoughts.

"She's right," Paul added. "I've seen her when she—"

"I said listen, all of you!"

This time Lorraine's tone slashed through their words, left them all staring.

She leaned toward Greg. "Just listen. All the time I was with you, you have to understand it was because I chose to walk through all the dinners and the trips and the laughter that went with being part of your life. Being Curtis's student meant I could be anyone, and I wanted to be your wife. You've seen how happy I've been, just not all the reasons for it."

"You... you read my mind?" Greg said.

Paul said "She'd never—"

"Quiet!" Lorraine cut in. "Really, Paul. You're the one who taught me to be more careful." She tapped her finger to her lips.

Right, they'd been talking about the power itself.

"But the police aren't listening," Greg said. "We keep checking, and they never do. Besides, whatever they come up with, we'll beat it. We'll find ways to use your talents too. How about... We know the charges against Paul. So we line up some lawyers, and march up to the police and *demand* they show us if they have any sign you were ever involved in any of them. Unless—"

Unless she *had* been going back over Paul's cases and covering them up. And Greg had just spent the day asking them if she'd been seen there, waving a spotlight around the idea.

Paul forced his mouth to open. "Uh. *Can* you come forward now?"

Lorraine smiled. "I'll be fine—"

Something hammered on the door.

"Police! You better be there, Ms. Schuman!"

For an instant Paul felt his world splitting, tearing away into separate truths all screaming at the same time. The police were here, now—his brother's look at Lorraine, sheer incomprehension—his own forgetting to keep watch—Lorraine telling them to be quiet, to let her speak—how the police *expected* her here—

Lorraine sighed "I thought you'd want to talk me out of it. So I called them before I came."

The door swung open; she hadn't even locked it behind her. The police swarmed in, Reid and *four* others clomping along behind him.

Reid glared at Lorraine where she sat. "You're actually here."

"Of course." Lorraine wrenched herself to her feet, letting them see every wince her injuries gave her. "Let's get this over with."

Greg stepped in front of her, eyes on Reid. "You're not taking her anywhere."

The uniforms behind Reid shifted in place, ready for a fight. *So that was why Reid brought so many.* Paul grabbed at his brother's arm.

"He's not arresting me. Or are you?" Lorraine turned from him to Reid. "It's mostly answering some questions, isn't it?"

"That's right. And my lieutenant wants to talk to you herself."

Greg glared back at Reid. "Then... if it has to be right now, we're coming with you. And if I see you take one step toward railroading her like you did Paul, I'll sue everyone whoever touched the case. Her case or his."

Lorraine hobbled around her husband to join Reid. As she moved, she shot Greg one look of tight-lipped irritation... but as she did, the expression softened.

"Railroading?" the detective grumbled. "You're always so sure you know everyone, aren't you? Come on."

"Of course." Lorraine's calm made her words the final consent of the person who'd brought them all together. The whole throng filed out the door.

Except, Paul found one cop blocking him from the doorway. "And where do you think you're going, prisoner?"

Damn you—

Pressure, doubt, confusion and loss all came roaring up from the pit of Paul's stomach to pour into his clenching fist and leave him standing, shaking with the need to smash something...

His father moved in behind the cop. "We'll keep it quick. And we'll stay in touch, here," and he passed his phone around to Paul. He added "Greg needs to get this house a landline. And a new floor, the way all of us are piling up."

And they walked away. Reid, Lorraine, and the rest of his family, and the cops simply walked to their cars and drove out into the lowering sun, leaving him standing in the doorway until the last of their engine sounds moved beyond his Opened senses.

Cold had already poured into the house before he shut the door. His thoughts still couldn't settle.

Lorraine came back. So much for her only wanting the easy choices... *so Greg really does know her better.* Or he thought he did—what was she doing calling the police before them? *I guess she would've warned us, if we'd given her a chance...*

He stared at the phone in his hand. One call to Greg and he could start getting updates, as many and as fast as he wanted. Even if it would sound desperate.

Or, it was getting late. He could start dinner for them, if he had any clue when they'd be back. *Or how many of them would be.*

He flung himself down on the soft sofa, staring at the phone.

His finger moved on its own. Sarah's number was right there.

"Hello?"

"It's Paul. Get this: *Lorraine* just walked in, and she had the cops take her away for their questions. And everyone's gone to help, except I'm stuck here."

Silence. The way he'd just unloaded all that...

Then Sarah laughed, a husky, rueful sound. "Just another day, isn't it? But listen: I'm glad you told me. I bet that if Lorraine set that up, she has it all planned. We'll talk soon," she added.

"Ah. Okay." She hung up.

Of course Sarah would be in the middle of something. Paul stared around the house, feeling the stillness that hung around the walls now. He was actually alone here—*and when did that start bothering me?*

At least Sarah had put her finger on what mattered now. Lorraine was off following her own plan. Reid had mentioned his lieutenant wanting in; was that one piece of how she'd set this up?

But Lorraine didn't know cover-ups and persecutions, not the way he did.

Please, be alright. Lorraine isn't like me, she didn't choose to help a few people and take on the risks for it, her goal was to never hurt anyone, ever. She doesn't deserve this...

Finally the phone chimed in his hand.

"We're here." Frustration thickened Greg's voice. "And she's already in that interrogation room with Reid and his 'lieutenant.' Never let us get a word in."

"Yeah." What did it mean, if they swept her out of sight that fast? "They may let you see her soon. Maybe."

"No. Paul, they're right on the other side of the glass now, but *we can't hear them,*" he finished in a whisper.

"What?"

"You have to find out *your way.* They're right there waiting for you."

Pick up sounds through soundproof glass, through a phone? The thought brought a headache squeezing at the back of his skull, but he said "I… I'll try."

He Opened.

A flood of sound crashed through him. Voices, footsteps, Greg's breathing—the whole world within the one tiny speaker. All crammed together with no location, no way to aim his senses except to strain to listen through all the layers of roaring.

One voice, one woman's voice among so many, was saying *Do you know why you're here* and it was Lorraine that answered: "I know it's about Paul's—"

The sound slipped away into the torrent. Paul held his breath, focused.

"…appreciate you coming in," said the woman, the police lieutenant. He caught "…know he's been conducting a one-man war of spying and breaking into any business he thinks is corrupt."

"A one-man war? I never knew that. And ever since I found out, I've been wishing I had known." Those words ached with regret Paul knew was real.

"So you could help him?" snapped Reid's voice.

The sudden blast made Paul's ear ring, and the sound slipped away.

Then he heard Lorraine again: "He's family. If you heard your brother-in-law had been running a 'one-man war,' wouldn't you want to know if it was true? And why?"

"You're saying you had no idea."

"I only saw him a few times when those LifeLab accusations were in the air. He was certainly interested in them, but I never saw him breaking in anywhere."

"LifeLab disagrees," the lieutenant said "They have surveillance systems around their lot. And pictures like this."

Something slapped onto a table. It rattled like a printed photo, but the sound still felt more like a steel trap closing. The room went still.

Then Lorraine said "That's not me." She sounded perfectly calm. "What that shows could be me, but from that timestamp... I was out trying to find Paul that night, yes. But I was never near LifeLab."

"You're sure about that?" The cop's voice tensed into a threat.

"Of course."

"I see."

And the lieutenant *stopped* there. Lorraine had fooled her—no, he realized, the picture must be a bluff, and her powers had seen through that and let her simply, safely deny it all.

"The lab has been... inconsistent in pressing charges about this," the lieutenant added. "Anything else you can tell us here?"

"I wish there was. Is there anything else you need?"

"You can tell us about Arthur Quinn and his death."

Oh God. Didn't they close that case, they don't know Dad shot him—

"I should have known that was coming." She let out a slow, pained breath. "I love Greg and his father, but it turned out they'd taken money from that loan shark. We ended up meeting him, and it never really went wrong until that big man stormed in."

Meaning Vernon, Councilor Bennett's aide and protector.

"What man?"

"He was huge, and talking like he was out of his mind. And he had a gun. He kept making threats, and then Quinn shot him, and... I just know that when it was over, Quinn was dead and Ian was shot too. I know going near Quinn was trouble, but once that man showed up..."

"I understand," and the lieutenant's tone softened. The next moment it went sharper than ever: "So you ran away? You saw a man get killed, and your reaction was to get out of town?"

"He was *killed!* Of course I ran, I needed to think. Please, did you ever find out about that maniac that broke in on us—"

"We've been investigating. But believe me, none of us have any tears for Quinn."

Paul might have sighed in relief, back in the place so far removed from the sounds. Was that it, the police wrote the case off as a loan shark with a gun getting what he deserved, to be sure nobody looked too closely at the Councilor's man Vernon there? Lorraine was making use of every thread of this tangle.

The lieutenant went on "So you ran. Clear across the country, to your home town of Cedar Springs?"

"That's right. Because it was my home town."

"Of course." Again, that moment of sympathy in the cop's voice. One more spark of emotion that Lorraine's powers could find and feed.

And Reid cut in "Then Paul came to the exact same place? And you're telling us you weren't conspiring together?"

"I told Paul about the town. Detective, you saw how much of a history I have there. If you want to suspect our both ending up there means something more, you go ahead. You can even blame us for exposing Chief Thiessen and her vendetta. But they were calling us heroes there, and you too."

"*Heroes?* So you ran away from custody, and now you felt free to come back here and start poking around Paul's crime scenes? How is that not a cover-up?"

"What cover-up?" Lorraine said. "Just where did I go? What did I do?"

"According to your husband, you were all over the scenes."

"Is that your evidence? That Greg wanted me to be there?"

"You *were* there!" Reid said.

"No," the lieutenant sighed. "She has a point. At the moment, that's all we have on her."

"And that's it? You're just... going to take her word for it?" Reid had to be on fire with rage. This was exactly what he hated about the power, all playing out before his eyes. Did he think Lorraine could make *anything* sound real now?

The room went silent. The other sounds closed around it, and Paul strained to catch anything more.

He got one whisper, from the lieutenant: "—another factor."

Then a chair scraped. Feet moved, and pulled out past the screening glass into the open room where the phone waited, where Greg's feet turned to meet them.

And Paul could let his power ease back, lay down some of the weight of keeping his hearing forced open so far. He still had a low ringing lodged in his ears.

Greg said "So what's next?"

The lieutenant said "Based on the evidence, there's no reason to hold you now. But there is one other factor here—oh, good to have you here, Doctor."

" 'Doctor'? What's this?" Greg said.

"Dr. Fish is here about what might be another side to your brother's surveillance habits—Mr. Schuman, who is on the other end of that phone? Your brother?"

"Does it matter?" Greg countered.

"Mr. Schuman, I need you to hang that phone up and hand it over, right now."

"By what authority?" their father said. "Are you arresting us now?"

Paul's fingers tightened on the phone. Whatever this was, they wanted to keep it from *him,* and right this minute.

"There are no charges for you yet," the lieutenant said.

"But...?"

"But," a new, dry voice said "I'd appreciate you Schumans all coming with me, along with your youngest. Our lab can test you for traces of... certain electronics that might explain what's been reported." Dr. Fish, they'd called him.

"Electronics?" Reid snapped. "You think this is some kind of new bug design?"

"I'd *appreciate* you coming with me," the doctor said again. "It might involve our national interests."

Oh God.

The words, the tone... *Why couldn't I be hearing something safe, like gunfire?*

That's a defense contractor there, or even a spy, the way he throws that talk around as magic words. He's trying to "explain" our powers—and when he doesn't find the "electronics" he expects, he might keep asking until he puts it all together.

And he said "your youngest" because they'll be coming for me too.

Paul bolted for the kitchen. Knives, knives... he'd known where they were a minute ago. He had to hack the anklet off and *run.*

"We have rights."

For an instant the insane words seemed to come out of thin air. Then Paul remembered the phone, still crushed against his ear. It was only his father's voice.

"I think..." Lorraine said slowly, "I think we might as well get it over with. If we can do those tests here, with the police watching over it. And Paul, I mean you too."

His name froze him, with his hand on a knife. Lorraine wanted to let them test him? What had she seen in their heads?

"We're not your babysitters," the lieutenant said.

"But Doctor, *could* you do the tests here? Us walking into a strange lab is... it's enough to make anyone paranoid," Lorraine said.

"Are you refusing to cooperate?" Fish said.

"Are you just handing us over, Lieutenant? This doesn't sound like you police making real charges. He's only dropping hints and telling us to jump through every hoop he wants. Ian and Greg aren't even accused of crimes, but he's dragging them in too. Does that mean anything to you?"

Paul yanked the phone away from his ear. No matter what they were saying, he had to check... the street outside was still quiet, the nearest car well up the block.

Back on the phone, Lorraine was saying "Or do they just take over? This 'doctor' is so important you have no say?"

"She's got a point," Reid said. "This time."

"She does," the lieutenant said. "I don't see any risk of them being marched into some black-hole secret lab, but... you test them here. Any findings you get are part of our case."

The doctor sniffed "You're not serious."

I could hate that voice, so sure everything's just an irritation in his way. But Lorraine thought his tests were safe.

A sound rumbled outside the house. A car pulling up to the driveway.

He had the knife against his ankle. He'd have to saw the strap off—no time, they'd be inside long before it parted—*have to run first, then cut it off before they closed in on the signal, no time...*

Paul set the knife down. Trusting Lorraine was the only choice he had left.

He moved to open the door, on suddenly shaky legs. Two uniforms were walking toward it. Had they gotten the last order, to keep him under police custody and away from the doctor's own lab?

He brought up the phone again. The line was dead.

The older cop just looked at him. "Alright, time for a quick trip," was all he said.

"I heard. To the station, right?"

They didn't answer. Instead one moved to each side of him and they cuffed his hands behind him.

He couldn't even try to run now.

Paul trudged toward the car, keeping his gaze away from the street and the night he could have vanished into... he sank into the back seat. Cold had begun creeping through his flesh.

* * *

The ride passed in a daze. Somewhere on the way he moved beyond fear, and felt himself drifting, floating, as if he'd already fallen and splashed through into icy water and could only wait to feel whether he rose or sank. Into his worst nightmare.

Lorraine thinks it's safe, Lorraine thinks it's safe, one part of him kept repeating.

The haze thinned sometimes when the car paused on the street. Paul would look up into the night and wonder if this time they'd arrived, or if it was another stoplight and a chance that he might have tried getting through the locked door and bailing out, if he'd been uncuffed. *Lorraine thinks it's safe.*

Then the car took a sharp turn around a cluster of signs, and the building outlines stirred the beginnings of relief. Finally the police station's silhouette loomed ahead—they *weren't* dragging him off to some private lab.

They came to a stop. Paul stepped out under the parking lot lights and into the scattered noises, and his knees went weak for a moment. The older cop grabbed his arm before he lost his balance, but then that hand stayed locked on him.

All of it, *all* of it, came down to the next minutes. Letting "Dr. Fish" run his tests and not showing they were blundering right past a bigger spy secret than any "electronics."

The cop started him toward the station door—then pulled him back. A van stood near it, and two men were wheeling a heavy crate from it to the door. "That's them. Let 'em get their gear in first," one of Paul's guards said.

Paul remembered the phone, that he'd shoved in his pocket when they cuffed him. If they'd just cuffed his hands in front he could have filled the time trying to call Greg back, to keep his thoughts on something besides how he should be looking for the darkest hiding hole in the city.

The men rolled their crate inside, and the police brought Paul in behind them.

Right away they took a turn to the side, and with every turn Paul saw the crowds around them grow thinner, as they headed to a side area of the station. Paul focused on keeping his chilled limbs moving, and on believing all the sweat he smelled was from the halls. As long as he *looked* like some ordinary, nervous blackmailer to them...

Reid marched out of the corridor ahead.

As he joined them, the detective said "She won't be 'talking' you out of this one."

How strong did he think Lorraine's powers were? "All Lorraine said was that you had no evidence against her. What if the police just believed the truth?"

Reid's frown deepened, and Paul realized his mistake. He'd all but told Reid he'd heard the whole interrogation.

"I never wanted these tests," Reid said slowly. "Still, maybe the doc's the only thing that can control you."

Paul blinked, looked at Reid again. *He wouldn't, he* couldn't *be using this research as a chance to reveal their powers... no, that wasn't his style...*

The escort's hand on his arm tightened. Paul kept walking, feeling the blood draining from his face.

They'd just passed the evidence locker. He realized he could have been keeping track of their way in, weighing every twist he might take if he tried to slip out, one last chance. He'd missed that too.

They stopped outside the door of a police lab—a lab with several lab techs standing outside it, grumbling about their work and interfering interruptions. The thumps and clatters of equipment came from inside.

Paul Opened to listen.

"How much longer?" came the lieutenant's voice.

"So protective of your suspect?" Dr. Fish answered. "That you'd side with her over me?"

"Actually it was the two older Schumans that bothered me. They were never suspects, but you wanted to sweep the whole family up."

"They were connected." That was all Fish said. An electric engine hummed softly, then the sound rose and steadied. "Bring them in."

The door opened.

The lab inside was crammed with heavy testing machines all along the walls, alternating with cabinets for holding samples. Squeezed in along one side was a heavy arch of plastic on the floor, just big enough for part of a person to lie under—some kind of undersized MRI scanner?

Around it stood a woman right where the lieutenant's voice had been, the two men who'd wheeled the scanner in... and one figure almost seven feet tall looming over its controls. How could Dr. Fish have such a small voice with that huge chest?

Paul reached for his thoughts. Fish's inner image leaned down, staring only at the machine's panel.

A door at the far end of the lab opened. Greg, Lorraine, and Ian Schuman walked in. They looked across at him, but none of them did more than nod to him with the others watching.

"Under there. Lie down," Fish snapped.

Paul's father took the first step forward. He walked up and laid himself down, slowly with his wound, on the floor with his head just below the scanner. Fish began sliding it down over his body.

That *was* an MRI, some kind of portable field model. So they were... scanning for some kind of gadget a person might have implanted in their body? That would be one way to hide a bug's receiver or some other spy-tech. For someone who used tech.

Another look at Fish's thoughts showed the doctor only fixated on the readings. One moment he stared fiercely at them, the next he waved his subject aside.

Greg moved in for his turn. This time Paul was sure, the whole scan took less than a minute.

Lorraine stepped forward. For one instant, a flash of fear showed on her face.

Why... *Wait, MRIs scan brain tissue too. Does using our power actually leave traces in our brains?*

Paul jerked backward. His side hit a counter, and a few bits of glass chinked a moment in the stillness. *I'm really losing it now.*

"Problem?" Fish said to Lorraine.

Greg warned "She got knocked around by a dirty cop last week. Be glad she came here at all."

Lorraine settled into place, face pale. Paul mapped the layout of the room from the corner of his eyes: the two cops, two techs, the lieutenant, Reid himself, and the massive doctor... if he even thought of making a break it would be on his own...

The doctor's eyes were watching him. Peeping up, sneaking a look away from the console, to study him. *Why'd I have to bump that table?*

Then Fish was waving Lorraine away. Barely noticing her now.

Paul kept his face a mask as they removed his cuffs, and he walked across. When he settled himself on the lab floor, bits of dirt left from the others' shoes brushed at him.

The magnetic scan felt like nothing at all, of course. Paul had a sudden urge to Open to Fish's thoughts to guess if the test was even real... or to catch the first reaction to any traces in his brain, even though *using* power right under the scanner had to be the worst risk of all, and the sheer crazy danger of trying it tugged at his focus and made him fight to *not look, not look...*

The scanner slid past his chest, down his legs. Fish stopped it a moment at the anklet, then slid it clear. Paul took a slow breath.

"No implants," the doctor grunted. "Brandt wasted my time."

Paul locked his face still. Slowly, smoothly as he could move, he got to his feet and stepped out of Fish's way. The machine gave a deep electronic sighing sound as it shut down, and Fish turned and stalked out of the lab without a word.

Don't think about the name. Don't ask how Brandt could be part of this.

The doctor's techs began packing up the scanner. The police in the room were still silent. Fish abruptly walking out had to have them stunned too.

Lorraine took a step away from her family, toward the lieutenant.

Before she spoke, Paul had his voice under control. "That should be it, right? We're done."

"You're done," the cop said. "Put him back in the house. The rest of you, you're free."

CHAPTER ELEVEN

TIES

When they got back, Sarah was waiting. She sat in her car as though she'd been there all evening—or at least after whatever she'd been doing when he called her. She trailed quietly behind them all while the police checked Paul's anklet in again, and finally left.

When the door closed, she said "What's wrong—"

Paul raised a hand to quiet them, and Opened. He made a long, slow sweep through the nearest rooms for any humming electronics that might have been planted while they were gone, and then listened around the street for anyone who might be lingering with a long-range mic. After the last days, he'd come to accept that the police simply wouldn't bother spying on him... now he wasn't so sure.

Finally he slumped in place, and said "The cops questioned Lorraine. And they let her off, yes—until this Dr. Fish dragged us all in over his suspicion that we might have some kind of spytech implanted in us." His family's eyes were on him, and he realized he'd just taken charge to silence them and then bring Sarah up to date.

" 'All' of you?" Sarah said. "All four?"

"All of us," Greg said.

Paul added "That came up empty, of course. But Fish mentioned that it was *Brandt* that sent him. In spite of everything he and LifeLab did to help us."

His father said "Although, the question is whether we believe that kind of off-handed remark."

Lorraine said "That casualness may be a reason to trust it. It seemed to me that Dr. Fish…" and she paused as the implication of her own senses hung in the air, "really did have his nose too deep in his work to bother lying. No matter how helpful Brandt's been."

Paul said "He keeps asking *how* I got at their secrets. Of course there were no bug-tracking implants or anything in us. But the thing is, Fish turning up sounds like another sign of Brandt wanting to know about me."

"Then we'd be right to worry," his father added.

Lorraine let out a slow breath. "We can't let him see anything more. We can't risk it."

Greg said "We keep our heads down. No signs, no hints. We don't need Brandt's deal to beat this—we insist on the police finding real evidence, *just* the way you did tonight." He motioned to Lorraine, as if she could charm their way out of anything. "And we start going on the offensive with our own campaign that crushes their accusations and makes Paul the whistle-blower who's looked out for this city."

"That might work," Lorraine said. "Or it might get more serious than that. If it comes to that, we have to be ready to do what we have to."

She pointed to the door.

Greg took a step toward her, fists curled. "Lor, you just *got* here! You can't—"

Paul flung his focus into probing the street outside. Still no police or anyone to hear her talking about running again. He let his attention slide back and caught the end of Greg's outburst:

"—can't believe you're thinking about disappearing again!"

She said "We may have to. If they get much closer to this, our lives are over, finished, there's nothing that can *ever* unring that kind of a bell. And did you ever think of coming with me?"

Greg froze. "What? But—"

She swept right on. "Did you ever think that I've had more time to think this through? You're still standing here with your favorite hammer looking for nails."

"But... before, you just ran—"

"Will you *listen* to her?"

Sarah stepped in front of Greg.

"Can you really stand there and forget how she's been through all this? Can you? Why don't you get out of her way, just once?"

Greg's frown curled deeper. He opened his mouth.

She added "No I *will not* shut up and leave this in the family. But you—"

Sarah spun around to fix her glare on Lorraine.

"Is it that easy for you? With all the ways you can twist people around your finger, you still fold or run away when you see one hint of trouble..."

Sarah halted, and the rest of her breath whooshed out like a broken whistle. Her hands flew to cover her face.

"I'm sorry, I'm sorry—you're right, I'm only an outsider that knows you just well enough to get it all wrong. None of this is my place to say..."

Paul looked at her, standing shaking and flushed in the middle of the room. Worry, sympathy, embarrassment all coiled in his stomach.

Greg was the first to speak, slowly, feeling his way toward the right words. "Well, thank you for that much. All the same..."

The silence stretched one heartbeat, two.

In that stillness, the still-watchful part of Paul heard it: a car engine, gliding toward their driveway, a soft sound that would be clear to anyone whose thoughts weren't sucked into their narrow surroundings.

"Quiet! Visitor!" he said. All four of the others froze.

He Opened to track the intruder. That purring engine was no police car. The car door opened, and a single person stepped toward the house. Paul knew that stride.

"Hello? You're all back?" called Eugene Brandt.

"That's how he wants to play it?" Paul's father muttered. "Play along," and he spread a warm smile over his face and started for the door.

All around the room, smiles went up, postures smoothed out to something that could pass as calm. Paul saw the Schuman PR family forming their front, and he remembered again where he'd learned to hide secrets behind his face.

"Welcome! Come on in."

Brandt strolled in, a ruddy-faced portrait of frankness.

Oh no you don't. Paul Opened to his thoughts.

Brandt's image wavered, seemed to walk a fraction faster toward them. His gaze studied them all, but it lingered mostly on Paul and Lorraine.

"You must be Lorraine," Brandt said. "It's good to meet you, and to know why the police were suddenly so interested in what charges LifeLab was pressing. Because you were back on their radar?"

Was that his excuse for coming down here now? Did he not know Fish had given him away?

Lorraine said "They said you were... 'inconsistent' about charging us. I guess that means, not as tough as they'd like."

"If someone had been working to save our company from a scandal, of course we'd more interested in helping them than in punishing them for how they went about it." Brandt's lips moved in an easy smile.

Ian Schuman returned it. "So you're here to argue for your offer, even coming down here at night." No mention of how he might be following up the scare Fish had thrown into them.

"In my defense, I did want to see if you needed anything. But yes. we do want to learn what we can from how your son... may have... gotten into our systems. Security does take any vulnerabilities it has seriously."

Paul reached for his thoughts again. Brandt's outer face stayed on the oldest Schuman, but his inner gaze was locked on Paul.

"We're glad for the help," Sarah said. Tension tightened her voice, where the others had been smooth.

"Sarah Gomez, isn't it? We're all grateful to you for tracking down Van Howe and poor Ms. Claire, even if you couldn't arrive in time. Still, I hear you found them all by yourself. Quite impressive."

Paul Opened again. Brandt's inner eyes stared harder now, flicking between Sarah and Paul. He suspected who'd been there, alright.

"Reporter's tricks of the trade," Sarah grinned. "That and being stupid enough to go out there myself. I've learned my lesson there."

"As to your offer," Ian Schuman said, "we'll be glad to discuss it tomorrow, but this is simply not the right time for it. Much as we appreciate your coming out here."

"We do," Lorraine added—and Paul knew the signs of someone trying to keep one finger on a conversation they'd lost control of.

"Tomorrow it is," Brandt said. "I hope we can agree soon, before the authorities take it out of our hands." This time, his voice darkened into the beginnings of a caution. Or a threat.

Their father didn't miss a beat. "Naturally. And thank you again."

And he was walking Brandt out, smoothly taking charge of it all. It wasn't even his house, he was supposed to be Greg's guest while he recovered. But Paul watched him lead their "ally" out and shut the door.

When Brandt's car drove away, Paul could feel the breathing in the room ease. His father turned toward Lorraine, one eyebrow raised in a question.

She answered "He's hiding something. I'd say it's probably about the doctor, yes. Did you guess that yourself, when you *decided* Paul would keep bargaining with him?"

"If we keep engaged with him, we have a chance to learn more about what he wants from us," was the calm reply.

Before anyone could reply, Sarah cut in "Like you said, it's late. I should go." She moved for the door with too-quick steps.

"Don't go too far," Greg said. "You're always welcome here, you know."

"Thank you." But she didn't quite look back at them, as if she could hide the embarrassment on her face.

The door was closing when he scrambled after her.

Cold air slapped at him. He glanced around the dark, afraid she'd already crossed his anklet's perimeter around the yard—but she stood in the driveway, looking back to him.

"Yes?"

He trotted the last steps to her side. "Greg, Dad, Lorraine... they're grateful you spoke up there. If Greg says it's fine, he means it."

Sarah only looked at her shoes, like she hadn't heard him at all. "How could I *do* that? How could I just tear into them? And to defend Lorraine too—the one person who'll never need it."

Paul looked at her slumped in uncertainty, and felt he'd run out here too far beyond any string of words he had in mind. A voice sounded back in the house, raised for an instant and then blocked by the walls.

He tried "Never mind if she needed it. You were trying to help."

"I don't have the right to tell you how to run your family. I only made it worse."

Paul shook his head. "Sure, they can take a thing over sometimes. Lorraine was pushing back against that. I'll bet she was glad someone came to her rescue." *Like you came to me, after just a hint that I'd gone to Cedar Springs.*

"Family. Going up against them's never easy." She shook her head.

"She'll be fine. They just need to get used to her drawing a line, instead of her finessing it away. They're already getting enough practice." If they could get used to Paul himself...

"They can start with forgiving going into journalism at all."

What? His gaze shot toward her. His family had been okay with his profession when it was just a job, before the power and his disappearance changed all that—

She said "It was my family that set me off back there—stupid of me. They hardly talk to me since I started my career."

Her family, when he'd still been thinking about his. Paul forced the awkwardness off his face. "They don't?"

"Then they hear I'm chasing after some crazy," and she flashed him a smile in the dark, "all across the country, and then I come back charged with assaulting a cop. Mom got me out of that before I could say a word. But they still won't believe any of it.

"Then last night I ask my brother to bodyguard me, and then I send him away and run off to track down a murderer... and tonight I still come down here to see you all. I guess there *is* no way to explain this."

A flush rose over her face, and she spun away to break into a run.

His hand caught at hers.

She stopped in her tracks. Their arms stretched out between them, connected by just the lightest grip of his fingers on her own.

He had to say something. "Or... you should try telling them. Somehow. Pick what you let them know and why it means you're not crazy, and talk to them. *Keep* telling them."

"You think so?"

"Sure. It has to be worth it, some time."

She smiled, a touch of gentleness shaping the dimness and softening her voice: "Aren't we a pair."

He stood silent, not willing to stir. His pulse pressed against the warmth of her fingers, stretching the moment out...

Then she pulled away. One flash of Opening showed the smile was still on her face, and a glimpse of a scar pale against that hand as it drew away from his.

The night pressed in, suddenly cold again. He could watch her walk to her car and drive away... while he was still held in by the anklet's grip...

He turned and pushed back into the house.

When the door opened, he caught one murmur of his family's voices before it dropped into silence. From the way they stood facing each other, they'd just been working on their own differences too.

Lorraine looked up at him, and drew her coat around her. He realized she'd never taken it off.

Greg took one step toward her. "Don't you *dare—*"

"I'm getting myself a hotel," she said. "I swear to you, I'll be back tomorrow."

"What..." His voice died away.

She added "I think we could both use some space right now."

"I... see." A piece of hurt cut in Greg's voice, Paul could hear it. But he smiled back.

"I mean it, Greg. Tomorrow."

Then she walked away, past Paul, out the door and away and out onto the street. Just like that, she'd walked back into their lives and away again. She really left them again.

Greg's gaze swung around to catch his brother's. "What are *you* looking at?"

"Nothing." Paul let a hint of a smile show.

From the corner of his eye, he saw their father grinning at both of them.

You're wrong, watching Sarah leave is nothing *like Lorraine heading out.* Except, Lorraine might have waited until the moment he came back before she made her own departure... to not break into his and Sarah's goodbyes.

The three Schumans barely spoke now. It only took a few words to push them into finally throwing a late dinner together, and collapsing onto the chairs. The lack of words was a relief now, to let them think only about the food and how much had changed.

Brandt and LifeLab, bringing Dr. Fish's lab in for the sake of what might be worse than curiosity. Reid and the police, still pushing their case. But now all of Lorraine's subtle powers were back on their side. That should give them an edge against anything, right?

But the night still felt cold, and tired. Even after everything else it had held.

* * *

Morning broke their silence. Paul saw Greg and their father were barely on their feet before the two were deep into talk about the business, their native tongue. Only this time each angle they discussed had an aspect about Paul's own case.

"I keep coming back to Estin Insurance," their father said. "We've been promoting them quite well using their reputation of fairness."

"What are you thinking?" Greg said.

"We drop a hint about how their honesty compares to where Addamson Abbot was, before Paul exposed them. One more way to keep the good he's done in mind."

Paul could only sit still and let them talk.

They were still at the breakfast table when Lorraine arrived. No calls, no explanations, she only walked through the door with a simple "I'm here."

Greg didn't answer her, only made room for her to sit.

"Greg's going to try to catch Estin with an early call," their father said. "It'll be the first step toward raising awareness in this town about the difference between honest business and the companies that 'someone' had to expose."

"Tell me that's not set up as blackmail," Lorraine said. "Would you bring up Addamson's past all over again if they don't drop the charges?"

"Of course not!" Paul said.

"Right," Greg added. "And you know that'd backfire anyway. This is about building a stronger public need for what Paul's done, and it starts with playing up better examples like Estin. I make the call, then go see them—with your kind of help, Lor?"

"Okay." She said it like her power, or her presence, would be just one more thing in another busy day.

"You need anything else?" the older Schuman asked.

Greg's answer was to reach for the phone.

Sure enough, even this early, the call went right through.

"I'll make it quick," Greg said. "We're thinking this is a good time to push your Fair Shake promotion."

"Push it?" said the woman on the other end.

"It's the right time. Think how your fair-price image has given you a boost. The way the market's changing, though, it's time to play up the fair *treatment* your clients get."

"What market changes? You've got research for that?"

"Of course, and we can show you. It's a city-wide current that's building. You get to ride that wave from the start, before everyone's talking about it."

About me. *They're trying to turn business trends into a city-wide focus on stopping fraud, that would celebrate anyone who fights it. Can they do that?*

The woman said "Say, about how we're different from Addamson Abbot? And how they're still trying to rebuild their brand?"

Greg's face didn't change, not in any way Paul could see. "What about them? Why'd you think of them?"

"We're good, they're bad—is that what you're setting up? But you didn't have someone go and out dirty up Addamson last year to make us look good, did you?"

Did she just say... Paul felt a chill growing in him.

"Sabotaging your competition? I know you didn't just say that," Greg said.

"I didn't. It was the detective here yesterday, he was asking all about you and our relationship with you, and the hit Addamson took."

Detective? Lips tightened, breath caught, all around the room at that word. Reid.

"Oh, him." Greg only lost an instant, before he took up the thread again. "We've been getting some harassment from him lately. Nothing to waste any thought over."

"Are you sure about that?"

Greg leaned forward, and his eyes narrowed in concentration, but his voice hardly changed from its unworried tone. "You know we don't work like that."

"Sure. Just weird hearing it, is all. You want to meet us later?"

"Sounds good."

The call wrapped up in a few more practiced words, and Greg sank back in his chair. "How many clients d'you think Reid went to?"

"He had all of yesterday," their father said. "You might know better if you'd spent it with them or in the office, instead of running around forcing Lorraine's hand." The words were sharp, but he softened them with a smile at Lorraine.

"I know—" Greg began.

"It paid off, though, didn't it? But now Reid's trying to ruin us." That frown turned to focus on Paul. "So that's his idea of investigation, drop rumors to destroy the people around his suspect? Scorched earth?"

"No!" Paul made himself meet that gaze, and rushed out the part he could explain. "Reid is... for him it's all about the worst case. If he says I might be sabotaging one company to prop another up, he thinks I really might go there. Or he wants everyone on guard that I might."

"Wonderful."

"We, we may really need a deal with Brandt now, more than ever," he added. "But then, Reid's also putting more attention on how many places I could have messed with, and that makes it even harder to keep the secret."

"Or makes it impossible." Lorraine's lower, intent words reached under their louder voices. "This could bring us too close to the kind of attention we can't put back."

"You're not saying—" Greg stopped, tried again. "Don't you talk about running again."

She glared back at him. "I can't even talk about it? It may be the only way."

The older Schuman slid his voice between them. "They've already forced us all under that scanner by waving 'National Security' around. That was quite a bluff then, but it's also a measure of the pressure they could bring if they were sure enough. Reid's already hinting at us and our clients colluding with Paul, and we could end up with no money or influence left to even fight back."

Greg shook his head. "All that to punish you breaking into some scammers' rooms, and never taking anything?"

Lorraine said "Reid doesn't want anyone ruined on that scale."

"But I told you, he only sees the worst of it," Paul said. "Or even if he won't push it to that level, he can't control if it happens anyway. We've got Brandt nosing around now. What if the next lab has an MRI that *can* spot traces in our brain?"

"No!" Greg snapped. "Nobody is running, stop saying that."

Instead they began working through the list of charges against Paul... with all three of his family crowded in at the table, turning each case over and over for any ways Reid might spin each whistle-blowing as a ploy to help Schuman and Son. Paul had to sit under their gaze and feel nausea creeping up in him, trying to reimagine how everything he'd done to expose lies could look like simply a way to make someone else money.

The worst was St. Central. He'd found his powers at that hospital and haunted it for answers—searching everything in it *except* Lorraine and her dying mentor there—and now he had to face the family about how he'd ruined their bargain to let the place's billing scam go.

His father mused "They might claim our deal was falling through, and so of course you exposed them. Or that you did it out of spite against us."

"It wasn't *like that.*" Somehow Paul kept his voice almost calm, even hearing his father try to twist his decisions.

"It couldn't be like that," Lorraine said. "Is he supposed to be attacking the family or colluding with us? They could at least accuse you of something consistent."

Ian Schuman winced. "Consistent? If you think that would stop them from using both sides of the coin against us, you haven't spent enough time with lawyers."

Paul watched them begin calling their clients again. This time it wasn't to raise his chances of staying out of prison, but simply to check the damage Reid had done to the people around his target.

The first client was friendly and hadn't heard a word against them. The second had had her own visit from Reid, and sounded ready to cut ties with the firm, until Greg talked her down. The third had met with Reid just an hour ago.

"That *does* it."

Greg said it the moment he hung up. He tapped a key on his laptop and eyed the file it brought up.

"I've told the bastard I've got a list. He's harassed us for days, now he goes after the firm—it's time to sue Reid up to his overstuffed eyebrows."

"That won't stop him." Paul leaned over for a look at the file. "And it's even more attention on just how much I've gotten done. One step closer to when I have to disappear."

" 'When'?" their father said. "Let's not give up yet—let me see those."

Greg slid the computer around, to him and away from Paul. "It's all there. Constant 'inspections' of the house arrest, compared to industry standards. His harassing calls to Paul. And these insinuations to our clients? Is he going to claim that's part of the investigation too?"

Their father hunched in to share the screen. "Also, he traveled all the way to Cedar Springs when he heard Paul had been caught, and remember that was before he knew about his power. Not that that goes in the lawsuit, but it shows Reid's obsession isn't always about those gifts."

Now they're even talking about my power like I'm not in the room anymore—

"Well it is now," Paul snarled. "And this isn't always about the business either. Even if it did take a threat to that before you decided Reid was a problem."

The air went still. Paul saw Greg's face frozen, Lorraine's eyes closed—*did* I *say that?*

Ian Schuman turned slowly to Greg. "You and Lorraine have been cooped up in here long enough. Are you ready to get back to the office?"

Greg glanced between him and Paul, and got to his feet. "Um. Right. And I'll start that lawsuit for Reid—"

He stopped, looked at Paul again.

"Well, I'll start some groundwork for it. We'll pull the trigger when we're all ready."

When he said that, Lorraine took his arm.

Greg's eyebrows shot up, but then the couple fell into step and only needed a few moments more to scoop up their things and slip outside.

His father didn't make a sound. He only watched Paul, with a stony poker face Paul could never have matched. His hands resting on the table showed the slightest tremble.

His father. The man Paul had gotten *shot,* who'd had to *kill* Quinn because of Paul's mistakes. *The absolute heart of all the damage I've done, and I can't get away from him...*

"Paul, do you think anyone's listening?"

Paul let out a breath, and Opened to the sounds outside. A quick sweep showed nobody lingering in the street, or even lurking in one of the yards. Unless the police were driven enough to take over a nearby house to get a mic on him.

No, it wasn't the police that had him hesitating. He pulled his focus back and his father's face formed in front of him again.

"No, nobody out there."

"Paul…" The eyes of that lined, sharp face closed. "I've done everything I can to help you. Bail, lawyers, influence. Everything."

"I know!" Paul caught the pleading before it could gather speed. What had he told Sarah about family, to just talk to them? He settled for a simple "And I'll pay you all back some day. I know I can't fix all the rest that I've put you through."

"And you pulled Lorraine away from us. Even now that she's back, she doesn't fit in the same way."

"You can't blame me for that too—" Paul froze. Just seconds after choosing to listen, *that* came lashing out?

"I'm *not blaming* you. I simply… don't know how to help you."

He leaned slowly toward his son.

"I've tried to give you and Greg the life you needed. I've held this family together after your mother died. We had the firm, and it was all Greg ever wanted. You had your own plans, that's fine. And then you run off and start saving the world and won't tell a living soul where you are or why—"

"For two years. There must be dozens of cases Reid doesn't even know about. Aren't there?"

"Hmm." It was all he could say. *How can I defend myself to someone I've hurt in so many ways?*

"About that power, now… are you still saying that was what drove you to run off, now that we see how Lorraine was living quietly with her own all that time?"

"I…" Of *course* he saw that. Paul squirmed in his seat. "When I got mine, I couldn't even remember the night clearly. I was sure there was some secret to find about it, and then I kept looking for other secrets and all that was safer away from you." The words sounded as hollow as the hole in his father's side.

"Was it like that for Lorraine, when she first got hers?" Those eyes missed nothing.

"Um. I don't think so. And for Reid, he ran wild and almost beat my head in once, but all that was over soon. How it works for anyone is… just *different.*"

"So you don't know. It's part of the reason for how you've been living, but you don't know any more than that."

"I guess I don't." *There* is *no defense, none at all.*

"Then that's one way you're the same as me. Because I don't know how to help you."

He slumped, sagged against the table, his gaze sinking to the floor. Paul found himself leaning toward him, but the words kept coming:

"All I know is work, Paul. If that's no use for you anymore, I've got no ideas left. So please, please… if you don't know how you got here, help me find a way I can make it right. What is it you need, under it all, right now?"

Paul stared at his father's face, lined and tired and not even looking up, but still trying to help him find a way.

He wished he had an answer, some kind of excuse. Still, he reached into himself and told the truth, the wishes that were beyond impossible now.

"I just… I need to believe I've done the right thing. Or at least, that I haven't been pushed into the whole world coming after me and all of you because of this power."

His father looked up.

A smile worked slowly over his lips.

"Understood. Then, why don't we try to deal with Detective Reid our way, just the two of us? That can get us started on your second wish.

"As for the first… I still don't know how you managed it, but you've done more of that than any of us."

CHAPTER TWELVE

THROUGH THE GLASS

"Meet you?" Reid said. "Why? I know you won't be confessing."

Paul shifted his grip on the phone. "It's about some questions I have. About me, not for Oliver and his prosecution."

"Can't change a thing. You really think it'll get you anywhere?"

Paul glanced at his father, watching, trusting him. *Alright, let's see Reid turn* this *down.* "I want to understand what's driving you. How can locking me up be so damn important?"

"You still don't get it? I'll be there."

The call cut off, and Paul leaned back on the chair.

Now all he needed was a way to convince Reid to ease up. He turned it all over in his head, everything he'd seen the detective do… but one thought stuck in his head: when would Brandt call about his own offer? What if those two walked in on each other, the one trying to bury the secret and the one who was dangerous just knowing part of it?

The worry nibbled at him from one side, then another, as he tried to plan his arguments. Until he heard the car outside, and Reid walked in.

"Alright, where do we start?" Reid walked up to the table.

Paul's father sat still, letting him take the lead.

Paul reached for the pitcher of water. He poured Reid a glass, and his hands stayed steady.

Reid only sat down, arms folded, not touching the glass.

Okay, I remind him of the first thing he sensed with his powers, it's no surprise he refuses. Or he even thinks we'd drug someone like Chief Thiessen did.

Paul tried again. "I know there are no police listening to us."

"Of course not. Or did you want to read my mind and confirm that?"

"Thoughts aren't as clear as that." But he could have *tried* that trick, if he'd thought of it... That made two tries to connect with Reid that went sour. Still, Paul tried to build on what he'd said: "You're so sure our powers just rip what we want out of people's minds? And you still risked coming here?"

The edge of Reid's mouth curled in a faint smile. "I'm not afraid of you."

"No? I hear you're running all over town, even scaring whoever my family does business with. All that to put me away. What else would you call it?"

"It's not fear. What you do is a loaded gun pointed at the city. So I'm putting that threat under lock and key."

"And that makes anyone Schuman and Son helps a suspect? You know my motives better than that. I'm interested in frauds and liars, not business rivals."

"How do we know that?" Reid leaned over the table. "One minute you're catching a scam, the next *second* you could be reading someone's ID code or some secret nobody knows. And Lorraine *makes* people do what she wants, but at least she's got some respect that keeps her from doing it every minute."

"She also had her home town's police chief locking her up out of sheer hatred." Paul leaned forward to match Reid. "And we stopped Thiessen together, all of us. But after all that, you're just taking over the hate from her?"

"I don't hate her. Or you."

Sure, lie to a mind-reader. But Paul bit down on that answer. He needed a way to calm Reid down from his worst, not antagonize him.

His father broke the silence. "So you blame Paul for the crimes he might commit, instead of what he's done. Isn't there a rule about 'innocent' and 'proven guilty,' or are you making your own decisions about the law?"

"I'm *within* the law." Reid locked his gaze on Paul. "You rack up trespassings and B&Es like you think every door is stuck open for you to use. I don't have to tell them you can rip their world open *with your mind* because we can catch every time your body goes over the line. And we will get every time."

His hand brushed his jaw.

"You *hit* me. I'm giving you that one, because instead... that computer of yours you hit me to destroy? We're rebuilding it. And if we don't get enough out of that, we'll look every other place you might have been. You'll do your time for each one of them—before it gets worse. Before you get worse."

His voice shifted, went softer.

"You just lost CC. Lorraine's been through her own hell, your father's taken a bullet... and you don't see where you'll all headed, just for being around this twisted thing you can do?"

The hardness in his glare had faded, leaving only pain. He'd known CC too.

Paul forced himself to not look away.

His father's steadier voice spoke up. "So, we take responsibility for the worst that we've done?"

He reached out to brush the untouched glass in front of Reid.

He added "Then, what about the best? What about all those swindles, cheats, and violations that you see Paul has put a stop to?" He picked up an empty glass and began pouring water in. "He's found crimes none of the police did. Are you so sure which one outweighs which, when you balance them?"

And he set the second glass down in front of Paul. The water in it looked just about even with Reid's.

Reid's eyes went hard. "When I balance them? *That's* the danger—thinking we get to balance anything."

He caught up the pitcher. And began pouring, into Paul's glass.

"You talk about the 'good' you've done. And you ignore the laws, you keep shoving the world into what you want. You go behind our backs, again and again, and still you're making excuses, until—"

Water spilled over the rim.

Reid shoved the glass with the pitcher, sending it toppling over. Water poured along the table and splashed coldness onto their laps.

"Look at me!" the cop roared. "Can you look at me for one second and even say that you were wrong, and how much you have to pay for?"

"Is that what you want?" Paul flung back. "If I said it, would you see it in my head and believe me?"

"You think I'm that easy? And I know you'd be lying anyway. You see *everything*, but never how goddamn wrong it is to know!"

Paul could only stare. *He believes that, he thinks nobody should have this power even though he took it himself. But the one thing I know is that we all found the power because we* needed *it...*

And I need...

"I see how much is wrong out there, Reid. I know CC got killed because someone spied on me and I was stuck where I couldn't warn her. And that kind of helpless wrongness—"

He snatched up a third glass, empty, and slammed it down on the table.

"I'm *sick* of it!"

Reid glared back at him. "Still a slow learner."

Paul's father laughed. "He has nothing to learn from you. As I understand how these abilities work, there must have been some part of you that wanted to see what the world keeps hidden. And when you got your wish, your takeaway is that nobody should see a thing?"

"Nobody *should.*" Reid stood up. "And you're going where all you'll see is what's left of people that think like you do, where there's nobody worth saving. Prison."

He spun and walked away.

Paul grabbed for a cloth and began mopping up the pool on the table, as the door slammed.

"Sorry. I was starting to think I'd reach him. Or that I'd get him to leave the business out of it."

"Stop worrying about that. What did you get from his mind?"

Oh. He thinks I could have…

Paul had to shake his head. "It doesn't work like that. I can get bits that help me, but it wouldn't do much with someone I already understand. Lorraine's better, but she only gets so much too. And Reid, he really is stuck on stopping me. So we got nothing."

"Maybe. Or sometimes, it's the pitch that doesn't work that teaches you the most."

Paul set the cloth in the sink. "Oh? About him or about me?"

"You're the mind-reader. You'll have to tell me."

He smiled and glanced at his phone.

"But, I think that was the rehearsal. Brandt says he can be here in an hour."

Great. At least with Reid there'd been no way to make it worse…

Paul moved from the table to sink down onto the familiar sofa again. Behind him, his father was calling Greg and Lorraine to join them.

He stared at the front door, trying to think whether he could give Brandt any of what he wanted. The best plan had been to explain those "security gaps" as him being a master of simple stealth. *Or even use that to make the same kind of deal if Addamson Abbot or the rest wanted in, anything to bring the number of charges down.*

But with Brandt talking with spytech people, with Fish? One slip could show them all everything.

A car roared down the street outside, passing on by. In prison he could at least hear reminders of the outside; if people like Fish took over they'd dissect him, one way or another.

He slumped lower in the sofa. If nothing changed, Reid would only keep finding more charges to pile on him. And if he could rebuild Paul's computer... forty-eight scams and secrets he'd exposed, that Reid would only see as more violations.

Those had put Sarah in prison, briefly. Gotten his father shot.

Paul gritted his teeth. Those forty-eight times he'd won had to count for something. And he'd told Reid he was sick of being help-less.

Sure, except I'm facing prison and worse. Not the way to take con-trol back.

But the worst threat was still Brandt and the rest learning the truth, and that one was closing in right now. Whatever else he did, he had to convince Brandt he *wasn't* some great game-changer for Dr. Fish to pick apart.

He shifted his weight on the cushions. As long as he kept up an underwhelming front for Brandt and his questions, that one danger would fizzle out. Reid would still keep adding to his accusations, but the worst couldn't touch him, or Lorraine.

And he might still beat Reid's charges. Or endure them in prison, knowing the real nightmare had passed him by.

Except...

That cell...

It crept up around his sides, his shoulder blades, even slouched on the familiar sofa. Cold, helpless dread, that worked cracks into his resolve at just the first thought of prison. *Can I really risk going back into years of that, just because I'm playing by someone else's rules?*

Planning would be easy. Running would be easy—he'd already beaten the anklet once. To simply get *out* of this vise he was in.

And leave his family stuck with the bail, the accusations. He looked up at his father.

The phone chimed. His father glanced at it.

Paul breathed "Please be Lorraine on her way." His nerves still tingled with the risk of saying one word too many, or not saying enough while Reid pieced his whole history together from that computer. He wasn't ready to face Brandt, not alone.

"Not quite," and his father slid the phone into his hand.

Sarah.

"Hi," he said.

"Hi. Everyone alright still? It's been a whole morning." She spoke lightly, and the joke stilled some of the shivering in his sides.

He laughed "No arrests yet. No runaways, no—"

Deaths. The laughter faded.

"Just checking in?" he added, still able to keep it casual.

"No. It's about the lab."

"Which lab? Dr. Fish's, or Brandt's LifeLab?"

"Yes." Sarah's own laugh only lasted a moment. "I found Fish's operation. It's a small spot, but LifeLab Medical is a major investor in it. Here."

A picture flashed on the screen. A single door on a small industrial building, seen from far enough across the street that he could just make out the so-bland name "Operative Solutions."

Operative could mean *practical*—or *agent*, or *spy*.

"You think that's as big as the company is?" He tried to stop, but his mouth kept going. "Everything depends on how much else they're tied to. Or they could be just a small specialized lab, that simply gave Brandt a string to pull to scare us."

"Small and connected. From what I see."

So Dr. Fish wasn't as threatening as he seemed, but Brandt knew enough to be working with him...

The doorbell rang.

"Morning," came the familiar voice.

"Brandt is *here*," Paul hissed.

"I'll keep looking. And yes I'll stay safe—watch yourself too." She hung up.

Her quick, honest concern sent a wave of warmth through him. *One reason not to run.*

His father led Brandt inside. "Coffee, water? Anything?"

"No, thank you. I'm hoping there's only so much of this left to set-tle, since we all have so much else on our minds." He waved a sheaf of papers, copies of the agreement again.

They settled around the table, laying the pages where Paul had mopped up Reid's spill.

Brandt added "You can bring in your lawyers now or later, or any-one else you want here."

Paul's father said "For the moment, the three of us should be fine."

If it could ever be *fine* to start bargaining without Lorraine's pre-cise power. But he'd never let that need show to Brandt.

"You've already looked through this. The bulk of it," and Brandt flipped past the first two pages to look at the half-dozen remaining, "is mostly definitions and limitations, so both sides can make an agree-ment without embracing any kind of lawbreaking. Of course your lawyer should confirm this later."

"Of course," Paul's father nodded.

"Still, you did say that CC liked the terms here?" and Brandt's gaze swung to Paul.

I should dodge that question, it would give us more wiggle room. But CC *had* approved of the terms, and with her dead, telling the truth was the least he could do for her.

"Paul?" Brandt said again.

I just have to be sure of one thing. "CC liked them more than we did. We might have solved all this before, if she hadn't gotten am-bushed outside your gate." And with that subject in the air, he reached for Brandt's thoughts.

The man's face softened into regret, sympathy, and a faint trembling—fitting for reactions of honest pain and a fear of being misunderstood. Too little for Brandt to have a hand in CC's attack.

Like Brandt said, he'd only picked Van Howe to do his dirty work and never guessed it would spiral out of control. *And now I'm trying to keep limits on a deal with him too.*

"—what about?" Brandt was saying when Paul unfocused.

"My son and I found a number of issues we could discuss, to be sure neither of us is incriminating—"

"It's about the details of what we're trading," Paul cut in.

"Of course. Here." Brandt slid the pages around to view the first two again. "Basically, you satisfy LifeLab security with your explanation of the ways you 'might have' accessed our resources. Which includes the details about any contacts of yours in the company, sad but necessary. In exchange, we drop any related charges in the past and future—'any' as limited by those later pages, that is. Which shouldn't be a problem since nobody's accusing you of attacking our guards or passing our secrets to competitors."

"I see."

And there it was: could he *satisfy Security* and hide his real tricks, from someone as savvy as Brandt?

Brandt added "Still, dropping the LifeLab charges only does so much when someone is facing as many others as you are." He smiled. "So I thought of sweetening the deal."

"Very kind," Ian Schuman said. "Of course 'sweetening' is also what someone says when they're baiting a trap—but then, we've all had a bad experience or two." His grin made the moment's warning a casual thing, just part of the background of doing business.

"Naturally. Paul, you once wondered if any of your other accusers might be open to the same arrangement with you. I'd say that some might be. Not all…"

As Brandt spoke, his fingers darted between the pages. He slid out a small note, angling it for Paul to read the bold, handwritten words:

not St. Cedric's.

"...so you'll need another way to cope with those, if you can," he finished.

Paul watched the note vanish out of sight again. Was Brandt... afraid of being bugged? And he'd had that message ready, written?

Paul caught at Brandt's thoughts. The inner face that stared back was sharp, locked onto him—

The next moment it began narrowing even more, fierce, *greedy*—

"—in here about a possible job for you," Brandt was saying. "If anyone's interested in you, we had to be sure we got first dibs."

And he slid out another note: *you'll like it.*

Paul kept his face still, utterly still, anything to hold off having to answer. The silence stretched.

So Brandt had some plan to hire him, some scheme that had his thoughts hungry to get him. *How do I back away, what do I say...*

The front door rattled open.

Greg stepped in, with Lorraine right behind him. "Sorry we're late," he called.

Lorraine, here, right when they needed her most. Paul felt a rush of relief so great he couldn't risk looking at her, certain the joy would break through onto his face.

Brandt grinned "I'm just glad to have you all. This ought to be a family decision... as long as Paul says yes," and his smile widened to keep it a joke. Or seem like one.

The older Schuman waved them to sit. "We were talking about Paul demonstrating any methods he might have used, both to LifeLab and some of the other accusers, in exchange for dropping the charges and possibly taking a job with them."

"Now there's an offer," Greg said. "I just hope he stays free to try it. Last night we were almost all locked up by some spytech scientist."

And as Greg said it, from the corner of Paul's eye he saw Lorraine's gaze sharpen a fraction. She was probing Brandt's reaction, to the news Greg had raised for her.

"Seriously?" Brandt said. "I... I guess all I can say is that the terms here won't be adding to that kind of risk. Paul, you understand the back pages here that keep us from incriminating each other? So we're left with essentially the front pages and the quid pro quo itself. Is there a part of that we should discuss?"

His gaze tightened, showing just a hint of the eager look his true self had.

"Or, you run it by your lawyers but right now we agree that you're in?"

Paul forced a tiny smile, pinned under that gaze. *I have to go along. I need to prove I'm nothing special—but, a* job? *for* him? *The more I say now, the harder it'll be to refuse...*

"Ah. I really need to talk with my family, and the lawyers. Before I say anything."

Brandt nodded, but the edges around his eyes stayed sharp. "Of course. But is it their choice or yours?"

Paul's stomach roiled—did he have to put it like *that?* Still, he said "It's complicated. We'll talk soon."

Now that gaze softened. "I'm sure we will. And I think my time's up, so I hope we do make it soon."

Then he was on his feet, walking out and trading more pleasantries with Paul's father, as if the silent notes and demands had never happened. Paul forced himself to simply breathe, ignoring the razor-edged tension in the room, until the door closed and Brandt drove away.

"We're so sorry," Lorraine said. "We tried to get away in time. But then traffic... we should have been here before he showed up."

"It happens," Paul said. "Like Brandt said, same trade as before. Security demonstrations in exchange for dropping charges, only this time he might be bringing more people in. But here's the thing: he showed me a *note,* that St. Central Hospital wouldn't be in on them."

"Note?" Greg scowled. "What... oh, in case we were bugged, or we were recording him."

"He had another note ready, about me taking that job. The way I read him…" the euphemism was good enough, even though he'd given up worrying about bugs himself, "I think he really wants me to sign on."

"Oh, he does," Lorraine said. "He isn't thinking small, I'm sure. And I'm more sure than ever that he called Fish's lab on us. You can't take the deal."

"Can't?" Greg said.

"Paul, you keep saying you want a quiet life now. Brandt's shown he's got too many schemes to ever let you have that."

"I didn't say *quiet—"* Paul began.

His father cut him off. "There has to be a way. Could you meet their terms without giving them a glimpse of anything more? You have to have choices beyond living like a phantom again—or a chameleon."

He glanced at Lorraine for that, and she winced.

"Stop it, all of you!" Greg said. "What do *you* want, Paulie?"

Paul could only shake his head, and groan.

"Okay, then think it over. Listen, Dad, at least we got some of the clients talking to us again…"

Paul leaned back in the chair, as the others fell back into line with Greg's change of subject.

A quiet life? Lorraine's words still sounded wrong. That was her own style and her power, that liked smoothing away what was already easy.

But it's never *easy for me.* He'd hurt them all, he had Reid shoving him into prison—with his files on all forty-eight cases, if they had any luck rebuilding those—and now Brandt trying to sink his own hooks into him.

If there was any strip of safe ground between the two traps… it was still in satisfying Brandt just enough.

Paul stood up and walked to the living room, smoothly and silently as his feet could lay themselves on the floor. A board creaked gently, but he glided on to the front hall, then back.

In the dining room Greg's chair had its back to him, and he crept up. Quieter, softer, enough to convince Brandt's people he used only simple stealth...

Or I'm practicing for going on the run.

His shoe squeaked on the floor.

Greg spun around in his chair. "Huh? What's that for?"

"Practice."

He padded out again, back and forth, again and again, quieter with every minute. Of course, in a demonstration, he wouldn't have time to Open to feel every muscle moving, but he knew them and how to make them flow together. He only had to show he could creep up behind Brandt and his security people, to stop them from thinking he could do any more.

A phone chimed.

"Ian Schuman here." Surprise twisted his father's greeting.

Paul paused to look over to him.

"—No, not at all."

The surprise deepened, clashing with his father's usual grace in managing people. Greg and Lorraine were eyeing him now too.

"—But you think Sarah's here?"

Sarah? *Think* she was here? That could mean anything, but Paul closed the last steps between them in a moment.

His father passed the phone to him.

The name on the screen was *Marina Gomez.*

"Paul Schuman."

"So you're the convict my daughter's been chasing after." The woman's voice was rich, and she measured it like gripping a weapon ready to draw.

"You have to know I'm not a convict," he said. *Yet.* "And I never asked Sarah to get involved."

"I guess you wouldn't have." She sighed slowly. "I know the last time she did what she was told to do. That never goes well."

"That does sound like her."

And her rage at Lorraine trying to bend her emotions, blaming both of us... Paul shut his eyes as he felt his understanding of her deepen a touch.

He added "You were saying you thought she was with us?"

"Sarah asked me to meet her, to discuss something. Now she's late."

And she'd been looking at Fish's lab—no, no, that didn't mean trouble— "I'm sorry, she's not here."

"She already sent her brother away to see you, after specially asking him to sit with her. But this? This is the first time she's ever asked to see me, and she's late."

Missing, she meant. Paul felt his fingers digging into the phone.

Somehow a steady, unhurried voice came from his lips: "I'm sure it's important to her, then. She's probably just delayed, and she'll join you when she can."

"I'm sure you're right," she said. "And, a word to the wise: you'd better beat those charges, for her sake."

She hung up.

Paul tried to ease the tension out of his grip. This wasn't CC again, Sarah really *could* just be held up.

He shot her a quick call. No answer.

The others were looking at him. He handed the phone back—*and I am so* tired *of borrowing phones from people.* "She's just late."

He turned back to practicing his step, back and forth, searching for silence. All it took was controlled balance and care, and knowing where to step on floorboards, or snow or whatever it would be. His feet glided faster now.

Practice. He slid in and out of Opening to track the other people's breathing, to spot any moment that they might be about to move and look around. Not that he'd need to that to convince Brandt, not when his plan was to seem just sneaky enough.

He was *not* training to go after Sarah. Certainly not with the early afternoon sun still glaring in the window.

And Greg and Lorraine were still here. None of them mentioned it, they only kept passing Brandt's papers around and staying on their phones with clients and lawyers, but none of them mentioned leaving. A kind of bunker sensibility had closed around the house.

Finally they stopped to throw a late lunch together, and he broke his silence. "Any news from the lawyers?"

His father said "CC's associates are doing their best to pick up your case. The prosecution's reported a new round of evidence against you, all scrupulously within the requirements for disclosure."

"What've they got?"

"More witnesses that think they saw you at... Vitamintastic." His lip still curled at the name. "Nothing much there. They found more people who might have spotted you at St. Central."

"Just like Brandt's warning said. I spent enough time there, so of course it's the worst spot or me."

"You better hope they don't find any fingerprints," Greg said.

At least that helped him smile. "Me? *Please.*"

Practice came faster and faster now. He ghosted up the stairs and back down, more smoothly each time. Sometimes on the quieter stretches of floor he began scuffing his heel, just so he could show Brandt he wasn't flawless. And none of it helped check on Sarah.

He only noticed the phone call when his father held the cell out to him.

Sarah's name was on the screen. A moment of pure, sweet relief gushed through him, and then he brought the phone to his ear.

"You alright?" he asked. The same question she'd opened with last time.

"Of course I am. But do you believe it—they just *grabbed* me!"

"What? They?" *She said she's alright—*

"I was outside Fish's lab. Not going in, not anything. And their security just grabs me off the street. Not even cops, they simply haul me inside and ask what I'm doing. I bet if I didn't play so scared I'd still be in there! Guess if you take one dollar from the 'intelligence community' you think you've bought off people's rights."

"But, you're okay." It came out as a release of breath, close enough to a sigh to make a listener feel the weight of worry he'd been carrying.

It didn't even slow her down. "Fine. You know they ran that scanner over me? Said the scar on my hand could mean I'd had something done there—like they couldn't see it was five years old! But, you don't need my temper now, do you?" she added.

"Give me a minute, I'll be mad enough for both of us. Fish did that to you, I bet Brandt allowed it..." He tried to let the thoughts settle. "What're you doing next? You ready to see your mother?"

"So you know about that." Now the outrage left her voice, leaving only calm. "Paul, do you really think I called you first?"

"Oh. Right."

Then she said "I did," and the call ended.

He froze, and the last lilt of her voice echoed in his ear. *What is happening with her, and me? Right in the middle of everything?*

The phone in his hand pinged

The screen showed an alert for an email—it had to be someone important, to stand out from the mass of messages his father must get. Paul was walking the phone back to him when he saw the sender: *EBrandt.*

His father read it aloud:

Ian:

I heard you're having more trouble with your son's case. And an increase in collateral damage, that is likely to get worse.

Like you yourself said, we might have solved all this before, if CC hadn't been ambushed. Mr. Schuman, I think you understand.

If you do, I'd like you to meet me alone, at LifeLab at eight tonight. It may be your last chance to gain an ally that can keep your family out of danger.

Greg scowled. "What's he up to now, Dad? He wants you to go behind our backs?"

"I... don't think so," Paul said. "That bit about almost solving this before? Dad isn't the 'Mr. Schuman' who said that.

"Brandt sent this to me."

CHAPTER THIRTEEN

BETWEEN THE DEVIL AND THE DEEP

"That's insane!" Greg was on his feet, just a step from Paul. "We can work with Brandt without you running off for some arrest-breaking visit because he snaps his fingers. Or we can beat the charges without him."

"And how do we do that?" Lorraine edged around past Greg.

"We've got our secret weapon: *you,* Lor. You find ways to go to their witnesses, and you do what you have to make them doubt what they saw. And we keep promoting the good you've done, Paul. We can do this."

"Witness-tampering my way to freedom," Paul sighed, and he saw Lorraine wince as he went on. "Is that safer than working with Brandt? Is it *better?"*

"We're assuming Brandt's sending this request to you in the first place," his father mused. "But yes, words like *Mr. Schuman, I think you understand* are too clumsy to be anything but a signal to us. And after those notes he flashed us in the meeting, we have to accept that this is another way to speak to you without being traced.

"Which also makes it a more effective trap. If you break house arrest to meet him, he can record you there, but there's no evidence he solicited your escape. He gets more leverage on you than ever."

Paul shook his head. "More leverage than what? He's already got control of the LifeLab charges against me, and maybe some of the others. Now he's got Fish checking us for classified surveillance gear. And going after Sarah."

"Hold on! About that," Greg said. "You notice how Brandt's invitation came in *right after* Sarah told you what she'd been through? How'd he do that?"

"He..."

Paul only needed a moment. Then he reached for the phone again, and his father handed it over.

Sarah's phone went to voice mail. He forced down the worry that he was too late, and said "Careful! I think when you left Operative Solutions, they had you followed. Or bugged your phone. Watch yourself."

Lorraine said "Brandt's pulling out more tricks all the time. He really feels like an honest man, but he's learning fast."

"One more reason you can't go see him." Greg thumped Paul's shoulder, then turned his gaze to his laptop. The mouse clicked back and forth gathering files together. "We just have to beat down enough charges to keep you out of prison. We sue Reid for harassment, and half of that'll be done. Trust me, nobody's running away here. Nobody," and he glanced at Lorraine.

Paul shook his head. "That won't stop Reid. Nothing will. And he's rebuilding my computer, with all my files."

Slowly, Lorraine said *"If* you *did* believe that... you'd run anyway. Hypothetically."

Hypothetically? Like it's only a matter of time before Reid is asking them if they'd heard us planning our escape? After all their open strategizing, her sudden caution slammed down between them like she'd thrown down a packed suitcase.

She went on "It must be hard to keep worrying about what the police will find next. Much harder than just making plans and getting what you'd need. Or what any of us would need, if we thought we'd only be next on Reid's list."

She glanced at Greg. Shock and denial were struggling in her husband's paling face, starting to pry his eyes wider.

No, no... Paul shook his head and scrabbled for any other ideas. "Wait... Brandt won't stop either, but maybe..."

The phone was still in his hand, the number still right there waiting. Paul put the call through before he could hesitate.

Reid didn't waste time either. "Schuman? You've got more excuses for me?"

"Did Sarah tell you yet?" Paul rushed out. "I saw how you don't trust Dr. Fish and his spy people. Well, they just grabbed Sarah off the street and tried interrogating her. Like they were actual cops."

"Off the street? Sounds more like she was doing more of your dirty work and got caught, inside the premises. Too bad she's way past being scared straight."

He's still *not listening?* "Stop it! You know there are worse things out there than me. Or someone trusting me. Remember when I tried to tell you about Eckles?"

"So you want to warn me about Fish?"

"About Eugene Brandt, and LifeLab. You said they were up to something when they backed out of charging me. Well, *Brandt* told Van Howe to watch me in prison, and that led to Eckles trying to use it. Brandt gets more ruthless the more he finds out about me."

And that was the man I was thinking of sneaking out to meet. The thought sank coldly through him. The last thing Brandt needed was more proof about what Paul could do.

Reid only said "And he grabbed your computer too, I bet?"

For a moment the words made no sense. "Computer?"

"The pieces of your machine we were fixing. All gone, straight out of the evidence locker—just like you almost got into the place at Cedar Springs. You and Lorraine did that, and she doesn't have a tracker on her. You want to tell me who else could have done it?"

"I... I did *not* steal my computer back." He looked at Lorraine, and she gave a quick shake of her head. "Not her either. I told you, try looking at Brandt, he must have done that too."

"It was her. And we'll get her."

Why would Reid let them know... oh. Paul remembered how the detective had worked before his powers: by bluffing clues out of people. He was waiting for him to defend Lorraine.

"Just look at Brandt." He hung up, set the phone on the table.

Lorraine smiled. "So that's the computer the police got from you? You know I wouldn't try going after something they had locked up. Too risky for me."

"Not your style, I know. Not when you're alone. But is it too much to ask that this once Reid listens to me?"

"It's enough to make someone wonder, why they'd bother playing Reid's games at all. Or Brandt's."

She was circling around the word *escape* again. Like there was nothing left to do but plan one and deny it... Paul slumped into his chair, and let his father take the phone back. He had no more ideas.

Still, they never sent Brandt an answer, either way.

* * *

The sun sank lower in the sky. When darkness came he would still be unprepared for any kind of sneaking out of town—but knowing he *could* go kept pulling his glance toward the fading light.

At one end of the table sat Lorraine. She brought up file after file on her laptop, never speaking but always tilting the screen toward him. Car rentals, buses, clothes, whole lists of ways to move and hide someone.

At the other end, Greg gathered legal arguments and promotion plans. He showed each one to Paul, always trying to build his own case for staying to fight. His gaze and Lorraine's kept avoiding each other.

At least Sarah had sent a quick text, that she was still safe.

Once when Greg and their father were talking with CC's law firm, Paul reached over to look up Eugene Brandt. Most of what he saw was familiar: a somewhat-known investor, hands-on about LifeLab and only sometimes being mentioned for his other connections. Known as an honest businessman, best known for being taken advantage of once or twice in the past. Nothing at all about Operative Solutions...

Greg slid the laptop away from him. "Brandt again? Is that for if he comes to us later, or are you still thinking of going to him? Even if he does have your records," he added.

"I don't want to." Not that he liked any of his "choices."

"Good. We can file the suit against Reid first thing tomorrow. That should slow his persecution down."

And cover my escape tomorrow night, if—when—I go? "Unless he arrests me tomorrow and it's all over."

"The lawyers can keep watch for that," and his father sent a quick email. "That should do it. One whiff of a motion to set the trial or re-imprison you, and we'll know."

For Lorraine's end of the table came a quiet, steady "And if there is? Can you admit that it changes anything?"

"Nobody needs to run." Greg stood up to loom over the table. "We can fix this. You could fix it yourself if you cared enough to look at—"

She didn't look up from her screen. "I care too much to waste my time on what's never going to work."

"Then get out of here! We'll save Paul without you. Hypothetically," he added.

Paul snapped "Slow down! Both of you—"

Lorraine's eyes locked into him. "What if, they come for you tomorrow, and you aren't ready? You'd... we'd... anyone who needed to vanish would need to disguise their look, maybe rent a car and drive far enough to change—"

"Oh, you've got it all planned," Greg smirked.

"You think there's one reason I *wouldn't?* "

"I guess not, you lied to us long enough!" His face flushed red. *"Give me that—"*

Greg clutched at her screen. One wrench yanked the laptop out of her hands.

Paul couldn't move.

"Greg!"

Their father's voice, sharp and certain.

Greg went still. He leaned across the table, trembling hands pressing against the wood. His breathing slowed.

He slid the machine back to her.

"I… I'm sorry. I know, I know, I can't *make* you do anything, even let me save you. But… do you even want me to try?"

Her face was pale. Her voice choked, as she said "You have no idea. I just, I can't *need* it…"

She stopped. Then she turned to Paul, and her words were clear again. "And you don't need me out there. I know I still owe you so much for not showing you how our powers work. But, you simply don't need me. And Reid and Brandt and the rest can't touch me, here."

Greg stared. "Did you just say…"

Her lips curved in a grin. "You heard me. Here."

Her hand closed over his, resting over the keyboard. The two froze there, Greg leaning across the table, neither able to move.

Paul pushed his chair back to clear the way. Long moments later, Greg finally moved around the table and pulled his wife into an awkward embrace. Awkward but real.

Paul looked away.

Lorraine made it sound so easy. Her way was to stay where she belonged, now that she'd gotten through the worst of the shocks. *I've got real crimes against me, and now I think Brandt has my hard drive with all forty-eight cases…*

Lawyers couldn't save him from that. But to simply run, before he even heard what Brandt was up to?

If I'm running anyway...

* * *

When the first layers of shadow began spreading over the street outside, Paul moved upstairs to Greg's room. He couldn't take the same clothes as when he looked for CC, but there had to be some combination that would be warm, and wouldn't draw everyone's eyes by flopping around on his smaller frame...

"Paul?" Greg was standing behind him. "So that's it, you're not even giving us a chance to fight for you?"

"It's not that simple." He kept his eyes on the closet in front of him.

"And you're sneaking out now? Then we just look up and see we never got to say goodbye? *Again?*"

"No! Not tonight," Paul gasped, anything to smooth the pain that cracked in Greg's voice. In the house below, other footsteps moved toward them.

Greg blinked, and he took a step back. "Oh. I get it, you're going to meet Brandt now."

"I didn't say that."

Lorraine stepped into the room. "You have to find out, don't you? What Brandt wants." Her lips curved in a small, sad smile.

Behind her, Paul's father added "It's no great surprise. So you're still considering staying?"

"I... might," Paul said. "Or you can call it a last gasp of curiosity, if I don't find something that changes it all. And it's not much of a risk—what does my breaking house arrest mean if Brandt has my records on all forty-eight cases anyway? It looks more like I'll leave tomorrow night."

"It *looks,*" and Greg took a slow, deep breath, "more like you'll be staying. Of *course* you'll let the court work out what to do with you, and tonight you're... getting to bed early. So we should let you sleep, right?"

Deniability. *He says I'm staying, because he admits...*

Paul grinned back. "Right."

He watched as the three of them trooped back downstairs, then set out the long shirt and sweatshirt he'd need.

He looked down at the locator anklet—he'd barely thought about how to remove the thing this time, he realized. Still, after having his family and his choices twisting themselves into different shapes all day, this was a kind of relief. One challenge that was all his.

The knife. The lamp cord. This time a couple of kitchen forks, that he might use to hold his wires in shape. This time he knew the innards of the system, and the rest would be only retracing what he'd done before. Unless it was that confidence that tripped him up.

The carpet was hard under him, as he sat back against the foot of Greg's bed. A few quick cuts readied a set of wires.

He Opened. Humming sound and engraved memory locked together to plot the inside of the device. Wires edged into shape, one hair at a time, aligning with where they'd need to be... In and out of focus he shifted, conserving his strength as they slid into place.

The case popped open.

He took a slow breath, and studied the web of wires he'd fitted on, for how to reach between them and undo the strap.

"Inspection!"

The word downstairs lanced through him and pinned him in place. *No, no, I can't even snap the thing closed without setting it off... Of course they're here, I had to go and piss Reid off today...*

The voice was higher than Reid's. Only one set of feet below.

Paul could only sit frozen, on the hard carpet, searching for sounds and any trace of an idea. He caught one whisper from Greg: "We stall, give him more time to run—"

"Alright, alright, 'm coming..."

Lorraine walked, *stumbled,* to the front door. What was she doing?

"Come on in," she said. "Can't have a drink with us, can you? Too bad. 'S a good night for one, and friends."

"Sorry, ma'am. I have to finish this check before the shift's done. But, you make it sound good." A softness crept into the cop's voice.

Oh. Lorraine was *making* the thought sound good, one of her distractions.

Distractions. He'd seen her hold people's minds, make them overlook what they saw. If she could hide something as obvious as the locator hanging open and all the wires he had bristling through it.

The wires quivered in place, waiting for one jostle of Paul's leg to set it off. At least he could cover the thing up and make it less conspicuous; he reached for the sweatshirt.

It lay just beyond his fingertips.

"He's up here," Lorraine was saying. "Take your look, do your job and call it a night. You deserve it…"

His leg had to stay flat on the floor, his hips couldn't risk one twitch. Instead he slowly lifted up his shoe and gripped it by a lace, tossed it over the sweatshirt, and fished the shirt toward him.

It rustled over the carpet, a few inches. Into his grasp.

Then he laid it over his legs, hands under it to keep it tented above the anklet and its wires. An awkward, absurd position to sit in, but he could only hope covering the sight of it would be enough. He shut his eyes.

Lorraine opened the door. "Here he is, sound asleep. And here's the room if you want to search it, and then the next room and on… until… you're… finished."

Her own words slowed, not with her playing drunk but with her total focus on her power. Anyone would have noticed.

Anyone but the person under it. "That's… enough," the cop said.

They shuffled out of the room. Paul heard them move downstairs, downward, and down to the front door.

"Thanks. I need a drink."

He was gone.

Paul lifted the sweatshirt off his leg, and pressed his fingers to the rug until the shaking left them.

From below he heard Greg whistle. "Is that how this thing works? We need to talk, Lor."

As long as they're talking. And staying downstairs, not up here with me.

He went to work on the strap, until he could slide it off and make his way into the night.

* * *

The LifeLab building might have been waiting for him, for his first glimpses of its broad blocky shape through the other buildings. The place where he kept going back to pay off Quinn, or untangle Sarah from the story he'd given her about it. It was where Van Howe had grabbed CC.

And one car sat up the block, with what his Opened sight picked out as the crouching silhouette of someone inside it watching the place. Sarah.

His sight lingered on the edges of her face. *She's still putting herself in danger... but where else would she be?* Brandt's people had tried to scare her. Of course she went to watch the source of the threat.

Paul swung around toward the far side of the building, out of her view. The less he saw her the easier this would be.

And if she stayed out here and got caught? He spun around and jogged back toward her, swinging wide around the building to stay out of sight. He had to tell her to go home.

How well does that ever work?

He slowed as he neared the car. She sat up and opened the door.

"You're out here again?" She stared hard at him. "Who's in danger this time?"

"It's not that. Brandt wanted a meeting, here."

"And you came? What's he got?"

"Everything." He leaned down against the car, cold against his hand. "My records of everything I've done, I think. And every chance left that I can stay in this town."

"Oh. Then why are you wasting time out here?"

There were no arguments, not from her. No doubts.

He leaned in.

His balance swayed, his hands scrabbled on the car to steady him, her own face moved so the kiss met the corner of her mouth—

Warm.

Warm, soft, afraid to move an inch—

Hands, *her* fingers, locked behind his head and held him in.

When they did pull apart, the flush and the sweat throbbed on his skin.

He turned away, walked away. His voice couldn't work, and there were no words that wouldn't blunt the moment.

I can't believe I did that.

I can't believe I ever doubted that she'd kiss back.

He walked faster; focusing on each step, step, step was one way to pull him back to what was waiting ahead. Around one sidestreet, then another, until he came in view of the LifeLab back door.

Hanging back behind a corner let him peer across at the lock panel, twenty yards ahead. Keycards were the worst kind: no combination to spot, no tumblers to turn, and this one was too out in the open to let him work on the wires. He glanced at his watch—just fourteen minutes before eight.

Only a few lights and voices moved in the building, and fewer still were around them outside. He knew all the ways around, but it was always harder with less preparation.

And that kiss—*I kissed Sarah...*

No good, no way through in time. Unless the locks were all off. Or he simply knocked on the front door. Brandt asked for this meeting, what did it matter who else here saw Paul outside?

A man was walking toward the door, keycard in hand.

I could just walk up with him, and ask Security to take me to Brandt. Or... He felt a reckless grin tugging at his lips.

Paul angled around behind the man, in his blind spot twenty yards back. The man—young, unhurried—was just nearing the door when Paul broke into a silent run.

Every step smooth. Let the balance flow forward. Measure the distance. Control the breath—no sound...

The door swung open. The young man stepped inside, and Paul slid in half a step behind him.

For one instant all his momentum had to *float,* caught on his feet without a sound and halted just inches short of the figure ahead. The door swung in toward his back.

The man took another step and another, and Paul had the space to edge in before the door thunked closed, not even slowing it for that one second that would make someone look back. They stood at a stairwell, and the man was plodding away down the steps. Paul sidestepped in his blind spot to start on the stairs upward.

The building thrummed with the quiet energy of its evening shift. He stretched his senses around the floors. The lockers that kept the janitors' clothes were only a floor away, a simple way to blend in.

No time. He needed to settle this now. *I don't have Lorraine's influence, no money or badge or anything with me, but I have to face Brandt my own way. See if there's any way left I stay in town.*

If it went bad, he'd escaped from this building before.

He emerged onto Brandt's floor, a level furnished with understated brown carpets and mostly empty now. Tracking each set of footsteps let him avoid the first two people he passed, and move past the third one at thirty feet away, too far for her to take much notice of him. He kept his face off the first camera he passed, but ignored the second— Brandt shouldn't see him ghosting past everything.

Brandt's office was the only lit one in that corner, and he heard a single person inside.

His watch put him more than a minute early. For a moment he thought of waiting to time it to the second, then brushed the idea aside. He pushed the door open.

A large room, mostly open space, with the walls crowded with a mix of medical pictures, news stories, and more kinds of art than Paul could follow. The single desk was bare except for its computer, a half-dozen glass bowls filled with what looked like poker chips, and a featureless closed file.

Behind the desk, Eugene Brandt's flushed face looked up in surprise. Then he pushed his keyboard to the side, and folded his hands over his plump stomach.

"You're here. I hoped you'd understand my message."

"I'm here." Paul swung the door closed, but stayed where he stood.

"You snuck out of your arrest, and you made it here." His smile grew. "And you slipped out before to search for CC, didn't you? Except you arrived too late, because we didn't notice her abduction in time."

"We don't know how that might have gone." *Keep it neutral.*

Brandt sighed. "Paul, I am sorry about Van Howe, and Eckles too. I only asked Van Howe to keep an eye on you. I never guessed he'd involve that unstable Eckles, and I certainly didn't think he'd take it out on CC for suspecting him."

As he finished, Paul Opened to his thoughts. Brandt's still, regretful face only creased itself with deeper regret, no hidden evasions there.

One frisson of tension eased away. Brandt wasn't part of the worst of this, if he could trust his own mind-sight without Lorraine's to be sure. *No, I can't have Lorraine around, Brandt hasn't noticed her "talents" so far. I'm doing this myself.*

"Nobody could have expected those," he said. "I wish we could."

"Or you wish you could prevent it." Brandt motioned to the chair in front of his desk. "And, thank you again for stopping Koenig's attempts to smear LifeLab before. I'm delighted if I have a chance to return the favor."

Paul settled in the chair. "Do what's best for everyone, you mean?" Brandt would have his own terms for getting him off the hook, and

Paul could let him work his way up to revealing them. *I can wait here for hours if I need to.*

"Best for you and for others, both? Is that really how you balance your life?" Brandt leaned his weight forward, eyes searching Paul. "Or is it that you simply try to... do some good, where you can?"

Where was he going? "It's an easy word to say, 'good,' " Paul hedged.

"I hear some of the stories you broke got you a finder's fee. But tell me the truth: if none of them made you a cent, would you have done them anyway?"

I never quite *had to make that choice...* but avoiding it had meant years of scraps and flophouses to live on what he could get. Why deny it? "I think, yes, I'd have done it for free."

"That's what I think!" Brandt leaned back. "After all, this is a medical company here. We're trying to help people—the profit just helps us keep going."

Easy claims to make, too easy. "Profit from Dr. Fish and Operative Solutions? That act like they own everyone around them?"

Brandt's gaze dropped to his desk. "I am sorry about that. You're right: supporting some toys for the intelligence community did make us good money, and contacts. But I never liked the arrogance some of them have—to simply *demand* they scan you and your whole family because they'd had some tech stolen!"

They'd come closer than they knew by including Lorraine. And Brandt hadn't mentioned Sarah with them—better not to remind him.

Brandt shook his head. "Now they think some of their own staff pocketed the tools and sold them. I do hate that."

"Anyone would," Paul nodded.

Brandt's gaze only sharpened. "So yes, I told Fish about some of your achievements. Call it a lapse in judgment—at the time I thought you really might have taken their gear and be using it. It was a relief to know you weren't. You're really no part of that world, are you?"

Paul shook his head. Even that was too much of a hint of *how* different his methods were from any gadgets.

Brandt went on "You aren't in this to cheat anyone, or rob them. You're trying to uncover those cheats. Again and again and again."

My computer records, has he read how many I've done? Paul Opened to Brandt's thoughts, but only the same intense, appreciative look stared back at him...

When he pulled his focus back, Brandt was starting to frown at him; he'd taken too long. *"Alleged* again and again," he said to fill the pause.

"But you made it here, I see that with my own eyes. And they 'allege' that you've blown whistles on insurance, health, and so much else. I suspect you've done much more, and nobody appreciates it."

Did he have the computer or not? Paul kept still.

"Well, I appreciate what you've done. And I want you to help us tighten our security here."

"You always say that," Paul said. "But when we talk about this, I never seem to meet your security people. Is the 'T Johnston' on your letter even real?"

Brandt threw back his head and laughed, for one long second. "You got me. I am trying to manage this myself, yes. You see these?"

He motioned to the side of the desk, where the bowls of chips lay.

"I keep these around to give me a sense of how many favors I've earned from people, and who I owe. This bowl here," and he touched the largest, nearly empty, "was half full in the years I started out. Until I lost most of it."

"Lost?" The prompt was too easy to not take.

"I made several... agreements with other companies, that gave us a chance to get more of our medical benefits into the world. And several of our partners simply robbed us. We were almost ruined."

He wants revenge? Paul grabbed at Brandt's thoughts again... but even now his face was more closed-off with regret than sharp with anger.

"Since then I've tried to be more cautious. I try to fill this bowl up with our resources and with favors we earn from other companies. But I've had to clear too much of it out when we were robbed, and then more trying to bargain our way back."

Favors. Paul looked at the bowls, so many of them with their little plastic markers. *He wants to trade my work for influence with other companies... and how long does that stay about "medicine" before it's simply industrial espionage?* And his own power would be the biggest bargaining chip of all, if anyone guessed.

"Quite a philosophy," he said.

"I'm trying to help everyone. And I'd like to use some of it for your benefit. I can drop the charges against you from LifeLab, and from a few others that are willing to talk." He drew out several chips from the bowl.

Then with his other hand he scooped out more, leaving just one chip left in it. "And, I think I can just about find which strings can get Detective Reid relieved from this case, and help you deal with what he's found."

"You can?"

"I think so. If you're willing to work with me." Brandt let the chips clatter back into the bowl.

"Work." Paul tried to keep his voice even, to keep the rising dread from showing.

And Brandt smiled, wide. "Like I said on my note, you'll like it. One of the groups that robbed me was St. Cedric's hospital."

Paul could feel the trap closing around him, as Brandt reached over to open the file on his desk.

"Yes, St. Central's also the worst of the holdouts against letting you go. And they think you made so many visits there. But on my side... we'd developed a type of stent to implant in certain patients, to pipe blood through where it's blocked."

He pointed to the first page of the file. A report, with a diagram of a short tube on the side.

"We partnered with the hospital for some final tests. And they managed to copy and steal the design. They even ignored the last findings, that it had begun to look less safe..."

He flipped to another page, of columns of statistics. Paul eyed the line at the bottom. What did that summary figure mean, the design was *20%* more likely to need replacing? What would that cause in extra procedures, patient costs, risks? Lives, the longer they used it?

Brandt jabbed a finger onto the report. "Does this sound like some of the people you've tried to stop?"

"It does." *And I know St. Central cheats people. Hell, my whole new life started when Lorraine and her power tried to limit one of their scams...*

Brandt grinned. "You can find evidence that they stole this, and I can shut it down. Or that it's unsafe. And as part of that, we'll get rid of the bulk of the charges against you. Is that a perfect win?"

"It could be." *Too perfect*—he felt shivers moving up him at the thought of what it could lead to, but it was too good. "So you want evidence against them. Before the trial goes through and it's too late to change my charges?"

"Yes. And of course, the sooner you finish, the less time Reid will have to make it worse. Tonight would be ideal."

Of course it would. "You're... expecting a lot. The police can't even know I'm outside."

"You'll find a way. Between us, we can make *all* of this right."

"You do make it tempting. And after that, I walk away?"

Brandt's smile wavered. "Why would you want to? Think of the chances we'll have to find other frauds, and give honest business the edge it needs. My resources and your skills—you've already done it forty-eight times."

The soft-spoken number hit like a fist. Brandt might as well have slapped Paul's reassembled computer onto his desk, with Reid's cell number next to it. He knew exactly where Paul had been, everything except how he'd done it.

"So it's a threat." A growl rose in Paul's voice—why hide it?

"I don't want it to be," Brandt said. "But I don't want you out there alone. You've been arrested, persecuted…"

His ample form leaned forward over the table, just a fraction.

"And I think your father had to shoot a man. Yes, I think you want to work with me."

CHAPTER FOURTEEN

HARD COPY

Sarah drove silently, guiding the hybrid through the night streets toward St. Central. Paul peered through Brandt's file by the dim pool of the passenger's seat light.

—A research project at first, yes, and he knew the ways the hospital managed that. If digging into that would help put it right.

—Doctor Glen Imamura, the man in position to steal LifeLab's design, and he was still using it. The name opened up its own other routes to investigate. If taking Brandt's case was anything but a mistake.

"So you're doing this?" Sarah could have been speaking of anything, and her eyes never left the street ahead.

"I'm going to try."

"But, do you think you can?"

"Probably. I see a few angles here."

And if I can't get it, I simply run. He'd only be in the same position he'd been in after Quinn's death. Except, burning even more bridges from his family and everyone.

"This is a chance, anyway," he tried again. "If I miss, I've got nothing to lose."

And what did that make Sarah? he realized, an instant too late. He had to keep his own eyes forward, on the red tail-lights passing by.

"I mean," and her voice went sharper, "can you let Brandt use you this way? Chasing his enemies?"

"I've peeked at his mind. Every chance I could. When I put the glimpses together, I think under the wheeling and dealing he's still a good man."

"You could be wrong."

"I know that."

"You're giving him more chances to figure out you're something more than a burglar."

"I know that too." Did she have to dig through all this, right now?

"He wants to keep using you, after this. That means even more chances to get noticed. By more people."

"I *know!*" He slammed the file onto his lap, hard enough to bruise. "Asking questions is easy. What would you do with this?"

"What?" She stared at him, like she'd never even *thought* of—

"Say you're someone who... who wanted more than anything to believe you weren't wasting your life and your gift." The words came flooding out. "And to *never* let someone like CC get hurt again because you were just *stuck*, helpless. But—

"But you're *scared,* too scared to even look at it, that doing *anything* except running and hiding will leave you with nothing but years and years in prison hearing how every step could be someone coming to stab you in the back. How every choice you ever had about it is gone the moment Reid shows up with his handcuffs. That or you're sliced up by someone like Dr. Fish to find out where the power comes from.

"So tell me!" When had his voice gone so hoarse? "How could you *not* take the last chance you still had to ever see the people you cared about again?"

"Oh." She let out a single breath, before he went on:

"What *would* you do? You're the one driving anyway. If at least one of us doesn't think this scheme is a real way out, you might as well take me to the bus station right now—"

She turned the car to the curb. One pull on the wheel, with a smoothness that shocked him out of his shouting. The car settled to a stop.

Quietly she said "Did you just ask me to decide for you?"

Paul let out a slow breath, and his head steadied. "Sorry. Forget all that—it's not fair to put it on you. Wouldn't work anyway; I never let someone else make choices for me." He felt a laugh bubbling up inside him. "Even if it's choosing between a life under Brandt's thumb and one marching around under prison guard, I have to pick my own cage."

"You do, don't you?" Sarah's lips curved. "I never liked taking orders either."

"Your mother said that."

The words slipped out on their own, drawn into the stillness hanging between them.

Sarah flinched back. "She would."

"Sorry," he said. "And… again, sorry I let Lorraine try to twist your mind once. I'm sure she regrets it too. Even without knowing how long you've hated anything like that."

He looked down at the file again. If Dr. Imamura was still at St. Central… no, why would he be there at this hour…

"It was a boy."

Sarah spoke at a whisper.

"We went to one of those high-school things together—" She stopped, turned and smiled to Paul. "Oh, he never hurt me or anything. He only tried to, when he didn't like me saying no. That was over and done. Really, what mattered was my family afterward: all they could say was that he'd been so low-class I should never have expected anything better from him.

"That was the last time I gave them a vote in my life." Her voice was back at full strength now.

"I see," Paul breathed, all he could say as he tried to let the new pieces about her fall into place.

She went on "I'll tell you the whole story some other time—"

She stopped.

"If we have one together," she added, suddenly hushed.

Yeah.

He started with a grin, before he answered "I... I'd hate to miss that."

"Then you better get that St. Central evidence and see if it lets you stay."

She started the car humming forward.

But, she kept them along the curb, gliding slowly along. She added "Or if it doesn't... don't think you'll get to tell me if I'm coming with you."

A joke. It had to be, with her smile a little too wide, her voice too brassy to be serious.

She was just keeping that door open, probably. And she was right—if it came down to that, nothing he said would make her stay, or leave.

If it came down to that, I'll sneak away, so this woman never gets to waste her life.

* * *

The St. Central building framed the night at the end of the parking lot. It could be just another part of the hospital complex's western wall, but they called it the research wing. Brandt's clues were most likely there, not in Surgery next to it.

Just looking at it again, stretching his hearing and sight around to search it... *I found my power in there, and lost my memories, and spent the next months sneaking in trying to get them back.* Of course finding or losing his last hope would happen right here.

It also meant, he knew its ways better than any place in the world.

"There are several routes in, and it sounds like nothing's changed." Having someone to say that to was a pang of pleasure. He folded up the papers from Brandt's file and stuffed them in his pocket. "The trick will be in being careful enough that I get to make a long enough search, without being interrupted at all."

"Meaning you don't need me sitting out here?" Sarah said.

"Best guess, no. It could be all night, and I won't be making any sudden escapes."

"Oh, I'll still be here. You've been wrong before."

"True…" That easily, she volunteered for staying out like that?

There was nothing he could add, and the urge to grab at her hand and delay was weighing him down more every second. Paul stepped onto the pavement, with one last glance at her thumbing through her phone.

He circled left toward the maintenance access. Every step stretched his legs and brought long-honed reflexes prickling to life in his glances, his timing. Shadows and lines of cover lay all around him.

Even at night, maintenance and deliveries had to drive in and out. Paul tracked each worker and searched the corridors beyond them, until the moment came and he darted past them and inside.

Using maintenance back corridors at night was about patience. He could hear steps and equipment dispersed around the paths, never still but always easy to predict. He took cover in one room, wrinkling his nose as the faint smell of cleanser swelled and tangled there, then when the way was clear he slipped on to another shelter, on and on.

Passing through the edge of the surgery section took more judgment. Even at night it clamored with doctors and staff busy at their work, but now that attention mostly swirled around a few areas. Paul swung wide around most and avoided the rest of the eyes, but he kept watching in case he came across some nurse logging into a computer.

He had no luck spotting passwords there. But, he did grab a couple of surplus pens; he'd have a use for those soon.

He was at the edge of the research section itself, when one of the voices far behind him called "Dr. Imamura?"

She had to be speaking to the thief himself—here, now? Paul glanced back, knowing he should dodge on to the quiet research wing;

what would a random glimpse of the doctor say about a project stolen years ago? Still, he slid into a closet.

Footsteps pounded past him, a nurse chasing a larger man with a stiff older gait. When they passed Paul's hiding place, he cracked the door and Opened to Imamura's thoughts.

The pudgy man's stride shifted. In Paul's sight, those steps looked fluid, knifing him straight down the corridor like some machine, utterly deaf to the pleadings of the woman behind him. But no machine would have that pitiless, sharklike will driving them...

"Eh?" An orderly looked toward Paul and the sliver of open door at the closet.

Clumsy! But St. Central closets were big and crowded down here; Paul slid back from the door and folded himself behind a cart, hoping he could slip around it and out if the orderly entered. The orderly strolled up, shoved the door open a foot... then pulled back and shut the door.

Paul slumped in the darkness until he heard the corridor clear. He headed out and on to the research wing, with the feel of Imamura's mind still clinging to his senses like a splash of cold.

Those thoughts were different from reading Chief Thiessen's layers of resentment, Van Howe's rage, or Dr. Fish's self-absorption. With a man that heartless, Paul could believe he'd steal Brandt's design, or use it whatever the risks. *The doctor could be risking another patient in an hour, or the next minute... how many other people are like that...*

Paul locked his gaze on the corridor ahead. He'd still had years to observe how there was only so much real evil in the world, so seeing underneath that to thoughts shouldn't change that. The world might be dotted with minds like that, unpleasant but not doing the kind of damage they threatened. Something to ask Lorraine about.

If I get the chance. I need to finish this soon.

The corridors of the research "wing" were thick with true silence, with only a few scattered people awake tending one late study or another. Paul worked his way between them toward the records room. He watched each person he slid past for a chance to catch them logging in to the computer system, but there seemed to be no shortcuts tonight.

The heavy door of the records room still had its simple key lock. Paul took the clips from the pens he'd grabbed, and a few tinier bits of metal, and went to work. He Opened in brief, testing probes, to feel the shape of the tumblers—and leave no scratches outside—and then check around him for anyone passing near. When a pair of doctors came within two turns of him, he slipped easily out of sight, then back to finish learning the door's secrets.

It swung wide, and he stepped into the past.

There they were. Rows of file cabinets, St. Central's compromise between keeping hard-copy backups and throwing nothing away. Dozens of them stretched into the blackness, with only the crack of light under the door to hint at how far they went, except when he chose a patch of darkness to Open to. Two years ago he must have glanced at every page here, in the search for some clue about his senses.

They were sorted only by their customized subject system, with the archivists hoarding their copies of its index in their own rooms. What Paul did have was his memory, if he could sample the files enough to work out their patterns again. He dug out the thick-folded notes in his pocket one more time, Opening to make them out in the darkness. Then he began sliding drawers open.

Drug tests here—one glance at the stuffed-together pages showed that. ER records there. Components for surgery should be further back... what was the pattern here again? He rolled out every eye-level drawer all the way down one row, and walked along them, peeking in at each. The whole row was still nothing but drugs.

He was closing that row when he heard the footsteps outside.

Two drawers left, one—he shoved the last in with a low thump, and heard those feet move a step faster. *Damn!* He dove behind the back end of the row as the door swung open.

The guard smashed the dimness by bringing up the rows of fluorescent light.

But then he only made a brief stroll into the long lines of files. Paul scurried behind their far ends out of sight. *This was supposed to be the whole night with nobody glimpsing me at all.* The guard switched the lights out and walked off, more luck than Paul deserved.

Paul leaned against the cold metal cabinets. That close call meant he should leave the room alone for an hour, or come back tomorrow night... The cold of the cabinet brought back that cold sense of Dr. Imamura, and the thought of what he just might do with every hour he still had patients. Fear.

Instead, Paul stepped toward the next row of cabinets and let the memories well up. Like the days he'd been willing to take forever to work through all these, with no rush—and all that time only made it easier now.

And this time I'm not so afraid of finding something about myself. Sure, there's what Imamura could do or which future I'll land in, and who's with me. But at least I know what I am. He smiled in the darkness.

This row still wasn't surgical components. He must have overshot it... or...

He knew it before he slid the lower drawer open: "Surgical Sources." And the dates from Brandt's notes meant their project started right about—

Nothing. All through the project's timeframe, he found no actual traces or hints about working with LifeLab's stent design. Instead he found one set of summary papers where the hospital claimed they built the stent themselves—even the sharper, newer ink on the paper said "forgery." He stuffed those pages in his pocket.

So they'd cleaned out their records that completely, just crudely. If there was more, it might be in Dr. Imamura's office or computer... if that was worth the risk.

He played his hearing around the corridors toward the offices. They weren't busy enough to be a true challenge... or instead, he could rest and plan for it tomorrow night. And give Reid another day to decide the case was ready and drag him back behind bars.

In the wide net of footsteps, a determined tread—*three* of them—strode toward the records room.

A few turns lay between it and them, but Paul slipped out the door while the corridors were clear. He put one, two, turns between him and the records room, then ducked into a side room. He crouched behind a chair with a lab coat hung over it.

Behind him, the three guards descended on the records room. They only spoke a few words, but one *he's not here* told Paul they weren't just checking out stray sounds. They knew they had an intruder.

He threw on the chair's lab coat and marched outside. Every quick, soft step brought him further away from them, with all the familiar back corridors of the hospital to lose himself in, and now he had the coat to throw off casual glances.

Imamura's office was most likely one floor above. He walked slower, quieter, searching the sounds for the quietest way forward.

"Hold on... okay." The words came from far ahead, where someone paused a moment and then moved on. Paul angled sideways to take another corridor, but as he did he heard another set of steps being paused at the next intersection down. Checkpoints.

He leaned past a stretcher around a corner. Sure enough, a guard stood there—right by the stairs, and where he could watch the next intersection over as well as his own. A doctor passed by, and the guard glanced from his phone to the doctor's face.

They're looking for me.

They still had only so many checkpoints. Paul edged back to the second corridor, the intersection the guard had to watch from a distance. When an orderly walked past the guard's own spot, the moment's distraction was all Paul needed to dart through his own crossing unnoticed.

A quick stride and the lab coat's cover got him to the next stairwell, and he raced up to the office floor, hoping they couldn't spread out much further.

How'd they know about me? Brandt had sent him here—but no, nothing in Brandt's mind had looked ruthless enough for that kind of double-cross. *I should have pulled back half an hour ago, but here I am again, sucked in by the excitement once I get close to anything.*

He paced past rows of lightless offices, counting on his brisk, confident walk to get him past the few people on this floor. The map on the wall was right where it always was. Imamura's office was sixteen doors down.

He held down the urge to walk faster. Sure enough, no guard came near him. None of them knew St. Central the way he did.

Someone moved in one of the offices ahead, maybe Imamura himself; how could he use that...

"You, head up there. You with me." The voice was right at the elevator onto the floor, and it was Reid's.

Paul dove into the next room. He crouched down behind a set of boxes, tracking as Reid and two men started down the corridor.

Reid was *here*—he'd been in St. Central waiting, or he came running at the first hint of an intruder? *Am I really that predictable?* Reid's group marched toward him, one of them stopping to keep watch at an intersection.

Reid. If the detective just *saw* him out of the house Paul would be back in prison, or they'd seize his family's bail for running, or both. Paul crouched lower and let his long-honed memories of the floor's five rows show him the way out. His position was beside the first row, with Reid marching along that.

And Reid and the guard with him tromped right past his door.

Paul waited, breath steady, tracking every step as the two moved toward the other end of the wing. When he heard them shift from the 10-row over to the parallel 20-row, he stepped out and moved up along the path Reid had come from.

The other guard had been posted far up on that same path. Paul stepped casually around the next turn, sheltered in the crossway out of sight between the first row and Reid on the second.

Reid whirled around. He started back up his row, and the guard with him split off to head back along the first, boxing Paul in within the crossway. Reid *knew* where he was.

He spotted me... because he tracked my steps with his power.

Paul's fists clenched. All this time of Reid cursing him and his senses, and *now* the detective used it again?

Reid closed in the row to Paul's right, the guard moving in on his left. Trapped.

The guard's radio squawked.

"Sir!" the guard shouted. "They spotted the thief, on the top floor!"

"Wha..." Reid stopped, took a step toward the guard.

One chance.

Paul charged across the row, a single burst of all the speed his legs could make and fighting not to think what would happen if one frantic step was anything less than perfect silence, or if Reid simply didn't look away—

An instant later he crossed the row. He swept on past another couple of offices, then slowed, still silent, and ducked around into the third row, out of sight of the crossway. He pulled up there, pulse thundering in his head... and locked his lungs still as they screamed for air. *Can't breathe, can't make one sound that Opened hearing could catch...*

"The thief's up there!" the guard called again. "He attacked a woman, we gotta cut him off—"

"No!" Reid snapped. "I've got him, he's here!"

What thief? The thoughts fought with the pressure on his empty chest to let in just a hiss of air. How could someone be up on the top floor, how could it be right now?

Reid advanced up his row. His feet were loud, quick, desperate.

"Got you—" Reid lunged around the corner, right at the crossway where Paul had been. He froze, and Paul caught a shocked choking sound.

Don't breathe! Somehow Paul held his lungs still even with that tantalizing gasp of air in his Opened hearing. But even Reid couldn't be listening for him every moment...

He held on as Reid yanked open an office door. Then those feet turned, headed around. Down the crossway, toward Paul's row.

He guessed! Have to run...

Reid's steps shifted, loud mixing with soft... *or that's my head going gray...* but he did hesitate. One step forward, one back.

The guard's radio spoke again. "Get up there! There's a guy at the desk yelling about thieves. Shut this down!"

"Detective?" the guard said. "I gotta go!"

"I... show me!"

Reid screamed it like giving up his last hope, and he whirled away from where his power had pointed him and charged for the stairs with the guard. The other guard, further out, called "But if he's here—" but Paul lost that as he finally let his own breath whoosh out.

His head cleared, enough to listen again. Reid and the guard with him were still racing up the steps and away.

Two rows from Paul, the last guard began marching through the turns, but he was no threat on his own. Only one other set of feet moved on this whole part of the floor.

That clear, safe space was all that mattered now. Paul forced the questions about the "thief" down and pictured the floor, the two people on it, the stairs at the far end away from where Reid had gone.

Dodging the guard was simple; Paul circled in behind him to close on the stairs, then ducked into an office before the other man came near.

When the door was closed and he ducked safely down below its glass window, the questions in his head broke loose. *How is someone else here right when I am? The only ones who knew about me were Brandt and Sarah—*

Stop that. He locked his focus on the corridors around. The guard was far away, and the other man strolled closer, but as soon as he'd passed by the way to the stairs would be clear.

The approaching man… something about his stride, familiar…

He walked past Paul's hiding place and entered the office three doors down. Paul stole one look out: Dr. Imamura himself.

Here. Right now. Was he tied to the "thief upstairs," or just his own late-night work?

Paul took the first step toward Imamura's door before he realized it. Then he padded to it and peeped through its tiny window, and Opened his sight.

Desk, man, walls, gleaming pictures, the shine of the monitor… but the perfect reflection was the one off of Imamura's own glasses. The faint image in them gave a clear view of his password as he logged in.

And it was all too late.

The insight crashed down around Paul, and he stumbled pulled back to the office he'd hidden in to get out of sight. It *was* all too late, nothing about Imamura and Brandt's mission and the "thief" could change how Reid only had to go to the house and prove he was missing to lock him up.

He crouched down into the office, trying to steady his knees and check the routes out and downward again. Reid hadn't *seen* him, maybe he could make it home in time…

"Are you catching this guy or not? How many ways out can a top floor have?"

The voice leaped at him from the sounds below. *Greg.*

Greg, here... demanding they catch someone whole floors away from Paul...

There never was a "thief." Greg must have started that outcry, probably *Lorraine* faked seeing someone and then her power made the distraction huge...

Sarah must have told them. And they swooped in—

How dare they... but it's working... they were safe... this is my job*... when did they learn to...*

Imamura's door opened. The doctor stepped out, walked away.

It's my *job!* The office was only a few doors away, and he slipped inside in moments.

The guard was still at the far end of the wing. Paul logged in with Imamura's password and glanced at the programs there. *That* one would be their archive, *this* would be the data spreadsheets, all familiar... He ran a simple search for "stent," and logged on to one of the online data sites he kept ready.

One drag of the mouse started dozens of "stent" file copying out to that storage.

He left out the largest files, so the progress bar flowed smoothly across toward completion. Thirty percent, fifty...

Sound blasted through the hospital. The fire alarm.

They're going all out with the distractions. Paul felt a crazy laugh trying to rise in him, and kept his eyes on the transfer. The moment it finished he cleared the browser history, closed, and logged out.

No more stalling. Opening let him spot the guard's footsteps even through the ear-aching sound.

Paul made for the stairs.

The way was wide open. Better yet, people streamed down the steps—grumbling, tired, looking everywhere except at him. Paul followed the beginnings of the crowd down to the ground floor.

That floor was a slowly-filling pool of confusion. Deep in the thick of the crowd, he spotted Reid pushing toward the front door, hands over his ears and staring wildly around. Like his powers couldn't focus in the chaos.

Paul turned and headed the other way from Reid. All he needed was to move within the crowd, until he reached the next door. He even passed a laundry cart, and dropped the lab coat into it. He didn't steal.

He stepped outside.

Soft night pressed around him, even with the bright hospital lights trying to push it back. More people churned around him every second, too many for security to keep in line, and the parking lot and its maze of shadows were only a few steps away. The brisk air on his face felt like freedom.

One car in the rows stood out: Sarah's hybrid, and it looked empty. He trotted a few steps to look at that row from the other side—good, that angle confirmed she wasn't crouching in the car. Giving him a ride would make her an accomplice if Reid spotted it.

Another car rumbled to life behind him. That silver BMW had his father at the wheel, and it glided right toward him.

No, no, not right here... Paul stepped back through the row of cars to block it off from him. That hint should be enough for anyone: *don't come near me.*

The car swung around through a gap in the row and moved up behind him. His father waved him inside.

Too late. Gritting his teeth, Paul grabbed the door and climbed in.

"I've got him. I think this is what's called Mission Accomplished," Ian Schuman said on his headset. The clipped, conspiratorial tone clashed with his smooth voice.

They pulled out of the lot, at an easy, inconspicuous pace. Paul snapped his belt and Opened to search the milling figures behind them.

One man dashed from the building and darted in among the cars. Reid—*of* course *it couldn't be simple.*

"That's Reid! Get down the block fast, and I'll bail out. He's not after you."

His father pushed them forward in a roar. Shapes raced past them in the dimness, one block, then a second. No sign of slowing down.

Far behind them, a black car came closing in fast, with Reid glaring through the windshield. A glint of blue beyond that was Sarah's car, and he saw Greg and Lorraine riding with her...

"Reid's catching up! The next right, try that!"

They raced through the night. Paul twisted his neck, back and forth between watching for the black on black of Reid's car on their tail and searching the dark street ahead. He called out directions, but his father only raced on toward some goal of his own.

Blocks later, Reid wobbled and fell back. "He's slowing down! Turn the lights off, the next right is clear!"

The headlights winked out. The car turned, skidded a moment, and slid into the blackness of the side street.

Paul kept his sight Open, struggling to lead the night-blind man through the dark spaces between the streetlights. "Okay, it's all as clear as it looks, just get through the crossing in time... okay, okay, ease back—*left*, just a bit, that's fine—"

He stole a moment to search behind them. No sign of Reid; maybe driving with a sense Open was too much for his rusty control.

They began to slow, to a steady pace and then an easy prowl. Paul looked back again. Blocks back, Sarah's car was still with them.

He let out a breath. "I think you can turn the lights—"

A black car burst out of the intersection.

"Go! Go, the next right looks clear—"

They lunged forward, Reid sliding in behind them. The next turn raced up and they swung wide ready to duck into it.

Paul saw the moment Reid's car wobbled on its course. An instant later it barreled forward, still veering drunkenly as it lunged through the gap to them—

The impact spun his senses, spun his head, spun the car spinning sideways. *Still moving, we're moving, he only clipped us,* a wild thought came, as an airbag flared out in his face.

Then he heard Reid crash.

CHAPTER FIFTEEN

TRAPPED

Head ringing, motions slow and dreamlike, Paul stared around. He reached past the airbag to the driver's side... his father brushed his hand off and struggled with the belt.

Out in the night, orange flames gathered.

He wrenched the door open. *Can't walk right, where's my balance...* he staggered toward where Reid's car lay crumpled against the wall.

Power worked fine, he realized as he pushed his vision through the night. Reid lay motionless in the seat, and the driver's door beyond him looked twisted and jammed where it had hit the wall.

Flames were licking around the car's rear. He hauled the passenger-side door open with a squeal of metal, and dragged Reid out across the snow.

"Mmmf... what was..." Reid's voice was strong.

"You alright? I think you crashed from trying to drive while Open—"

"Damn you!"

The shriek came before Reid's body twisted, before he rolled to a crouch and leaped at him. Paul was already jumping aside.

From the corner of his eye he saw his father stumbling toward them. "Hold on..."

Reid's gun was in his hand.

"Out of my way!" the cop yelled, and he spun toward Paul.

Paul bolted. He dove past the wreck of the car—*maybe the firelight behind me will screen me*—and scrambled over the snow. Behind him he heard Reid staggering, steadying and gathering speed with every step.

He dashed down what looked like a narrow alley: high walls, dim shadows and dustings of snow. Something hit his foot and sent him stumbling, sending trash rattling out under his step before he charged on. His father had to be safe, the way Reid was closing in.

Bang! The shrill sound, the crack on the brick beside him—shock flooded through him. *Reid never shot at me, never!* He twisted out the end of the alley.

Somewhere behind him came a shout of "Hey! What was—"

"Stay back! I'm a cop, he's dangerous!" Reid made the chase sound normal, but the raggedness in his voice was as vicious as the gunshot.

Paul kept running, twisting, dodging through the back streets, with one small part of his mind insisting that no trick would throw off someone else with Opened senses.

A heap of old newspaper flew up under his feet, with a whiff of whatever garbage had been in it.

An old man watched him run past, another observer that Reid only waved aside.

He dodged around a corner. Ran along a chain-link fence, too high and noisy to think of climbing. Reid fell back again and again, but nothing seemed to shake him off.

Then a voice called out, from a corner he'd rushed past, as Reid closed in on it: "Don't you get it? He's trying to *help* people!"

Sarah. And Reid's steps twisted, swung toward her.

No! Paul slammed to a stop and looked back at him. "She's only telling the truth," he said. "Tonight I was tracking down a faulty medical device, something that has to be stopped." Saying that felt like a small victory. At least if Reid locked him away, they just might follow up—

"It always is with you." Even in the darkness, the lines of Reid's scowl were clear. "It's always *them* that needs stopping, right?" He took a slow step toward Paul, gun pointed at the ground between them.

"I told you, the thing's unsafe! You know when I do this, there *is* a reason."

"And how long will that last? How long before you're peeking into everything there is, and twisting our heads?"

Behind Reid, another voice gasped "And that's why you want him? A witch deserves a witch hunt, is that it?"

Panting, gasping, but still clear as he ran up—*Greg.* With his father closing in behind him, leaning on Lorraine.

Paul yelled "Stay back. All of you!"

Greg only moved in, and his voice steadied as he got his breath. "You've chased Paul for how long? How many real criminals have gotten away while you rooted through everything he *might* have done? How long before your lieutenant takes the case away from you—"

"They don't know!" Reid said. "That man is a walking violation of every boundary we live by. And he's *infected* me. It takes everything I have to stop seeing it all, because he did this to me…"

Reid froze. His gun swung up, at Greg.

"He got you too? You're one of them now?"

Greg looked right back at him, like the gun didn't exist. "No infection here. I just know my brother."

Reid's voice rose. "That's what you *would* say."

"Don't do it!" Lorraine shrieked.

It was the kind of urgent, desperate scream she'd fling at someone who'd done more than put a finger on the trigger—*what did she see in his mind?*

She closed in, circling to the side and drawing Reid away from Greg. "You know shooting anyone won't stop the pain. Locking them up won't either."

"Get out of my head!" Reid yelled.

Paul edged around, toward Reid's back. Greg was on Reid's far side, but maybe he could move around to him...

Lorraine said softly "I wouldn't dare get in your head. Detective, don't you think you'd feel it if any of your pain or fear started to fade away? I'm not doing a thing."

"Liar!" Reid leveled the gun straight at her face.

Greg said "Listen to her, will you? She's been through all this, she understands."

"I'm not in your thoughts now," Lorraine said. "That's what you keep missing. *You've* got the power, and that means these are part of your head now."

Reid only snarled. His knuckles whitened on the gun.

Paul yelled "Stop!"

Reid spun around, toward him, toward Greg.

"None of this is about them!" Paul said. "You know, you *know,* they aren't part of what I've done. And Lorraine... when we found out what Chief Thiessen was, you worked with Lorraine, with me, to stop her. But I'm the only one who's been breaking laws—"

Greg muttered "Shhh. Let Lorraine do this, she's better than any of us at—"

Paul snapped "Quiet!" and he glared at Lorraine too, before focusing on Reid again. "Sneaking around breaking secrets is *my* life. All of them are just sticking their noses in, like always."

"That is enough, Paul." His father's voice had a cold edge. "We're trying to help you—"

"By throwing yourselves into all of this? The moment I got the power, I left you, so you wouldn't get dragged in. Or so I could have *one thing* you weren't taking over!"

The words tore out of him, and the flinch in the others' faces showed him there was truth in them.

A part of him thought, *Lorraine can still get to Reid better than we can.* But he could never slow down now: "Reid, this is about me! I'm the one sneaking over all those lines you love."

"I know what you are." Reid's eyes bored into him. "Running through hospitals, interfering with police… how long before you have that curse reading every thought around you?"

Quick and harsh, Paul flung back "And what have you been doing tonight? You say the power's nothing but trouble, but you can't resist using it yourself. That's how you kept up with me." He finally felt the idea taking shape.

Reid took a step toward him. "You think you're that good? Of course I caught you, I'm a cop."

Does he really believe that's all? This just might work. "You think *you're* that good? How'd you find me in the dark? Why couldn't you keep your eyes on the road when you drove? You keep talking about how you hate our power. But you already know you can't touch me without it. Just try."

He spun on his feet and bolted up the pavement. A roar and a sound of footsteps told him Reid had only lost a moment in starting after him.

Paul wrenched every muscle in his body into flinging him down the street. Lungs gasped, joints burned, but one low building and then another flew by him. Reid's steps began to fall back.

A twist around the next corner gave him a bit of cover. He had to keep drawing Reid away from his family. *And if I hold my lead enough to put a building between him and me, and he tries not to sense me moving, I can slip away on whichever side he doesn't take.* And keep running.

Never stop, maybe.

Far behind them someone else shouted, and a voice that had to be Lorraine's answered it, keeping whoever it was away.

But Reid... He could feel the sound, the *idea,* of Reid keeping pace down the street. The detective ran more slowly—and something in that steady pace promised that Paul's own wild speed would only burn itself out first. Was Reid's power tracking him at all, or was this simply some hunter's understanding of how his prey had to move?

Two blocks later he twisted around a turn and felt his wind giving out. Reid would be only out of view for moments, only one alley let him stay hidden—

Sarah was walking up it—

No time. He scrambled into it and wheezed "C'mon, then we split up," to her. She raced after him, already catching up too easily.

They reached the alley's far end.

Instead of splitting off, she caught his hand and wrenched him to the right. He scrabbled for balance, stared at her.

Reid burst around the corner. She stepped in his path.

"You always have to—"

Reid cut her words off, yanked her around and slammed her against the wall.

She only gasped "I've seen how you hate him. I saw you beating him in Cedar Springs, remember?"

"Let her go!" Paul said. "You know I'm the one who—"

Sarah hissed "But I'm still defending the enemy, aren't I?" Fighting for breath against the bricks only made her fiercer. "He got away once because I hit you, even if those charges got dropped. And you *never* charged Paul for the one time he punched you. Because you remember what this power can do to you if you let it."

"Quiet!" Reid said.

"I've seen how you get. You hit him again and I'll see you charged for all of it. And sure, I'll confess too. Power or not, we can all pay for losing control. We'll see how your charges against Paul hold up then. But I want you to see, what's dangerous isn't just this power—"

"Sarah, stop it!" Paul stared at her face, scowling against the wall. "You just got your charges dropped—"

"Just being fair. I never asked you to come take the blame for me, or anyone to get me out—"

"I never asked *you* to do *this!*"

And Reid's gaze looked as brutal as his grip on Sarah. Of course drawing Reid away wouldn't stop the detective from coming back for her, and his family, now that they'd helped him escape. There had to be a way to make him leave them alone...

He said "You don't hate her, it's the power that you hate. And you know you've been using it, because you *have* to."

"You're wrong." Reid's hands crushed her harder against the wall.

"Hurting her won't change that! And, you'll need your power to keep chasing me. You think prison's going to hold me?"

"For five years, ten? It'll do," Reid growled.

"Try *months,* if you're lucky." Paul forced out a laugh, tried to sound like he could endure that time. "Just months, before I know every secret in the prison. Of course I'll get out. And that's if your case even sticks. How many months do you think they'll give me?"

"Years. And you won't have your family running interference for you. Tonight gave me enough to put them away too."

"I know..."

Paul squared his shoulders, forced his voice to keep the words steady:

"But you want to get the guy with the power, not his supporters. You let them all go, and I'll confess. And I'll stay in there."

"Too late. We've got everything we need on you."

"And if I just run down the street, and keep running? You've got *nothing."* He kept his eyes on Reid, anything to keep from facing Sarah and what she'd do to his resolve. "What you want is a full confession.

"Of all forty-eight cases," he added.

Reid's grip on Sarah went limp. His face flickered in shock.

Then the detective's face hardened again. "More lies. If you did all that, all it proves is how fast you'll escape."

Paul stared harder at those burning, demanding eyes. "I won't escape. You know I won't." *Please, you have to know it.*

"Lies. You'd say anything to get them out of this."

"Yes! And I'd *do* anything, as long as it *keeps* them out. You know I would. You *know.*"

The detective's eyes narrowed to slits, tiny gleams in the dimness...

Only a faint ripple through his body showed it, when Reid Opened. When he had to see that Paul meant every word.

Then:

"No... you made me..."

Another, fiercer spasm went through Reid.

"You can't... you're *done—*"

His gun was in his hand.

Paul stumbled back. Reid's eyes were locked on him, blind to the world.

Sarah kicked off the wall and slammed Reid away. The shot screamed off into the night.

Paul felt Reid's gaze still on him, as he flung the last of his strength into reaching the corner, whole steps away. In the moment he rounded it he got one glimpse behind him of Sarah kicking the gun from Reid's hand, the detective spinning to look for it.

His breath stabbed exhaustion into his side. In some far-off place on the streets, shouts began rising. Sarah raced around the corner to join him, and for an instant he saw her eyes glance around them and wondered if she'd *led* him there.

Another shot tore through the streets, wild. Then Reid loomed up behind them.

I lost a moment, when I could have run further or readied to jump him—

"Up there! Take 'em!"

The shout from down the street they'd left made Paul steal one dark-piercing glance toward it, he saw the two men—*not* in cops' uniforms—raising rifles, and he threw Sarah and himself to the ground.

Shots split the night, several deeper, louder shots from rapid-fire rifles.

Paul hugged the pavement, stealing a glance up. Reid looked to have taken cover as well. The gunmen held their place up the street... guarding it. And now he recognized the building behind them: Operative Solutions, the place Sarah had found.

He crawled up the sidestreet, and Sarah moved with him. Snow and pavement scraped under them until they were out of the line of fire.

"You *led* us here?" he asked her.

"I tried. Didn't think anyone would start shooting."

The two guards' voices put them still standing at their building, nervous but ready for more trouble. Sirens howled from somewhere blocks away.

Reid moved up to crouch behind the corner. He peeped around it at the shooters, then back at Paul and Sarah. The rage had left him, and he sagged like a deflating balloon.

"Was that some kind of trap?" His voice was drained but uninjured.

"No," Paul said.

Sarah said "Not a trap. That's where Dr. Fish works. I wanted you to remember what some of the 'normal' people you're protecting can do."

Reid laughed weakly. "Opening fire like that? Those are maniacs, they think they're outside the law. And they'll pay for it when those cruisers get here."

"Or they *make* the law sometimes," Sarah said. "Enough government contracts and someone can think they've bought the country. Detective, do you think this power's the only thing dangerous? Before you heard about it, you had a whole world of crimes and abuses to keep in line. Now you've got something better to fight it with."

Reid looked right past her, to Paul. "Your power *is* the crime."

The sirens were drawing closer.

Paul said "Whatever our power is… it's an answer, for when people don't know who their enemy is. You can still keep me off the street if you let the others go. But after that you'll have to find a use for your own power."

"No. You're wrong. I'll stop it, all of it." Reid's voice was weaker now. His eyes were closed.

"Not all of it. But you can start by locking me up and letting my family go."

Paul held out his hand, hoping—fearing—Reid would open his eyes and take the deal.

"Or," he added, "you can stay here and tell Fish's men what you can do. Start the whole country hunting for anyone like me. But you saw what they just did, you know that's just giving them one more weapon."

"No…"

The sirens swelled, the police car engines ground to a stop up the block at Operative Solutions. Megaphone shouts of *Put down those weapons* and *Now!* blared through the street.

"Come on!" Paul waved to Reid and turned to go.

"All this *seeing*… it has to end…"

The lifeless, hollow sound in that voice stopped Paul in his tracks. He glanced back, saw Reid's hand slowly rising, bringing up his gun.

Toward his own head.

More metallic voices shouted up the street. Paul waved for Sarah to run and crept to Reid's side.

Reid's voice was so weak. "I'll never stop you. They'll hear about all my running and crashing around tonight… I bet I'm not even a cop now."

"Okay…"

Far around the corner, the police voices squawked *Okay, what happened?*

Paul said "You hear that? They're just letting those trigger-happy guards go."

Reid's eyes clenched shut. His fingers whitened on the gun. "You can't stop me."

Paul took a deep breath. "Then who's going to stop Brandt?"

"What?" Those eyes opened a crack.

"Eugene Brandt, owner of LifeLab." Paul flung the sentence out like a frantic reach of his hand, as if the intensity in his words could call someone back across some vast distance. *"He* sent me into St. Central to get proof about how they'd cheated him. But he's also making my victims drop charges against me, and he talked about taking your badge. He tipped Fish off about us too."

"You... told me that."

Up the block, the police had to be reporting the source of the shooting. Soon they'd be spreading out and looking for whoever the guards had aimed at.

"Sure, I told you when I called you. I said Brandt got Van Howe involved too, and that led to CC's death. And he *did* steal my computer from you. But the worst thing is, Brandt was a good man."

"He's what?" Reid's face twisted in confusion.

"He cares about people—or he did, until he got involved with me. The more he sees what I can do, the more he *wants.* He calls it getting back what was stolen, but it always lets him come out ahead. It's just like you said how the power twists us up, and this is just from knowing about it. No, he only knows a fraction of what I can do, and he'll only get more greedy."

He stabbed a finger at Reid's chest.

"Just like you keep saying. So who's going to stop Brandt if you die? Or I do? Or we get locked up?"

He took one more breath, and added:

"Who's going to watch me?"

Reid looked away. His eyes were unfocused, staring at something that had to be more personal than any shape in the night.

The voice was almost too low to hear. "I... someone has to... even if it means seeing all the..."

With one move Reid lowered the gun and dashed after Sarah, toward safety.

Paul ran after them. Reid's steps didn't have his own practiced smoothness, but they had a firmness in the night. Like someone who knew he could pause and see through any darkness he needed.

They'd put three blocks of safety between them and the police search, when Paul heard Reid slow and sigh "Why'd it happen to me?"

"The power? When you never asked for it?"

I said that to Chief Thiessen once. But it's not quite right. Paul gave the only answer he believed:

"You needed to know what you were seeing, Detective. You needed to, so you chose to Open your eyes."

Reid didn't say a word.

CHAPTER SIXTEEN

THE SENTENCE

One night later, Paul crept into the LifeLab building.

A bit of planning during the day made it easy, building on how well he already knew the place. He took his time now, gathering glimpses from each section for when he'd need them soon. A name here, a blind spot or a pattern there, some insight about each one.

Brandt was in his office, of course.

"Glad you made it." The pudgy man leaned back in his chair. "You made all that noise at St. Central, and they still didn't take you into custody."

Paul settled in the opposite chair. "How could they? I was at home, of course."

Brandt's grin widened, but even without Opening Paul saw his eyes narrow with calculation. "The hospital claims nothing was taken."

"It's a big archive. They won't miss these, and I'll be putting them back soon." He handed over the pages he'd grabbed. "These are the records they dummied up on making your stent design."

Brandt slid the pages around his desk, with a soft rustling sound. "Not much here."

"And then there are these." He passed Brandt a flash drive.

Out of all the files he'd copied from Imamura's access, the drive only held the few that would cast some doubt on the doctor. But

Brandt plugged it in and began clicking faster and faster, and his eyes grew wider with each click.

"I knew you could do it!" Brandt pushed the keyboard away and reached over to the bowls of chips. He picked up two from one bowl, and dropped them into the largest container. "We'll follow up soon, and make sure they pay what they owe. As for you, now I'm certain we can get the charges dropped from, I think, at least a third of the companies you've touched."

A third of the ones the world suspected, anyway. Paul kept his answer casual: "In exchange for a few 'security tips' to each of them, isn't it? I appreciate that."

Brandt scooped up a larger handful of chips from the main bowl. "I think I can pull enough strings to discredit Detective Reid too. But, he seems to be doing that himself, after crashing into your family's car last night."

He let the chips cascade back into the bowl. Paul kept his relief off his face, glad he wouldn't have to defend his "enemy."

Brandt went on "But here's something else you might have heard—or more than heard? Last night some of the Operative Solutions guards started shooting into the night. We may need something to get us a tighter rein on that place. After we follow up on what the hospital owes."

He gathered a mass of chips from one bowl.

"I wonder, if we play this right I could take partial ownership of St. Cedric's—"

"No."

Brandt looked up, and his chair squeaked. "We won't know until we try—"

"We're not trying." Paul locked his eyes on Brandt's, and kept his voice firm. "I got you evidence that they robbed you. That's meant to put things right, not help you take them over."

Brandt gave him a long look. Paul Opened, and saw the taut, hungry look on Brandt's inner face waver and soften.

"You may be right. Still, once you see some of the other ways St. Central has done business, I think you'll see the need for some changes."

I saw them stack their billing years ago, and I've seen Imamura's thoughts, and... But those were his secrets.

Paul smiled. "I look forward to it. But I think we have to look into Operative Solutions first."

"St. Central first. It has to be." Brandt's fingers full of chips tapped the edge of the bowl he'd lifted them from. "We are working together on this, after all."

"We are. I'm getting you back what's your right, and you're keeping me out of jail. You're keeping quiet about the casefiles on my computer, and I'm keeping quiet about who smuggled it away from the police for you."

Or we will know who. I know Reid and Lorraine can dig that out.

Brandt looked at him a moment. Then he carefully laid the chips down on the center of the table, still in play. "That's... for the best. And of course we keep your family safe. No questions about just how that Quinn person was shot."

There it was. *Just a sentence short of calling Dad a murderer.*

"Exactly. Or how a former LifeLab guard like Van Howe took such an interest in me, when the man was unstable enough to end up killing CC.

"But mostly," Paul pressed on, "you want me to help with your own security, don't you? For instance, right now do you think you're more worried about your front gate or your lab section, or somewhere else?"

Brandt shifted in his chair, uneasy now. "The lab. Or the storerooms, I think."

"Naturally—"

Paul Opened his hearing, one quick stab downward, enough to confirm what he'd seen in the store section.

"—since Mr. Ashlin is probably on the phone more than he's standing guard. And the lab has those old Nexeis cameras that need replacing."

This time Brandt's jaw dropped. Paul Opened to his thoughts and saw the same blend of shock and worry, but not the true tightening-up of fear or rage.

After all, the lab *did* have newer cameras. Brandt had to think some of Paul's tricks were bluffs...

But he was starting to understand who could make the threats.

Brandt swallowed. "I see it's going to be a pleasure working with you."

* * *

The courthouse only had a few spaces that could pass as conference rooms. But with Paul's two lawyers, plus his father and brother *and* Lorraine, all focusing their different forms of influence onto Reid and ADA Oliver, Paul suspected they could have gotten half the floor. They'd see the judge in an hour.

They all squeezed around the table, Reid at the back corner with Oliver leaning forward beside him as if he could hide him from his opponents' eyes. Some of the bustling sounds outside seeped into the room, so even Oliver's most diplomatic words needed him to raise his voice:

"I believe you understand that Reid's actions don't reflect the entire police department. Disciplinary processes have begun, that will weigh his conduct against his past service to the force."

"And I apologize, again." Reid looked at Paul's father, at Greg, at Lorraine, and his gaze slid past Paul himself. "I saw you driving away, and I assumed the worst."

Paul could all but feel the two lawyers tensing to strike back, but Lorraine cut them off. "It's hard to blame a detective for dedication. I hope you're getting some help with... whatever it is. But I don't think we'll be suing anyone."

Oliver smiled, a smile that had to mask torrents of relief. Reid looked calm enough too—he ought to be, knowing Lorraine would be bringing her talents to help him with that "discipline" process anywhere he let her.

And Greg reached up to grip Lorraine's hand.

The two lawyers from CC's firm looked somewhat alike, and they dressed as if they were brother and sister. The "brother" added, "Not that anyone's putting that in writing yet. There's still the question of your charges against our client."

"And still all the evidence that stands on its own." Oliver's fingers began drumming on the table, a muted sound not quite lost under his voice. "Mr. Schuman's presence at St. Cedric's over the past years is still confirmed by witnesses. We have the marks of lockpicks, that we will tie to him…"

Paul Opened to Oliver's thoughts. The man's inner gaze darted around the room, evading the others' eyes and pushing reluctantly back to face them. Definitely nervous.

Paul's father laughed. "Those would be the locks picked at the same hospital that just turned itself upside down hunting intruders that weren't there?"

"But *you* were there. Glass houses, Mr. Schuman."

"We told you," Greg said. "We got word that Paul's tormentor was chasing shadows in the middle of the night. We were… concerned."

The male lawyer added "Paul Schuman's relatives were observed the whole time they were on the premises. They were simply acting out of concern, until they left and 'Detective' Reid was the one who pursued them."

"I believe we were putting that behind us," Oliver said. "Another charge is Criminal Impersonation—"

"Your list used to be longer," the female lawyer said. "What is it, the more tax dollars you spend the less you have to show?"

This time Oliver simply pushed on, calm as if the smaller case had always been what he'd had in mind. "Several people have asked that

the charges be dropped. Now we have four charges of Criminal Trespassing, plus Criminal Impersonation, for a total of five years."

"Or…" Lorraine said, and gave the lawyers a slow look. The two
took the signal without even a glance at each other, only a questioning
look at Paul himself.

*If Lorraine has just weighed Oliver's confidence, there's no better
time for this.* Paul nodded.

"Second Degree Trespassing," the woman lawyer said. "All four
counts, and we'd agree to consecutive sentences if you agreed to home
confinement under less restrictive terms."

She spread her hands and slowly brought them together.

"That's twenty-four months, where Mr. Schuman has mobility but
his movements are strictly tracked, complete with regular checking in.
In addition to fines. If this case is about an alleged pattern of minor
lawbreaking, that arrangement is the one that protects society on all
counts without sinking more money into punishing nonviolent charges. And it's the best you can get."

Oliver's mouth twitched in a smile. "Still a bit on the soft side. The
fines would be full value of course."

Paul's father said "Whatever it takes. We can—"

"It's okay," Paul added. "I seem to have a job offer from LifeLab."

From the end of the table, Reid said "Acceptable. All of it."

Oliver waved him silent. "That's hardly your decision, Detective."

But Reid rose from his chair, leaning over the table and looking
right at Paul. "Just remember, I'm still a cop, so far. Someone's
watching you if you get out of line."

His gaze searched Paul's face. He could be probing his thoughts or
not, but either way the detective's fire was still there.

"Same goes for you," Paul said.

Reid's massive eyebrows twitched.

Then Reid smiled, and sank back into his chair.

*Neither of us will be out there without knowing there's someone
who can rein us in. Not bad.*

Oliver glanced between the two, clearly wondering how much was going over his head.

Then he said "I'll talk to the judge. We seem to have a deal."

* * *

The courtroom lay far behind them. The room for setting the locators was just behind them, and the cold plastic shape on his ankle had a whole new set of rules in place, with new instructions tucked under Paul's arm. It could be a while before he even needed to slip it off.

Reid and the police escort walked away, deeper into the building. The lawyers walked away.

At the edge of the busy corridor, the four Schumans stood alone.

His father gave him a grin, wider than he'd seen in some time. "You did it. You *did* it."

"I'm starting to." Paul grinned back.

Greg laughed. "Yeah. So, can we get back to work now? We've got way too much to catch up on, thanks to certain people." He linked his arm through Lorraine's.

Paul tried to match that tone. "Whenever you want. That's how you picked when to make time for me anyway—it's not like I ever asked you for..."

The laugh faded in his throat. His face, the easy, reassuring expressions he'd spent years working with, began to quiver.

"I think I owe you... everything..."

Lorraine said "I think *I* owe you something. You might even need it now."

She handed over a shape of plastic and silver. A simple phone.

She added "The first time I found you again and asked for *your* help, you said you didn't have one."

The shape felt odd in his grip, but it gave him something to look at besides those faces...

"What did I miss?" Sarah stepped out of the crowd.

Paul saw it in an instant: how small the smile on her face was, the tugging at the corner of her mouth that wanted to let it grow...

His father said "We can tell you while we're driving back. There's just about room to fit us all in."

Paul held up a hand. "You know, I think I'd like to walk."

He held that hand out to Sarah. She took it, and the two started through the corridors alone. That was all it took.

Voices crashed and rolled around the two of them—all the anxious, struggling, or stranded sounds that brought people to the courthouse. Bodies rushed or shuffled by, so many. But right now, not a single one of those words or frustrated gazes was for *him*.

For now, anyway.

Instead they reached the door, and clear winter sunlight flooded through him.

The sounds fell back around them; that was one part of the open air, and he knew it should make it easier to speak again, but the rest of him only wanted to stroll along and soak it all in. So many people, so many voices and motions and little gatherings, all going on their own business. And some of them would get cheated or robbed, unless he Opened to what the liars were up to.

"Hey. I'm talking to you," Sarah said.

"Sorry. I guess... I wasn't listening."

Her eyes widened, but then she shrugged. "Well, don't get in a habit of it with me. I said, what's next?"

"Whatever Brandt sends me to. But I think that'll be about Operative Solutions and what lines they're crossing. That and any... other needs that I hear about."

When had that smile started on his face? He hadn't noticed it at all. Instead he looked away down the street.

He added "Maybe I'll even get you to talk to your family."

"So now you think you can do *anything?*"

Sarah's laugh spread the grin clear across his face.

Her hand pulled at his. He heard her feet shifting beside him, and it was all the sign he needed to turn and open his arms for the kiss.

*****

Keep reading for a look at the Spellkeeper Flight series in:

The High Road

PREVIEW from THE HIGH ROAD

This time it couldn't be hide-and-seek.

Nine-year-old Mark Petrie trotted across the grass when he saw Angie break from the trees and run toward the park's edge. The way her father had dragged her out of the park that afternoon, he'd thought he'd never see her there again.

So he went straight after her. He barely gave a glance back to the picnic table where his uncle was arguing about that "politics" stuff with his grumbling friends, their dinner still not unpacked.

When the grass changed to hard street-side sidewalk under their feet, Angie glanced back at him, her face just level with his. "I'm not stopping. I'm not waiting for him to catch me."

"Your dad? But we were only—"

She rushed on up the street, dodging between the scattered people in her path. Mark followed her red hair in the deepening twilight, still trying to work out why Mr. Dennard—a cop, as much a hero as any of Angie's other relatives she talked about—would have turned so angry at their playing with some of the family's old coats and belts.

Mark twisted around an old couple and their yapping dog, trying to keep Angie in sight. He passed sizzling burgers at the food stand, and his stomach clenched, reminding him the day was late and his uncle had been putting off their dinner. He tried to hold the emptiness down by thinking of the fun they'd had that afternoon—

Playing *Defend Sha Ta Ruath*—wherever that was—and letting their make-believe tell him *anything* could be about to happen—

But he was just hungry, and confused.

They reached the street corner at the edge of Rosewood Park's huge block, before Angie slowed and looked around.

"Where're you going? What happened?" he asked as he reached her side.

"I have something to ask my mom." She started across the street.

The word froze Mark a moment and he had to scramble to catch up again. Angie was going to her mother, after... how had she said it once, that mothers could run out on you? He still remembered the pain in her voice then, like Angie was better off with her gone.

She glanced over at him and added, "This is the way? If we keep going it's easy to hit Heat Street?"

"You mean Heath Avenue? The rich place? I think so."

She only moved faster now, with the sidewalk clear of park-goers and only the thinner evening crowds to weave through. Streetlights glowed along their way, just starting to stand out as night deepened, drawing the line between them and the stream of cars on their left.

By the second block, the sidewalk was even clearer. Now and then Mark passed people wrapped in scattered conversations, wreathed in cigarette smoke that added to the stench of car exhausts. Even some of the summer laughter he'd been hearing around the park seemed to thin away, while the air cooled and his feet hurt. Again and again, he saw the people Angie raced past turning to look at her flight.

Mark had lost count of the blocks they'd traveled before he managed to catch her arm. "It's getting dark. You can't just—"

"He said," and she spat the words at him like a weapon, "Dad said Grandpa died in a crazy-house! But he was my *mom's* father, Dad must be wrong, he has to be lying about him—"

She stopped, looked around the street. She must have seen something behind Mark, because she slipped from his slack grip and twisted away, heading up a side street, out of sight of the main road.

Mark scrambled after her, his thoughts pounding harder than his feet. The way Angie always talked, all her games about her family and its exploration of Sha Ta Ruath, and its soldiers and leaders and all the rest, and now her father said the things she *lived* for only ended in something awful?

At least he's not in jail like my *dad,* came an even darker thought. *And her mother's alive.*

The air felt colder now. They trotted past a construction barrier in the street and on through the shadow of a tall brick shape, and their feet sounded louder as the noise of cars fell away behind them.

The buildings pressed closer here, but a block ahead Mark could see the skeleton of a half-finished building silhouetted against the night. His nose itched at the construction dust in the air.

"Mark—" Suddenly Angie was turning back, toward him, past him.

He couldn't see what she had, only lines of darker brick pooling shadows into the slightly-paler street ahead. But that dimness, and the street traffic sounds so faded away behind them, brought a new shiver to his skin as he followed. Her footfalls were slower than they'd been all night. Hushed.

Then—

"You just keep going."

Growling right in front of them, appearing from around a corner, a huge man with some kind of black cap and a snarl of teeth flashing—

Angie, stumbling a step to put herself between Mark and the stranger they were backing away from—

Dim streets, alone, but the cars droning by not so far away, *people*—

The man took a step toward them. His arm reached out.

"HELP!" Mark yelled, with all the power his lungs had.

The next second, the big man had an ugly, blocky tunnel of a *gun* barrel pointed at them.

"Now you done it," he grated. "Wrong night for that. So you keep your holes shut or…"

Don't look at the gun, Mark told himself, feeling his heart stampeding, trying to tear his chest apart. If he looked to the side he could see Angie staring around, and another man—with the same kind of black cap over his scalp—moving up from where they had been headed, with a knife in his hand. Dust, so much dry, dead dust filling the air.

The gun tilted upward, relaxing the threat for a moment, and the man behind it grinned at their helplessness and lumbered toward them.

Then the gun swung higher as something yanked that arm toward the sky and a shape that had closed in behind the gunman's back twisted, spun, and sent the big man slamming to the pavement.

The gun clattered away. The man with the knife swore and broke into a run toward them, only to duck away inside a door as their rescuer reached inside his coat.

Angie gasped "Dad—" and there was awe in her voice.

Detective Dennard roared, "Just *go!*"

His tone, there was something wrong, like it was too fierce to fit inside his throat. And his hand drew back from his gun holster and brushed the belt at his waist...

In the next heartbeat, Angie's hand had locked onto Mark's arm and she pulled him into a run. His feet flung him along the pavement with her, toward the open streets. But he still stole a glance back, for a glimpse at her father chasing after the other thug.

Except Mr. Dennard was gone.

They ran. Ran through the night, forcing already-aching legs to carry them, with nerves on fire from the danger they'd brushed up against. In the rush of his heaving lungs, Mark at first missed the booming sound far, far behind them, until he realized it had spread and cascaded into a wild chorus of gunshots.

Blocks later they met a police car screaming toward the sound, and their shouts brought the cops over and let Mark gasp out a few words of what they'd seen. As he did, he realized Angie's father was closing in on them, as if he'd been only a few steps behind.

Angie flung herself into her father's arms without a word, or a single sob. Mark could only stand back, struggling for breath and watching them.

"Listen to that!" one of the uniforms said, raising his voice over the gunfire. "There ain't enough backup in the city to get me in there. That's got to be more than one gang killing each other—and you almost walked in right when something set them off?"

Almost walked in? Right, Mark thought, the three of them must have been blocks away from where the shots had sounded like they'd started. They had to have been.

Then Detective Dennard said "I... don't think I can be a cop anymore."

He kept his face bent over his daughter as he said those words. But Mark heard something in his voice, something that sounded too bitter to be the fury he'd shown before. Was that—shame?

Mark felt the two pieces in his head, refusing to go together. Angie's father had been running with them while the gangs started shooting far behind them... but that voice now... he couldn't make them fit.

No matter how he tried.

* * *
* * *
* * *

Dammit, Angie...

Mark threw his weight on the pedals, legs pumping, fighting for any extra distance he could get from the gang closing in behind him. Through the rasp of his breathing, the Blades' pounding feet sounded like only inches from his heels. All because even on his first day of work he'd *had* to stop for her call.

The alley's end loomed up ahead, and he squeezed the back brake to slow and skid around the poster-covered brick corner. He heard one shrill "So what's in the box?" before he swung out into the Anchor Street crowd, safe.

Easy as that.

Swerving narrowly around two lumbering dockworker types, Mark lurched to a stop to answer their shouts with a breathless, "Sorry, sorry," before walking the bike on. His breathing settled as he worked through the crowd, maneuvering along a sidewalk full of people, probably some afternoon shift letting out—one of the thickest crowds in Lavine city. Darkening clouds thinned the light around them, and his sweat swam in the air, making him shiver in the growing cold.

Tired, but safe. "Beats telling Gene my new phone got me killed," he muttered.

But what was the point of him learning every street in town if he couldn't use the time he saved on a message run to stop in at Angie's—or when she wasn't home, pull over to take her call? That bit of slack in his day was supposed to be the good thing about this job, he'd figured on that benefit ever since his junk Chevy had died and started him thinking of options besides waiting tables.

Didn't matter; the danger was over. Just because it was the Blades again, or they'd been near Angie's, didn't mean the gang had any reason to keep after either of them.

He glanced back again, and his knuckles tightened on the handlebars. The punks were still behind him.

They were just strolling along, some twenty feet back. Two silent figures with their leathers and black do-rags, already drawing uneasy glances from the workers they passed.

Still on me? But only two of them, where'd Rafe *go?* Mark stared up and down the street, trying to think if they'd really bother staying with him much longer. Or, he could put his knowledge of the street routes to use again and lose them, if he could find one gap in the crowd.

At that moment a car pulled out from its parking space, leaving a hole at the edge of traffic, and Mark leaped forward. A woman shouted as he twisted his bike past her, and he barely swerved clear of a wrought-iron lamppost, but he broke through onto the street. Free.

Once his tires dropped off the curb he hopped onto the saddle and began pedaling, finally able to move. *Faster, faster, I'm lightning, I'm a bullet train, I'm the damn Sha Ta Ruath Express if it has one...* He swept down the narrow space between the honking rush of traffic and the parked cars, eyes alert for any door that might pick just that moment to swing open into his path.

The light ahead turned red, but instead of slowing he only banked for the corner and angled onto the cross-street's sidewalk to rush along the new angle. But just as he turned he saw the black-capped rider away to his left, roaring down at the intersection on his Harley.

The crowds wouldn't last... that motorcycle would get closer by the second... so, he could stop while he still had some witnesses and hope he could brazen it out without the Blades remembering his face later. Unless the gang really had been lurking near Angie's because after all these years—

Besides, he *knew* the streets. Another twist of the handlebars brought him up a side street, with a parting glance back that showed he'd have a few moments out of the biker's view. The way ahead was just as empty and riddled with alleys as he remembered, and he arced to the side and ducked into one.

With a van parked squarely in its middle. A battered red barricade.

"Of *course,*" he spat, and jumped down, trotting with the bike toward the narrow gap even as he heard an engine thundering in behind him. He heaved the front wheel up, twisting the handlebars to make as narrow an angle as he could, and pressed in... a tip just catching and scraping on the graffiti... then his heart restarted as it squeezed free. The low box bungeed over his back tire wobbled and almost came loose, but it didn't matter. Now he had only open space ahead.

The Harley's roar rattled off the buildings behind him, dropping to a lower growl as it crept up the alley like a prowling beast. Mark leaned back out of sight, against the van's rear, listening for any pause in that motor... but it only crawled slowly by and finally gathered force and roared away.

He drew in a deep breath and let it seep out. Even in the thick stormy air, he could smell exhaust from the van, still *fresh*—would the alley have been clear just a minute earlier? He reached down to tighten the bungees around his box. At least his old green Raleigh could wriggle past where their motors couldn't, and foot soldiers wouldn't bother chasing him for long. Just as he'd thought, he'd ridden rings around them.

"Mark?"

The voice from around the van was low, worse than a shout: the calmness itself told him who it had to be.

Rafe went on "Still running errands for small bills? I always said you need someone who's got your back."

Mark's fists clenched. *We're a year out of high school, and he still thinks he can make me one of his thugs?*

I can't let him rattle me. Rafe couldn't have seen him duck back here; he had to be bluffing, calling blindly up each corner to see if he'd get an answer.

Then Rafe spoke again. "*This* time, the best place you can be is away from Joe Dennard. This won't stop until it comes out the far side of ugly."

Dennard. The night of the gang war. Suddenly that was all Mark could think of—even after ten years, after most of the Blades who'd lived through it must be dead or in prison. What could Rafe and the rest of them know, or *care,* about what might have happened back then?

But if they did—Mark found he couldn't breathe. If the gang was after Dennard—and they'd spotted Mark for being outside Angie's— were they already closing in on the father and the daughter too?

Then he heard a footstep, then another, the sound receding as Rafe walked away, up the pavement, to be swallowed up by the sounds of the city. He hadn't seen Mark after all.

Mark stayed flattened against the van for five more long, controlled breaths. Then he crouched down to look under it—he hadn't been so well-hidden, after all, not if anyone stopped to look for his feet—but saw nobody lingering out there.

His hands were trembling as he started the bike up the alley. At least his tires were silent as they built up speed, not like running feet would be. But he had to go faster, faster, get some space to stop and call the Dennards.

"Bastard!"

The sudden yell twisted his head back, to see the other two Blades charging up the alley at him. He flung himself forward.

Then the handlebar lurched and tipped, and he wrenched it blindly to keep it clear of the wall, clinging for balance, still looking back at the Blades... seeing the bungeed-down box working loose from the rack...

It's dangling over to foul the wheel—

Somehow, somehow, he kept the bike steady as he leaned forward and kicked back wildly, then felt the box break free. He scrabbled for the pedals again, fighting to build speed and hoping the gang would duck away from the falling box—or even stop to tear it open to discover the sample suit coat some designer had been so damn eager to have delivered.

Push! The street ahead still looked empty, no barriers to him, but also no witnesses if they caught him. Still, the thought of racing blindly into the lane made him twist, sweeping around the corner onto the sidewalk past a flash of red hair that had to be—

He heard the curses first, so fierce he had to steal a glance back. In that one instant he saw two recycling bins falling by the corner in a mess of green and blue and strewn metal. And a door, closing. Angie must have already ducked through it after knocking the bins into the Blades' path.

Mark had to imagine the rest as he powered up the street: how the first Blade might twist around the bins, but maybe the other would slip on some of the scattered cans... his mind kept supplying the sound of bowling pins crashing down together, but of course what mattered were the seconds Angie had bought him to get up to speed at last. And that she had spotted the bins and the open door in the one split instant he'd raced past her. Of course.

He rushed past block after block, keeping to the clearer side streets and zigzagging between them when he could. As he worked on picturing the evening streets' layout he remembered his new cell's GPS tracker app; of course, when he had broken off his call with her to run from the Blades, Angie could have used her own cell to find him. That could have given her some little warning that he was doubling back here, enough to set her trap.

With that guess in mind, it was only a matter of time before he settled onto the bike lane on Garcetti, and looked back to see a motorcyclist wearing a familiar denim jacket and red helmet moving up from behind him.

The old relief at seeing her was colored with an odd stain of envy, now that Angie's nimble Kawasaki had held up while his Chevy's breakdown had sent him back to pedaling. *Not that that matters, if the gang* is *hunting her father.* He pulled over to wait.

As his feet touched the pavement he felt his head spin, tension suddenly squirming up and down his muscles and turning them to water. The Blades had almost... and Rafe had...

A sudden thought made him burst out laughing, sagging against the handlebars.

Angie pulled up beside him, frowning at him as he fought to get a full breath. "Mark? Did I miss something?" Concern softened her voice more than usual.

"Just realized," he gasped out, trying to show her he hadn't lost his mind. "Even without your help, they... they lost that chase years— years!—before they met us..."

Her eyes narrowed suspiciously. "And why is that?"

He hauled in some air, and tried to say it properly. "When the first punks started their 'club.' Motorcycles couldn't squeeze through where I did, and runners couldn't keep up... but e-e-ever since they named themselves the Blades…" The laughs broke through again and he collapsed over the bike.

A moment later he heard her finish "…they wouldn't dare chase you on skates!" and break out laughing herself.

When they both had their breath back, Mark drew himself up, his lanky frame looming over her compact one. The one friend he'd kept by him, the girl who'd gone from severe pneumonia to winning track records. The girl who still held on to even bigger dreams, if she could get away safe from what he'd just learned.

He made himself meet her eyes. "Except… it was Rafe Martinez himself. And when they spotted me, I think it was because they were watching your place, and… he said they're after your father. I mean, if they finally found out he was there, and he really did know something about how the gang war started—"

"He threatened Dad—and you think it's for *this* thing again?" Her simple features tightened in frustration. "For the last time, give it a rest." She spun away, glaring up at the blackening clouds. "And it's been ten years. What could Rafe 'find out' that can have dug all of that up?"

"I don't know. I don't even know why he warned me; I've already turned down enough of his damn *offers*. But what I *think*—"

Mark stopped and bit back the flare of anger; he should have known arguing this with her wouldn't be easy. He met her gaze and settled his voice to its gentlest, steadiest tone.

"I think *something* had them waiting around your place, when I rode by it, and they even knew me, all of them. And that means they'll be back for you again, if you stay around here." He stopped there; no need to say again how he still couldn't forget the fury Dennard's face had held that night—or the shame after, then and when he turned in his badge, after weeks of bloody inter-gang warfare.

But Angie must have guessed where his doubts led, because she sighed "But years back—while he was saving our lives!—he was a block away when the 66s opened up on the Blades, and yet somehow it's *his* fault? No, this has to be about what he is now. If they can control the park's guard, they control the park, control the drugs and God-knows-what else they can do there. And they want me as a way to get at him."

She glanced around the sidewalk traffic, as if the gang might already be creeping through the crowd toward them. In just moments, Angie had it all figured out—without blaming the man they both wanted to trust. And he had to admit, her answer did make more sense.

A car honked on the street beside them.

"Mark?" She was looking back toward him.

"Yeah," he sighed. "Look, maybe it doesn't matter what they want from him. If they were at your place, they want to use you against him, but you're leaving the city anyway—and you still are, right? Staying isn't supporting him, it just gives him more he has to watch out for. And don't think about putting your plans on hold, that's one more way the gang wins."

"I... oh of *course* I'm leaving, I know that. I should like it more when you're right." Her head sank, then straightened a second later. "But you both have to keep yourselves safe, too, or I'll just be right back here." And she grinned.

"Sure, *anything* to keep that from happening." The joke came as a reflex, while his thoughts scrambled to catch up to how she'd be safe again, free, gone. He added, "If they're watching your place, I can round up some reinforcements to help while you pick up a few things—"

"No, I should just call Dad and go, and work the rest out later. Besides, *you* still have to explain to your boss about that package. And aren't you seeing Grace tonight?" she added as she started her engine.

That's over; it's Lucy now. But he didn't say that, only smiled back and dug out his phone as he pulled onto the sidewalk. He only had to keep the smile up a few more seconds, and then she was gone.

She's gone off to learn to fly planes, and when I'm trying to show her I'm the fastest courier on a bike, I get shot down. "Nice going," he muttered as he dialed.

ABOUT THE AUTHOR

"Whispered spells for breathless suspense."

Ken Hughes dreams of dark alleys and the twenty-seven ways people with different psychic gifts might maneuver around each corner. He grew up on comics and adventures before discovering Stephen King and Joss Whedon, and he's written for Mars mission proposals and medical devices, making him an honorary rocket scientist and brain surgeon. Ken is a Global Ebook Award-nominated urban fantasy novelist, creator of the Shadowed Steps series, the Spellkeeper Flight, the Mirrorman, and many more series of supernatural thrills.

Don't get him started on puns.

Find more books and join the Overview newsletter at:

KenHughesAuthor.com.